Alistair MacLean's UNACO

PRIME TARGET

Alistair MacLean's UNACO series

By John Denis
Hostage Tower
Air Force One is Down

By Alastair MacNeill
Death Train
Night Watch
Red Alert
Time of the Assassins
Dead Halt
Code Breaker

By Hugh Miller
Prime Target

Alistair MacLean was the bestselling author
of thirty books including the world-famous
The Guns of Navarone and *Force 10 from Navarone*.

HUGH MILLER

Alistair MacLean's UNACO

Prime Target

HarperCollins*Publishers*

HarperCollins*Publishers*
77–85 Fulham Palace Road,
Hammersmith, London W6 8JB

Published by HarperCollins*Publishers* 1997
1 3 5 7 9 8 6 4 2

A catalogue record for this book is
available from the British Library

ISBN 0 00225548 0

Set in Meridien by
Rowland Phototypesetting Ltd,
Bury St Edmunds, Suffolk

Printed and bound in Great Britain
by Caledonian International
Book Manufacturing Ltd, Glasgow

To Nettie

Acknowledgements

I am grateful to Philip Brent for information about satellite networks, Nick Carpenter for advice on firearms and incendiaries, Edwin Moss for Moroccan intelligence and Rosa Barlach for the low-down on urban biking.

Especial thanks to Fiona Stewart, my editor at Harper-Collins, whose vigilance and overall savvy did my manuscript no end of good.

Berlin, 24 April 1945

General Albers ran up the last few steps from the bunker to ground level and had to stand for a moment at the top, catching his breath. It was his habit to do everything at the double, but a spinal injury and chronic emphysema made that kind of behaviour unwise nowadays.

'One moment,' he panted, 'I'll take a look . . .'

He pushed aside a camouflage screen of metal and splintered planks and peered outside, craning his thin neck. All he could see in the immediate area was rubble and a scatter of uprooted shrubs.

'All clear,' he said, turning back to the stairs and holding out his hand.

Hitler declined to take it. He braced himself against the side of the stairwell and climbed into the open without help. The young soldier assigned to guard him came clattering up behind, clutching his sub-machine-gun.

'Please wait, Führer,' Albers said.

He crossed the rubble-strewn garden, smelling cordite and the damp sourness of the earth. A large hole had appeared near the gateway to the street. He detoured around it, turning up the collar of his greatcoat against the rain. He strode out into the middle of the road and stopped, looking both ways. Twenty metres to his left an officer of the Leibstandarte, nearly invisible in his black SS uniform, raised his arm to attract the general's attention. Albers waved back and glanced over his shoulder at the Chancellery.

For a moment he was transfixed, shocked by the level of damage. This was his first time out of the Führerbunker in three days. When he had gone in by the stairs where Hitler and his guard now waited, the back of the Chancellery had been intact.

1

Now, caught by the sideward impact of Soviet artillery closing on the rail junction at Spandau, huge stretches of stonework had been gouged out. Interior support walls had split and the second and third storeys had collapsed on to the crossbeams of the ground floor.

Albers started back the way he had come and felt a sudden pressure on his ears. The ground shook and there was a salvo of heavy gunfire to the west. He dropped to his knees as a pediment on the Chancellery roof flew apart with a loud crack and hurtled down in a shower of fragmented black marble. He crouched and put his hands over his head, feeling shards strike his back and arms.

He stood up again and saw the SS officer leading a string of young boys from a burned-out government building across the road. Over at the Chancellery Joseph Goebbels had come up the steps from the bunker. He spoke for a moment to the Führer, then came limping across the garden.

'Are they ready?' he asked Albers.

'They are being brought now, Minister.' Albers pointed to the straggle of children lining up by the wall on the other side of the road. 'We couldn't get proper uniforms, but in the circumstances I don't think they look too bad.'

The boys wore identical black jerkins, buttoned to the neck, and black forage caps. The youngest, who was eight, was frightened by the gunfire and had begun to cry. He was being comforted by the oldest in the group, a lad of fourteen.

'I'll speak to them and prepare them,' Goebbels said. 'I will take two minutes, then I'll come for the Führer.'

Albers went back to the stairs, brushing at his coat sleeves, noticing that black marble-dust mingled with rain resembled smears of oil. He looked at the soldier beside the Führer and saw how scared he was. Everyone had been against holding this ceremony outside. Hitler had been warned it was suicidal, but he had insisted. An induction as important as this had to be performed in the open air under German skies. Even if the skies were black with the smoke of a dying Berlin.

'The Minister is addressing the boys, Führer.'

Hitler nodded and appeared to shiver. He looked weak, Albers

2

observed, and incredibly old. Four days ago he had turned fifty-six, but today he looked nearer seventy. He was stooped and weary, one side of his body in a perpetual tremor, his light-starved skin the colour of putty. Earlier in the day he had been taken ill and could not stop vomiting. His valet, Heinz Linge, summoned the doctor who administered the usual, an intra-venous narcotic that drained the residue of colour from the Führer's face and put a very unnatural glint in his eyes. But afterwards he was no longer so desperately sick, he didn't shake so obviously, and he had even managed to display a little plea-sure at the prospect of this ceremony.

Goebbels had finished talking. He came hobbling across the broken ground, smiling cautiously as he always did.

'Everything is ready, Führer.'

'Good, good.' Hitler rubbed one blue-fingered hand on the back of the other, an attempt at vigour. 'So we have thirty boys, yes?'

'That is correct.' Goebbels fished a sheet of paper from his coat pocket and unfolded it. 'I have prepared a summary of the arrangements which have been made for them, if you would care to read it. Everything is precisely as we planned, of course . . .'

'Just give me the main points again, if you will,' Hitler said.

Goebbels began to speak and a shell exploded a kilometre away, throwing a plume of black and yellow smoke into the sky. The four men moved closer to the Chancellery wall. Goebbels started again.

'This evening, as soon as it is dark, the boys will be taken from Berlin by military transport to a covert SS airfield six kilometres south-west of Tempelhof. At ten o'clock an air-freighter, flying in the livery of the Red Cross –'

'Will this be a genuine Red Cross plane?'

'No, Führer,' Goebbels said patiently. 'It is a Wehrmacht troop-supplies aircraft, suitably disguised for its mission. It will take the boys directly to Zürich, where secure short-term accommodation has been arranged in a converted pavilion in the sheltered grounds of a hospital.'

3

'Which hospital?' Hitler demanded, as if it mattered. He had a habit of using questions to break the flow of others' speech.

'The Schwesterhaus von Roten Kreuz, Führer. The cost of caring for the boys, and of all their material needs, will be met from the fund set up on your instructions by Secretary Bormann. No outside help will be sought, since none will be needed.'

'The boys will be completely safe in that place?'

'Perfectly safe, Führer. They will be moved to more permanent quarters within the month.'

'Where will that be?'

'A fine location on the outskirts of Bern. It is a large house on a truly vast estate. It will be their home, a place where they will grow together in an environment of wholesomeness and good fellowship.'

The man spoke like a prospectus, Albers thought.

'They will become brothers in every practical sense, and always, *always*, they will be shielded from harmful and corruptive influences. In every particular, they will be educated and nurtured according to the precepts and guidelines you have set down, Führer. In the fullness of time, they will return to Germany and mount the definitive onslaught against the infestation of Judaism.'

'I think we should get started,' Albers said. 'The children will be getting cold.'

Hitler nodded. Albers led the way round the edge of the garden and out on to the street. The wind had dropped but the rain was heavier now, falling in ice-cold sheets that numbed the skin. Hitler walked between Goebbels and the guard, his hands tucked in the pockets of his greatcoat, the peak of his cap pulled close to his eyes. As they reached the edge of the road a shell exploded three streets away. The others broke step but Hitler kept walking as if he hadn't heard.

Drawing near the line of boys, who all looked thoroughly miserable, the Führer took his hands from his pockets and straightened his shoulders. Immediately he appeared to grow a couple of inches. He raised his head and thrust forward his jaw, making it taut. He fixed his famous stare on the boys and smiled.

4

At a nod from Goebbels, thirty arms shot out in the Nazi salute. 'Heil, Hitler!' the boys chorused. The sound of it echoed through the hollowed-out buildings behind them.

Hitler stood on the pitted road before them and returned the salute. The SS officer raised a battered Leica camera to his eye and pressed the shutter, recording the moment. Goebbels nodded again and the boys stood at ease. General Albers cleared his throat and stepped forward.

'Führer, I have the honour of presenting to you the most recent and final group of inductees to the Hitler Youth. This is a very special body, made up of thirty appropriately special young men. They are orphans, every one, and each is the son of a hero of the Third Reich.'

Albers walked to one end of the line with a sheaf of notes in his hand. He waited for Hitler to join him, then he introduced the boys one by one.

'Erich Bahr, aged twelve years, son of Area Commandant Konrad Bahr, killed with his wife Frieda in the bombing of Dresden in February. Klaus Garlan, aged ten years, son of Panzer Commander Gregor Garlan, killed in the Western Desert in 1944, mother Louisa Garlan killed in a bombing raid on north-west Berlin in January 1945. Albrecht Schröder, aged twelve years, son of Otto Schröder . . .'

Hitler listened attentively and shook each boy's hand before moving on to the next. By the time he reached the end of the line the rain had soaked right through his clothing and he was stooping again, his head jutting forward from hunched shoulders. He continued to smile nevertheless, as if sunshine blessed their little ceremony.

As he moved to the centre of the road to address the boys two shells landed nearby within a split second of each other. The shockwave struck Hitler obliquely, making him stumble. Five of the remaining Chancellery windows blew out in a cascade of glass and metal and stone. Hitler watched clouds of glittering dust rise around the base of the building.

'A Jewish–Bolshevik reprisal for Kristallnacht, perhaps,' he said, trying to revive his smile.

He turned, straightening his cap, pulling the lapels of his sopping greatcoat closer to his ears. When he spoke his voice was firm.

'I am told that tomorrow, or at the latest the day after, American and Soviet tanks will meet on the Elbe at Torgau. My dear boys, in that dark moment the Germany I dreamed of, the Fatherland I fought with all my heart and strength to build into a living reality, will be dead. It will have been killed. It will have been murdered by barbarians at the incitement of the International Jew.'

He paused and took a long deep breath.

'All that we love most dearly will be turned to smoke, and the smoke will disperse on the wind. Yet I tell you, my young friends, in this moment as I look at you, my heart swells with hope . . .'

Hitler let his gaze travel along the line, pausing a moment on each young face.

'I look at you and I see the essence of my *Jugend*, my ideal of the Aryan spirit. I see it in every one of you, the bright promise of a race and nation, the natural enemy of those who lay waste to our beloved land.'

General Albers moved a fraction closer, just to be sure: he took a swift hard look at the Führer's face and yes, he could see, there were tears welling in his eyes.

'In your maturity you will bear many duties,' Hitler said, his voice rising above the rumble and crash of gunfire. 'The most important of them, the most sacred, will be to uphold and keep alive the spirit of the Reich, and to eliminate its darkest enemy, with no thought of mercy. This is a precious charge. You boys, as its bearers, are no less precious.'

He paused and looked along the line again.

'You are the young, pounding heart of Germany,' he said. 'You are the embodiment of Siegfried, the strength and hope of your race. You are the future.'

Several boys were smothering tears. Another shell went off, bringing down rubble at the end of the street.

General Albers sidled up to Hitler and spoke in a sharp whisper. 'We should get back to the bunker, Führer, as much for

6

the sake of the boys as for ourselves. The chances of us all leaving here undamaged must be slim by now.'

Hitler nodded slowly and turned away. Albers and Goebbels fell in behind him. The guard led the way back across the Chancellery garden, the sodden earth sucking under their boots. At the top of the bunker steps Hitler stopped and looked back at the street. The SS officer was shepherding the boys back into the gutted office building. Hitler shook his head.

'What a thing it would be,' he said.

Albers and Goebbels looked at each other, mystified.

'To be young again,' Hitler said. '*That* young, with everything still to happen.'

Later, as General Albers sat in his quarters, recording the day's events in his diary, he looked up at the agonized Christ on a large wood-and-ivory crucifix by his bed.

'Not long now,' he said quietly. 'A week at most, with luck.'

The realism of the crucifix sometimes struck him as grotesque, but he kept it by him. It was the only memento of his wife, the one item to survive the inferno of their cottage after a British bomb reduced everything else, Greta included, to ash and vapour.

'Perhaps, Lord,' he said, 'you will arrange it so I can surrender to someone with a sense of irony, and no great desire to punish.'

He looked at the diary again and thought for a moment before finishing the page. *The small, special brotherhood is established*, he wrote. *If the meticulous plans of Secretary Bormann and Minister Goebbels unfold in the way they are intended, the remaining Jews in Germany will one day feel the Führer's throttling grip from beyond the grave.*

He put down the pen and rubbed his hands together. The room was cold and damp. He pushed back the chair, got down on his knees and peered under the bed. There was probably enough schnapps under there to ease the chill. He pulled out the bottle and held it up. Three good drinks, maybe four.

'Enough for now.'

He stood up, took the tumbler from the nightstand and poured a measure. With the glass held out before him he felt an impulse to toast the future of the thirty bedraggled orphans. They had looked so downcast. Just pathetic, frightened, parentless children.

That was now. But years from now . . .

'God,' he groaned, 'all the black tomorrows.'

He looked at his row of treasured books on the shelf above the bed; at the framed snapshot of himself and his brother as children; at the ivory face of Christ hanging there, twisted with pain and despair.

'Why should I wish more calamity on the world?'

Outside in the passage there was the sound of shouting. The wise men in the map room were being outraged again, berating absent commanders for the failure of crazy stratagems to rescue the Nazi dream. Albers sighed and raised his glass to the crucifix.

'Shalom,' he whispered.

ONE

A policeman on New Bond Street pointed towards the corner of Clifford Street. 'Along there,' he told the attractive American woman, 'and it's the first turning on your right.'

She thanked him.

'First visit?' he said.

'Oh no, not at all. I've been coming here since I was in college. But I still manage to lose myself in Mayfair.'

She thanked him again and moved on, turning along Clifford Street and into Cork Street. At the first gallery she stopped, caught by the sight of a solitary canvas on an easel in the middle of the window.

'Impressive, isn't it?' a man said.

She nodded, coolly enough to stay aloof, not so much as to appear rude. She had reached a stage in her life where the ability to draw men's attention, without trying, was no longer a particular pleasure.

'Probably a fake, mind you,' he grunted, moving off.

She could see it was no fake. It was an untitled George Stubbs, another of his horse paintings, this one a grey stallion hedged around with menacing shadows, rearing back from an unseen threat beyond the edge of the picture. The fear in the animal's eyes was painfully authentic, a primal terror more vivid than a photograph could convey. She turned away and walked on, blinking against the cold wind, wondering how a person could live with such an unsettling picture.

Outside the Lancer Gallery she stopped and glanced at her watch. She had dawdled over lunch and hadn't intended to get here so late. If she went in now, she would have to make it a swift visit. Too swift, probably, to enjoy it. If she waited until tomorrow she would have more time to browse. On the other hand, her London schedule was tight; a visit tomorrow could only be a maybe.

She stood facing the window, not sure what to do. As she raised her arm to look at her watch again, a man on the other side of the street drew a pistol from his pocket and fired a bullet into her spine. The impact threw her against the window. The second shot hit the back of her skull and came out through her forehead, smashing the plate glass.

Her body jerked and twisted, a grotesque puppet in a hail of falling glass. Abruptly she dropped to her knees. A single glass shard slid into her chin and pinned her to the edge of the window frame. She stopped twitching and became still.

The gunman made off along Cork Street into Burlington Gardens. He ran past witnesses too startled to do anything but stare at the glass and the blood and the blonde-headed corpse, spiked on the edge of the window.

The policeman who had given the woman directions appeared at the corner of the street. He stood for several seconds, staring like the others, taking in the scene, then he turned aside and muttered urgently to his radio.

The Arab came out of Sloane Street station with his eyes turned to the ground, walking purposefully, not quite hurrying. He stood in a knot of tourists by the crossing opposite the station entrance and waited for the green man.

'Do you know the way to Oakley Gardens, at all?' a small woman said. 'I have this map but it's very confusing.'

'I'm sorry.' He kept his face averted, as if he was watching for someone. 'I'm a stranger here.' He saw her push the map forward and stalled the next request. 'I need glasses to read small print,' he said. 'I don't have them with me. Sorry.'

He pulled up the collar of his windcheater, hiding half his face without obviously obscuring his identity. He breathed deeply, telling himself over and over to be calm and take care to make no eye contact. He forced his mind to stay on the primary need, which was to get to his rented room as fast as he could without arousing interest along the way.

10

The green man came on and he stepped into the road, moving fast but no faster than the others, his hands deep in his slit pockets. His right fingers were curled around his gun. The barrel was still warm.

Hurrying past W.H. Smith's he could see the pedestrian light at Cheltenham Terrace was green, which meant it would be red before he got to the corner. He put on a spurt, just short of running, and cursed as the light changed. People bunched on the edge of the pavement. He eased in among them.

'Bloody traffic,' a man next to him said.

'Right.'

'It's no pleasure walking any place these days.'

'Yeah, right.'

The light changed. He tightened his grip on the gun, holding on to it like a mascot, and let himself move along at the centre of a group.

On the opposite pavement he accelerated again, striding smartly, turning left down Walpole Street and right on to St Leonard's Terrace. One of his many superstitions dictated that if he took the same route back to base on consecutive nights, something bad would happen. Last night he went straight down the King's Road and got to his digs via Smith Street. It was much quicker than this way, but what was a gain in speed alongside the chance of bad fortune?

Approaching the bottom of Royal Avenue he looked up and saw two policemen walking towards him. They were 15 metres away but he was sure they were looking at him. He checked his watch. It was twenty minutes since he did the job, long enough for a description to be circulated. He reminded himself his face had been half covered, as it was now.

But what if they were looking for an Arabic type with half his face covered?

He decided to go up Royal Avenue. He turned right sharply and bumped into a woman. He hadn't even seen her. His foot came down on hers and she yelped. He glanced at the policemen. They were definitely looking at him now.

'I'm so sorry,' he said to the woman. 'Please forgive me for being so clumsy –'

11

'Stupid idiot!'

He tried to move past her and she swung her folded umbrella at him, hitting his shoulder. He smelled whisky. Of all the people to walk into, he had to pick a belligerent drunk. He pushed her away, but she resisted and tried to hit him again. He stepped aside and she stumbled, swinging wildly. She missed and fell over with a heavy bump, howling as the contents of her shopper scattered across the pavement.

'Hoi! You!'

It was one of the policemen.

'I have done nothing,' the Arab called. 'She slipped and fell, that is all.'

'Just stay where you are, mate. Stay put.'

They were coming for him. His heart began to race. He jumped over the flailing woman and sprinted along Royal Avenue. Leafy branches of garden shrubs slapped his face as he ran.

'Stop! Come back here!'

He put his head down and pumped his legs furiously, hearing the voice of Ahmad Shawqi: 'Never be taken by the police,' he always warned. 'Avoid all police in all countries. There is no worse misfortune than to be taken.'

It was one of his superstitions, anyway. If the police ever took him, eternal bad fortune would befall himself and his family. As he ran it occurred to him that last night he had gone back to his digs by the route he had just taken; it was the day before that he had gone straight down the King's Road . . .

'Right, pal, hold it right there.'

Impossibly, one of the policemen was standing ahead of him, arms spread, clutching his baton. The Arab stiffened his legs, frantically slowing himself as he realized they must have split up and this one had cut through a garden to get in front.

'Don't do anything silly, now –'

The Arab ran off the pavement into the traffic, narrowly missing the front of a taxi. He spun away from the near-impact and found himself with his hands flat on the bonnet of a police car. As the blunder registered, the driver and his partner were out and coming for him.

He turned to run and saw the first pair of constables heading

12

straight towards him. He turned back, ran, and slammed into the side of a removals van.

'Right!' a constable shouted, grabbing him. 'Don't move a muscle!'

A strong hand took his shoulder, the other twisted his left arm up his back. He plunged his free hand into his pocket and grabbed the gun. There were four policemen and they were all close. Even if he worked at his fastest, he knew he could never get them all before they took him. There was only one possible course of action.

'Shit! He's got a gun!'

He saw frantic hands coming at him, fingers hooked to drag him down. In an instant the muzzle of the gun was in his mouth. He tried to think of something noble, an image that would define his life.

Nothing came.

He shut his eyes and pulled the trigger.

'It is Tuesday 27th February, 1996,' the fat pathologist wheezed into the tape recorder hanging on his chest. 'The time is sixteen-thirty-three hours. I am Doctor Sidney Lewis and I am conducting a preliminary examination on the body of an unidentified male. The body was brought to the coroner's mortuary at Fulham by ambulance from St Agnes' hospital, where the subject was declared dead on arrival at sixteen-oh-eight hours, this date.'

Dr Lewis switched off the recorder and waited as an attendant led two constables and a plainclothes policeman into the autopsy room.

'I'm D I Latham,' the plainclothes man said. 'These are Constables Bryant and Dempsey. They were in pursuit of the dead man shortly before he died.'

Lewis looked at them. 'You're the two who were chasing him when he panicked and shot himself?'

'If you care to put it that way,' the taller one, Dempsey, said coldly.

'And why have you come here?'

'I wanted them to look at the body and tell me it's the man

13

they chased,' Latham said. 'There can be identity problems with Middle Eastern types, and since this case could turn messy, I want basic facts established before everything gets obscured by jargon.'

Dr Lewis waved a hand at the corpse. 'Well, then, gentlemen, is this the man in question?'

'That's him all right,' Dempsey said. Bryant nodded.

'Fine.' Lewis grasped the handle at the top end of the tray holding the body. 'Now, tell me before we go any further, are there any mysteries here? I mean, do we know how he died, for sure? Was it the way I've been told? He took his own life, without a shadow of doubt?'

'That's clearly established,' Latham said. 'But there's plenty of mystery, just the same. We don't know who he is, we don't know why the gun, or why he shot himself with it.'

'Shortly after shooting a woman in Mayfair,' Constable Dempsey added.

'Not yet confirmed,' Latham snapped. 'But that's likely,' he told Dr Lewis. 'He appears to have shot and killed a woman as she looked in a gallery window on Cork Street.'

'Who was she?'

'We don't know that yet, either. All very confused at this stage. There's a diplomatic angle. American. We'll know more in an hour or so.'

'I see what you mean by messy,' Lewis said. 'Never mind, in the meantime we can generate paperwork.' He switched on a bright striplight above the autopsy table. 'I don't think we're going to find much that isn't obvious already. If one or both of you constables would help me with the clothing, it will speed matters.'

He saw Bryant scowl and watched Dempsey work up a look of affront.

'Is there a problem?'

Bryant shrugged sullenly.

Dempsey said, 'I don't remember signing up for anything like this.'

'Blame your own bad timing,' Lewis said. 'You drove this poor soul to kill himself at approximately the same time a debt collector in Parsons Green pushed two of his targets against the plate-glass window of a betting shop with rather too much force. The glass gave way and the debtors were cut almost in half. They're through in the other room being stripped at this moment by my only assistant – the bloodstained one who showed you in.'

'I don't think you have the right to say we drove this man to –'

'It was a joke, for God's sake!' Lewis said. 'A bloody *joke*, of which we need plenty in this charnel house.' He shook his head at D I Latham. 'A sense of humour should be a prerequisite for the job.'

The body was stripped and the clothes bagged for examination at the police forensic laboratory. The big tray with the body still on board was then transferred to the roll-on scales. Dr Lewis read off the weight, hooked a measuring pole over one foot and read the height at the point where the pole touched the head. That done, he moved the body back under the light, switched on his recorder and proceeded with the preliminary examination.

'The body is that of a well-nourished man of Middle Eastern appearance, between twenty-five and thirty years old. He weighs seven-nine-point-three kilograms and measures one-eight-five-point-two centimetres, from crown to sole. The hair on the scalp is black and wiry with a natural curl. The sclerae and conjunctivae are unexceptional, the irises appear light brown and the pupils are dilated and fixed. Hairline scars under the ears and on either side of the nose suggest extensive and skilful cosmetic surgery. Apart from considerable damage to the head, to be described below, there are no other apparent injuries.'

Dr Lewis picked up a length of wire and pushed it into the dead man's mouth. The end appeared from the back of the head with a grape-sized clot of blood attached. Lewis withdrew the wire and spoke to his recorder again.

'The head is normocephalic, with extensive traumatic damage. A visible bullet-entry wound to the rear of the hard palate connects, on probing, to a gaping area of parieto-occipital bone loss, approximately ninety millimetres by sixty, with significant absence of intervening brain tissue.'

15

He switched off the recorder and looked at D I Latham. 'That does it for the preliminary. Nothing more until we have an order for a post-mortem.' He put a finger into the dead man's mouth and felt around the edge of the bullet wound. 'What kind of gun did he have?'

'Austrian Glock automatic.'

'Nine millimetre?'

'Correct.'

'Registered?'

'Not in this country.'

'Foolish of me to ask. You've no idea at all who he is?'

'We fingerprinted him at the hospital and got several mug shots. The PNC is working on it, so is Interpol, and we'll be uploading all the details to ICON this evening. But the short answer is no, we haven't a clue who he is.'

The blood-smirched attendant appeared in the doorway and said there was a phone call for Detective Inspector Latham. Latham went to the office and was back in less than two minutes.

'Apart from some money and the gun,' he told Dr Lewis, 'the only thing the dead man had on him was a snapshot, a picture of two women sitting in a bar. Somebody has just noticed one of the women in the picture is the woman who was shot in Mayfair this afternoon.'

'Why do you think there's a hold-up on identifying her?'

'The American Embassy is involved. They probably know all about her, and no doubt so do our top brass, but they have an agreed process whereby information trickles down slowly from the top, and we can't rush them. Not if we know what's good for us.'

'Intriguing.' Lewis was examining the body again. 'He's very muscular.' He lifted an arm, hefting it, pinching the flesh. 'He probably worked-out a lot, or he's recently been in the army.'

He hoisted the arm higher and stared.

'What is it?'

'Abdul has a tattoo. It's just visible through the undergrowth in his armpit. Look.'

The pattern was indistinct. Lewis picked up a knife with a straight blade and used it to shave away the armpit hair.

'What would you say it is, Doc?'

'It's nearly spherical, it's orange and brown and yellow with a sharp blue border. It could be some kind of Egyptian talisman, for all I know.'

'Or a Muslim symbol,' Latham suggested.

Constable Bryant was standing at the top end of the table. 'If you look at it from here, it's not too mysterious,' he said.

Lewis tilted his head and inched around the table. 'I'll be damned,' he said.

Latham was still frowning at the mark. 'What is it?'

'The face of a cat,' Lewis said. 'And it's smiling, in a ghastly kind of way.'

TWO

On Wednesday 28 February at 10.10 a.m. Eastern time, thirteen hours after the Arab had been declared dead at a London hospital, a startlingly clear image of a cat-face tattoo appeared on the ICON information screen in the UNACO Command Centre at UN headquarters in New York. It accompanied a case summary with a picture of the dead Arab male, complete with an investigative précis and inset shots of the dead man's property. Tom Gilbert, the duty Newsline Monitor, made high-definition printouts and spent another twenty minutes gathering peripheral information. He then took everything to the office of the Director of UNACO.

That morning was as busy as any other in the complex of offices and technical suites that made up UNACO's headquarters. UNACO – the United Nations Anti-Crime Organization – occupied an entire floor of the Secretariat building which dominated the UN's East River site. More than two hundred employees, many of them highly trained specialists, handled the administration of the world's most efficient crime-fighting body. Thirty prime-rated field agents, drawn from police and intelligence agencies around the world, formed the core of ten teams known as strike forces which, by agreement among the majority of nations, were able to cross national boundaries freely. They could also bypass police administrations and, where necessary, override laws and the diplomatic process. The organization's avowed aim was to counter crime at the international level, using personnel and resources funded by the UN member nations. UNACO was not a secret body. On the other hand it did not publicize itself. Its offices were unmarked, all telephone numbers were unlisted and agents and employees never openly acknowledged their affiliation. The Director of UNACO, Malcolm

18

Philpott, was accountable only to the Head of the Security Council and to the Secretary General of the United Nations.

As Tom Gilbert entered the office, Philpott was staring at a letter printed on CIA notepaper.

'Hope I'm not intruding, sir.' Gilbert crossed the big room, his feet soundless on the carpet. He put the folder on Philpott's desk. 'This could be relevant.'

'So could this.' Philpott tapped the letter. 'Remember Tony Prine and his one-man mission to Bolívar?'

'Prine?' Gilbert thought for a moment. 'Specialist in industrial sabotage – that Prine?'

'The same. A highly resourceful chap. He's been trying to uncover a solvent-manufacturing plant, crucial to the production of cocaine, located somewhere in the region of Cartagena. Well, a satellite surveillance officer at Langley has spotted a big bang in the heart of the Bolívar region. He says if it's got anything to do with us, we should tell the people upstairs to get ready to counter complaints from the Colombian government about unscheduled anti-drug activity on their urban turf.'

'Looks like Prine found his target.'

'Let me know as soon as he makes contact. Some kind of pat on the back will be in order.'

At that hour Philpott still looked puffy, a side-effect of the beta-blockers he now had to take for his heart condition. Otherwise, he looked fit and alert. He pointed to a mini espresso machine on a table at the side.

'Help yourself to Milanese blend, Tom. Bad for the heart so early in the morning, but it does wonders for the soul.'

Gilbert poured himself a cup and sat down to wait. Philpott looked at the pictures he had brought and read the sketchy case details. He looked up.

'No identification on the Arab?'

'Not at present. He's had recent plastic surgery to alter vertical *and* horizontal facial alignment.'

'Perhaps a seriously wanted man then. Is there anything more than you've given me?'

'The woman the Arab is believed to have killed –'

19

'She's the one on the left in the picture he was carrying. I read that and I've looked at the picture.'

'Don't you recognize her?'

Philpott held the print under the desk lamp. The woman had a pallid, delicate face, small-featured and framed by soft-curled blonde hair. Her companion, no less attractive, had a strong face and rich dark hair.

'You must have met her,' Gilbert said.

'Really?' Philpott shook his head. 'I meet a lot of good-looking females. Nowadays it's never a memorable *frisson*.' He sighed. 'Her jacket is a Donna Karan, I believe, but I don't know the wearer at all.'

'She's Emily Selby,' Gilbert said.

Philpott thought for a moment. 'Political analyst on the White House press team. Yes?'

Gilbert nodded. 'Her areas of expertise are listed as Central and South-west Asia.'

'God almighty, I believe I spoke to her at a reception not long ago.' Philpott groaned. 'Maybe I'm losing it.' He read the details again. 'So, yesterday afternoon, right in front of the Lancer Gallery in Mayfair, Emily was shot through the spine and the back of the head with bullets from a Glock 17, identified as the gun found on the dead man. What was she doing in London?'

'According to a Reuter's bulletin, she was taking a month of her annual leave in Europe.'

'Do we know who this other woman is?'

'Yes, I got her identity on FaceBase.'

'Did you, indeed. How long did that take?'

'Three minutes.' FaceBase was a feature-comparator capable of identifying photographs from a database of three million images. 'It never takes much longer than that,' Gilbert added.

Philpott stared at him. 'Do I detect a certain smugness?'

'Well, it does seem to work every time, and I *did* argue strenuously for the installation of the system, even though certain people –'

'Certain people. You mean even though *I*, alone, reckoned it was going to be a waste of money and floor space.' Philpott shrugged. 'I was wrong.'

'It's magnanimous of you to say so, sir.'

'Tom, when you're right as often as I am, you have to be wrong some of the time or you start to look infallible. That would never do.'

'The woman's name is Erika Stramm,' Gilbert said. 'She's German, a freelance political journalist with vague terrorist affiliations. She's twice been refused a US visa.'

'But we can't define the link between her and Emily Selby.'

'Not yet.'

Philpott got up and stood by the window, looking down at the array of national flags fluttering on their masts in front of the complex. The office was on the twenty-second floor. From that height everything looked reassuringly tidy.

'So,' Philpott said, 'the bald fact is that a man of Middle Eastern origin has murdered a US government employee in the heart of London. I think that until we know more about the gunman and his motive, we should regard this as a matter for low-level UNACO involvement. I'll have the Political Intelligence office hunt for possible leads.' He turned from the window and smiled tightly. 'Thanks for bringing this to my attention.'

Gilbert caught the dismissal. He stood up and drained his coffee cup.

'What about the dead man's fingerprints?'

'They were transmitted on the ICON file, sir. Did you want to have them?'

'Pass them to Mike Graham, with the rest of the stuff. Tell him I'd like a detailed work-up as soon as he can manage one. You'll find him in the Interview Suite writing case notes. He'll be glad of the diversion.'

When Gilbert had gone, Philpott picked up the phone and told the UNACO operator to find the number for Riot City in Hounslow, England, and to give them a call.

'Sounds like a fun place,' Ms Redway said.

'If you don't find it listed as that, it's real name is the Public Order Training Centre,' Philpott told her, 'and its bureaucratic handle is TO18. It's a fantasy violence environment for police officers. I'm not sure I entirely approve, but their crowd-control training is the best.'

21

'They probably won't be open for business for three hours yet.'

'I know. Tell the security person who answers the phone that Sabrina Carver should call her uncle as soon as she gets to Hounslow.'

The six o'clock forecast had said it would be a cold day, but sunny. On the drive out through Chiswick and Brentford it was still foggy, and on the approach to Hounslow the fog thickened. Slowing down to negotiate the narrow streets on the outskirts of town, Sabrina Carver switched on the car radio to catch the 8.30 news bulletin.

The announcer was annoyingly upbeat for the time of day. He reported that Sinn Fein were to be promised seats at peace talks if they could persuade the IRA to renew their recently-ended ceasefire; a woman shot dead in Mayfair was believed to be an American tourist, but no details of her identity had yet been released; five students had died in a car crash at Milton Keynes; a serial killer had been given three life sentences at a Crown Court in Yorkshire; a British-led team of scientists was on its way to Pisa to help stop the tilt of the leaning tower.

That was it. No news from the States. For the third or fourth time since she arrived in England, Sabrina promised herself she would try again to tune her Sony to Voice of America. Some weird signal-screening in her quarters at the police hostel played hell with shortwave reception.

She stopped by the Riot City barrier and smiled at the constable in the security box, He waved as usual, but this morning it was different. Sabrina realized he was beckoning her. She got out and put her head inside the tiny office.

'Morning, Terry. What's up?'

'You've to phone your uncle,' he told her. 'Soon as possible.'

'Yeah. Right.' It took a second to sink in. Until two weeks ago, the alias had been Cousin Malcolm.

'You can use this phone if you want.'

Sabrina knew that would be breaking Riot City rules. She also knew Terry was happy to make that kind of gesture if it would gain him points with a hard-bodied blonde his own height. Over tea and biscuits in the canteen, he had told her she was wasting her time being a cop; she should be in pictures.

'It's OK,' Sabrina said now, 'I'll get to him later. I don't want to be late. If Uncle rings again, would you tell him I'll call back as soon as I can?'

Terry said he would. Sabrina got back in the car, drove on until she was behind the administration block and stopped. She took her cellular phone from her bag and tapped in three digits. There was a scattering of satellite noise, then a ringing tone. Philpott answered on the fourth ring.

'I got your message, sir.'

'Fine. It's nice to hear your voice, my dear. I've been looking over your team leader's evaluation of your progress over there. He believes his notes are for the eyes of his London chief alone, of course, so there are one or two racist, sexist comments about pushy Yank feminist tactics and so on, but on the whole you've impressed him. He says that your, er, what is it now . . .' paper rustled, 'your capacity for total focus in a Level One TSG situation was especially to be commended. I assume that's good?'

'Level One is the ultimate stage of public order training, sir. A TSG is a Territorial Support Group.'

'So what have you been doing in your TSG?'

'All kinds of things connected with crowd handling and public order control. Yesterday we did gasoline-bomb training on a simulated Battersea street. At one stage I caught fire, but a couple of nice Inspectors patted the flames out.'

'And do they buy your cover?'

'Sure, they think I'm a New York cop. I chew plenty of gum and I swear a lot. It's not the hardest cover to maintain. But I'm sure you didn't get me to call just so we could engage in chit-chat.'

'No, indeed. There's a little job I want you to do, while you're in the area.' Philpott explained about the Emily Selby shooting and the possibility of the case being taken up by UNACO. 'You know the kinds of fears a case like this can raise. Apart from the possibility that Emily Selby was a spy, there are other worries. The gunman could have been an irate Palestinian.'

'Was Emily Jewish?'

23

'She was. Think of the possibilities: a Jewish employee of the US government gunned down by a man of Arabic appearance.'

'It raises a lot of scenarios.'

'Well, for the moment it's enough to be aware of them,' Philpott said. 'Emily had a small suite at the Knightsbridge Lawn Hotel, and unless inter-governmental procedure has changed wildly in the past year or two, the rooms will be sealed off for a few days until it's decided who has the right to nose around in the dead woman's property.'

'You want me to pre-empt the search.'

'If you would.'

'Any idea what I might be looking for?'

'A journal, perhaps, cryptic notes, any item in her possessions that doesn't chime with the rest. Try to find out if Emily was less of a credit to her job than anyone suspected.'

Sabrina looked at the clock on the side of the main building. If she was going to get coffee before people started throwing bricks at her, she would have to go now.

'Should I do the job tonight, sir?'

'Not any later.'

'In that case I'll have to do some manoeuvring.'

'Why so?'

'There's a full-scale military-style kit inspection tomorrow morning. My stuff's in a foul state. Getting it ready will be a three-hour job, at the tightest.'

'You're an agent of UNACO, my dear, which means you count resourcefulness among your many qualities. I'm sure you'll manage. How much longer will you be at Hounslow?'

'I finish tomorrow.'

'Lord, time flies.'

'I hope to be back in New York Saturday.'

'By which time, I've no doubt, you'll be an even more finely-honed and efficient emissary of justice than you were before you left us.'

'Are you being serious, sir?'

'Not particularly,' Philpott said. 'Take care, Sabrina.'

'As ever,' she promised.

When she walked into the canteen three minutes later, the

usual silence fell. It was momentary, a one-beat cessation of talk and rattling as the sixty-two men and four women in the place stopped everything to register her arrival.

Sabrina was not embarrassed or discomfited. She had been attracting overt interest since a few months past puberty; also, at Hounslow there was the added professional factor. The blonde was an American cop – or so they believed – and since all dreams of slick law enforcement centre on the US police image, Sabrina realized she was as much a focus of envy as anything else.

'It's coffee, black, no sugar, right?' Plump Inspector Lowther was on his feet, pointing to the chair opposite his own at the table nearest the door. 'I was on my way to get seconds anyway. Sit down, I'll only be a minute.'

'Thanks.'

As she pulled out the chair a young officer at the next table said, 'Hey, settle an argument, will you?' He pointed to her black cotton coverall suit. 'You had that made special, didn't you?'

'Nope.' Sabrina patted the gold-and-blue embroidered badge on her sleeve. 'It's standard NYPD issue.'

'Really? Has it got special deep pockets for the bribes?'

Sabrina smiled back. 'You must watch an awful lot of bad movies. Get out more often in the real world. Bribe a girl to go with you.'

He blushed, and the jeering laughter of his companions obviously stung. He looked away and said no more.

'Here we go . . .' Inspector Lowther put a cup of coffee in front of her and sat down with his tea and a jam doughnut. 'I hope it's hot enough.'

'It's fine, thank you.'

He was a sweet soul, and even though he was on the make Sabrina found the attentiveness endearing. He had latched on to her from the start and had helped her over the early hurdles without once making a move on her. But she could tell the hope was there. When she left England she would not miss Lowther, but at least she wouldn't remember him with distaste.

'So,' she said, making small talk, 'today's the grand finale, huh?'

He nodded. 'Rocks, bottles, firebombs, burning buildings, the lot. Nervous?'

'Very,' she lied. 'How about you? Have you ever been in a real-life situation like this one? People throwing stuff, hating you, too far gone to hear reason?'

'I got a taste of it in 1990, at the Poll Tax riot in Trafalgar Square. A man with a broken chair leg and a hatred of the police put me in hospital for ten days.'

'Wow.'

'But you must get into some vicious scrapes in New York.'

'I never faced a mob.'

'Ever had to shoot anyone?'

'No,' she lied again, thinking, *More people than you'd believe.* 'Up to now I've dealt mostly with traffic violations.'

'Well, at least you have an exciting working environment.'

'I wouldn't say that. Frantic's a better word.'

And then, without any lead-up or warning, Lowther leaned forward and said, 'Would you have dinner with me tonight, Sabrina?'

That look, she thought: the wistful smile, the eyes telling her he'd be devastated if she said no. It never worked, she always saw it as emotional blackmail, something else about men to despise. On this man, however, it simply looked pathetic.

'I have an engagement already this evening,' she said, simultaneously spotting an opportunity.

'Oh.' He shrugged.

'But I'll tell you what – we finish at noon tomorrow, right? How about lunch somewhere in the West End? My treat. I'd have loved to make it dinner, but I have to catch an overnight flight to New York.'

She watched the flicker of changes in his expression, all desperately transparent. This was less than he'd had in mind; she had side-stepped the proposition, but it was better than rejection; what she suggested still wasn't dinner, it was unromantic daytime stuff, but it still wasn't rejection . . .

'Well, that would be great,' he said. 'But I can't let you pay.'

'NYPD pays,' Sabrina said. 'They're covering me for two goodwill entertainments and I haven't done one yet, so we can have a splash.' She gave him her friendliest smile. 'Is it a date?'

He nodded, thoroughly charmed.

'Oh, and by the way, I was going to ask you, it's presumptuous of me, I know . . .'

'Go ahead,' he said generously, 'anything at all.'

'Well.' She made an uneasy face. 'It's the passing-out kit inspection tomorrow morning. It's obvious they take it seriously. I wouldn't want to lose the points, but I'll be squeezed for time, because I have to go to this woman's place –'

'You want me to get your kit ready?'

'Oh, no! God, no, I wouldn't dream of imposing. I thought maybe you could find me somebody who would take on the job for a consideration.'

'I'll do it for you myself.'

'Really?'

'Consider it done.'

'But that's so –'

'Look, Sabrina, don't mention it. It'll be a pleasure.'

She touched his hand. 'You're a real friend.'

His gratitude was something to see.

THREE

When Philpott stepped into the semi-darkness of the Secure Communications Suite he found Mike Graham hunched in front of six computer screens, three on three.

'I know you said another hour.' The padded walls and ceiling muffled Philpott's voice. 'But I got fidgety.'

'I'm antsy myself, now,' Mike said. 'One damned detail has bugged me for twenty minutes. I'm getting nowhere with it.'

He leaned back and stretched. He was a lithe man, conventionally handsome with even features and an easy way of smiling. Philpott, never keen to admit that anything or anyone was without major flaw, often remarked that Mike's hair was too long.

'When will you have results worth examining?'

'I've got them now.'

'Excellent.' Philpott took the swivel chair next to Mike's. 'Do you have a tentative verdict?'

'Well this could certainly be UNACO's kind of case, because the dead man had a terrorist pedigree. His real name was Yaqub Hisham, and he was Arabic, as everybody thought. He was registered with the Department of Social Security in London as Kamul Haidar, twenty-six years old, living in rented accommodation in Chelsea, with a home address in Morocco. He'd been in London a month, allegedly studying history and English at the Monkfield Institute.'

'Never heard of it.'

'Scotland Yard's SO11 gave it the once-over. It's a couple of rented rooms off the Edgware Road, run as a school by a retired teacher. Plenty of students are registered with the Institute, but nobody seems to show up for classes.'

'Another dismal racket,' Philpott sighed. 'Something in the atmosphere of England nurtures seedy hustlers.'

'Aside from his scholastic work, our man was a part-time porter at the Wimcote House Hotel in Paddington.'

'But in spite of that, he could afford digs in Chelsea. All of this was a cover, I presume.'

'Oh sure.' Mike tapped a button on the console and a Mossad Criminal Data card appeared on the third screen of the top row. The Arab's picture was at the left with his fingerprints at right and a summary of his criminal record below. 'No information at Scotland Yard or Interpol, but the Israelis have the goods on him. The picture was taken a month after he had his face changed. His prints were altered too, acid and pumice powder they reckon. Mossad's fingerprint boys used a latency comparator on smudgy dabs they picked up in Hebron, and the comparator turned up this guy's original set of prints.'

Philpott peered at the text on the screen. 'It's in Hebrew.'

'I got a translation.' Mike held up a printout sheet. 'Courtesy of Mossad Criminal Records.'

'I'm impressed. You have better connections every time I see you.'

Mike ran a finger down the sheet. 'Hisham had sixteen listed aliases and was a known terrorist from the age of eleven. During his middle and late teen years he managed to study history as well as sedition and anarchy. He was a prominent graduate of the Jezzine terrorist movement in Lebanon. Known to be energetic, technically skilled, resourceful and, unusually, the guy was multi-lingual. He wasn't strong on ideology, but he got by on plain hatred of the Jews. He was made an honorary member of the Brotherhood of the Civet when he was eighteen.'

'Brotherhood of the what?'

'Civet. It's a kind of cat. The brotherhood are sworn to do harm to Jews in any way they can, which doesn't make them unique, but they *are* customized. They have a tattoo of a civet's head in the right armpit. The animal's supposed to be lucky and to ward off danger.'

'Every day,' Philpott said, 'I learn a little more . . .'

'In June 1994 the Israelis bombed a Hezbollah training camp

29

in southern Lebanon and killed forty guerrillas. Six people survived. Yaqub Hisham was one of them.'

'He was with Hezbollah?'

'The Israelis believe he was training them. For a while after the bombing he was treated like a living martyr, and he made a public declaration that he would double his efforts against Jews. Three weeks after that he ambushed three officers of Shin Bet at a checkpoint in the Bekáa Valley and butchered them. Mossad's been on his tail ever since. He was believed to be holed-up in Tetuán, Morocco, which isn't an easy place for Israelis to go looking for somebody. Mossad are very surprised that he showed up in England.'

'Indeed. What was he doing in London, shooting a political analyst from the White House? I mean, why him? Why a seasoned, Jew-hating Middle Eastern terrorist?'

'Emily Selby was Jewish.'

'Not the kind of Jew that Arab terrorists travel all the way to Europe to assassinate, surely?'

'If we knew the link between Emily and the other woman in the picture, Erika Stramm, I'm sure we would be standing in a brighter light.'

Philpott looked at the screens. 'What's the loose end you're chasing?'

'Yaqub's gun. I checked the serial number with the makers at Deutsch-Wagram, and they say it's from a batch of fifty bought in Vienna last July for export to the USA. Buyer's name was Albert Torrance of Denver, Colorado, which turns out to be a fake ID. But the guns did clear US Customs. I have the other weapon numbers from the consignment and I've been flagging law-enforcement nodes on ICON, but nobody has a thing on Glock 17s.'

'Am I right in thinking the Glock 17 is the gun people were making so much noise about at one time? The gun that panic-merchants thought could escape airport X-ray detection?'

Mike nodded. 'There's a lot of plastic in its construction. But there's enough steel to show up on X-rays. What really grabs the enthusiasts is the seventeen-shot magazine.'

Mike tapped a picture of the Glock 17 up on to a screen.

'There's a lot going for it. It's hefty, it's accurate, and it's got enough rounds to let you do shot-clustering if that's what a job calls for.' Mike looked at Philpott. 'I'm just intrigued to know how the weapon got from the States to Yaqub Hisham.'

'And I'm intrigued to know why he shoved it in his mouth and took the back off his head just because four London bobbies were chasing him.'

'He probably didn't want to be arrested,' Mike said. 'Superstition and obsession are primary components of a fanatic's mental structure. They're also the elements that can undermine him. In my experience, a terrorist's superstition and fear often take the form of an abhorrence of being captured, of being *contained* on somebody else's terms. Remember in Rome, three years ago? I cornered a bullion hijacker, a Lebanese guy –'

'Shofar,' Philpott said.

'Shofar. I had the drop on him, he could do nothing but submit and get taken away. Except he was a fanatic. He didn't want to be arrested, not at any price. So before I knew it he'd shoved his wristwatch in his mouth and rammed it into his gullet. A heavy-duty Seiko with a steel bracelet and a casing four centimetres across. And boy did it wedge. He went blue and he was dead in less than a minute. All because somebody wanted to restrict his movement.'

Mike stood up slowly, rubbing his eyes.

'Are you all right?'

'I think I should get out of here soon. I'm starting to like the cloistered feel of the place, and I'm getting sleepy.'

'A refreshment break, that's the thing.' Philpott took a tiny cellular phone from his pocket and tapped a button. 'Then you can get on with tracking that gun. I'm sure it's important.' He put the phone to his ear. 'Miss Wellington? I wonder if you could bring something to sustain Mr Graham and myself? We're in SCS-One. Thank you.'

Five minutes later, as Philpott was pouring coffee, he noticed a strip of surgical tape across Mike Graham's knuckles.

'Have you been punching something harder than yourself?'

Mike flexed the hand. 'I took a corner too fast and had to

31

correct in a hurry. My hand brushed a projecting stone.'

'You really shouldn't go tearing about on motorbikes the way you do.'

It was something appropriate to say, and it was said with little enough emphasis to be easily ignored, if Mike chose.

'I don't tear about, sir. You know that.'

'Do I? I must have forgotten.'

'Even when I'm in a race I strive for the spiritual dimension,' Mike said, deadpan.

'Ah . . .'

'My goal is *oneness* with the machine, so that I can be part of the transcendental *fact* of its speed.'

'I see.'

'It's art. What's a little lost skin in pursuit of art? I mean, let's face it, when I'm on my bike I'm expressing my deepest urges and polishing my karma at the same time.'

'Michael. It was foolish of me not to realize all that.'

They laughed. Philpott handed Mike his coffee. For just a moment an edge of stiffness intruded. At sociable moments silences between them were awkward, because matters which stayed unmentioned were nevertheless always there.

'Still enjoying the serenity of Vermont on the weekends?'

'More and more,' Mike said.

'And you still like being on your own?'

'Yep. Just me, my TV for company, my pickup for transport, and my bike for death-defying art.'

Some years before, Mike's wife and son had been murdered by terrorists. He had been devastated, and the grief of his loss damaged him brutally. For a long time he was beyond consolation. Finally, when grief had run its course, he moved from New York to Vermont, and there he took up the solitary domestic life. With time he had gained a measure of tranquillity, though some women liked to think they still saw pain in those dark blue eyes.

The agony of Mike's loss was now a thing entirely of the past, but he was changed, and serious risk-taking was a feature of that change. Philpott privately believed that it was therapy: any ex-policeman knew that jeopardy wiped out restlessness.

'What's your instinct on this case?' Mike pointed at the screens. 'Do you get think we could see some action?'

'Paperwork action, maybe. A ground-covering investigation, with plenty of interviews, then a long, detailed report to tidy the whole thing up.'

Mike stared at him. 'You certainly know how to lift a guy's spirits.'

'On the other hand it could be a thrill-a-minute caper.' Philpott sipped his coffee. 'Let's see what Sabrina turns up. I just have a gut feeling this might be much bigger than we realize.'

FOUR

The receptionist had the kind of relentless smile that would weather any opposition. 'I assure you, Madame Reverdy, there is not a problem.' She pushed a registration card and a pen across the mahogany desktop. 'If you would care to fill this in, I'll get a porter to take your bag.'

Where the card asked for the guest's name Sabrina wrote *Louise Reverdy*, the maiden name of her maternal grandmother. She put her address as *28 Rue de la Grand Armée, Paris 75017, France.*

The receptionist came back with a small, thin, green-uniformed man who took up a protective stance beside Sabrina's suitcase. He smiled and bowed.

Sabrina pushed back the registration card and took the key from the receptionist.

'Thank you so much,' she said, revelling in the way she could impersonate her mother's accent, 'and let me say again, although you insist it is no trouble, I am deeply grateful for the way you have accommodated me at such short notice.'

'Not at all, Madame. I hope everything is to your satisfaction.'

The porter took Sabrina up in the lift to the third floor. He led the way along a passage carpeted in deep green Wilton. Outside her room he made a flourish with the key, turned it smoothly in the lock and pushed the door open.

'*Après vous, Madame,*' he said.

Sabrina looked surprised. '*Vous-êtes Français, m'sieur?*'

'No,' he said, following her into the room, ''fraid not. But I was good at French at school, and now and again I can't help trying it out. Sounded authentic, did it?'

'*Absolument!* Top marks.'

He beamed with pleasure. Sabrina handed him a five-pound

note and watched one small pleasure overlap another. Priming him had been easier than she imagined.

'Tell me,' she said as he turned to go, 'yesterday a friend passed this way in a taxi, and she tells me she saw police officers. Has there been trouble?'

The little man's features seemed to clench as he came back, head tilted confidentially. 'One of the guests,' he said, pointing upward. 'An American lady. She was the victim of a shooting. Nasty business.'

'She was shot here?' Sabrina managed a note of alarm without having to screech. 'In this hotel?'

'Oh no, no, ma'am, it happened over in Mayfair. But she was a guest here at the time.'

'Oh, how terrible. There will not be police marching about the place all night, I hope? I am such a light sleeper . . .'

'Not to worry,' the porter said, 'they've sealed the room and for the time being everything's quiet.' He made his little bow again. 'Have a peaceful night.'

'Thank you so much.'

When he had gone she kicked off her shoes and sat on the edge of the bed. She checked her watch: 10.28.

The minibar looked tempting, but she decided to wait until work was over.

Getting here had been a struggle. Nobody had warned her the last operational day at Hounslow could run into the evening. She had come out of a hostage-taking scenario at eight o'clock and got back to her room at the hostel a few minutes before nine. Since then it had been breakneck all the way. First she had transformed herself from tousled squalor to the simulation of a chic Frenchwoman visiting London. In the circumstances a disguise had not been strictly necessary, but she enjoyed changes of personality, and tried always to conduct herself according to Philpott's Rule One of Subterfuge, which he confided to her one tipsy evening at a UN reception: 'Be somebody else whenever you can, my dear, and always tell a lie even if the truth would sound better.'

Transformed to her own liking, she drove across town, put the car in an all-night car park, hailed a cab and presented herself

35

at the hotel, looking as if the most strenuous thing she had done all day was sign Amex slips.

She looked around her. This was a nice place. And it should be, since the tariff for one night was the same as a week's rent for a cottage in the Cotswolds. She had called the hotel before leaving Hounslow – delayed flight, staying one more night – and the receptionist promised to hold the one remaining room until eleven at the latest. It happened also to be a double room and there was no concession for single occupancy. Philpott would bleat about that.

She patted the mattress. What she wanted to do, more than anything, was sleep for eight hours solid. But she was here to work. She yawned and made herself stand up.

By the wardrobe she slipped off her dark blue jacket and hipsters, put them on a hanger and opened the suitcase. Inside was one other change of clothes, her NYPD worksuit and three bath towels to make up the weight. She put on the worksuit and a pair of black Nikes.

From the lid pocket of the suitcase she took a tool roll, a fibre optic torch, a plastic box with FIELD KEYMAKER stamped on the side, a Polaroid camera and a pair of thin latex gloves. She put the tool roll, the box and the camera on the bedside table and slipped the torch and gloves into her pocket. She closed the suitcase.

'Two hours twenty,' she said aloud as she lay down on the bed. She put her arms straight by her sides and let her hands lie open, palm upwards. She closed her eyes. 'Two hours twenty,' she said again, then fell asleep almost at once.

She woke up in rapid stages, first clambering out of a dream about being pawed by a policeman with sugar on his fingers; then she was entering an ante room just behind her own eyelids. Consciousness came and she was aware of pink translucence. She opened her eyes and brought up her wrist, peering at her watch. Five minutes to one. Not bad.

In the bathroom she splashed water on her face, patted it dry and went back to the bedroom. She put the tool roll and the box in her side pockets and looped the thong of the torch around her wrist.

Before she opened the door she put out the light. She stood for a minute just inside the doorway, listening. The place was quiet and dark. This was a hotel with a special reputation, an establishment where ladies could stay on their own. By now all the guests would be in bed; when Sabrina arrived, she noticed the bar was already deserted.

She closed her room door and walked soundlessly to the staircase at the end of the passage. The porter had pointed upwards when he talked about the shooting; there were six floors so she only had two to reconnoitre, at most. That was one blessing. The other was the kind of door locks they used.

The sealed room was on the sixth floor, and the sealing was figurative. There was a strip of yellow-and-black adhesive tape across the top of the door, another at the bottom, and a notice warning it would be a criminal offence for anyone to open the door, or attempt to open it, without the express permission of the Commissioner of the Metropolitan Police.

Sabrina went to the switchbox by the stairs and turned off the dim night lights along the passage. If she was disturbed and had to run for it, at least no one would see her face. She went back to the sealed room and shone the narrow torch beam on the lock. It was exactly like the others, a straightforward Yale, and the police had added no locks of their own.

She unfurled her tool roll on the carpet and took out a tiny pick and a torque wrench. The key-making kit in the box might still be needed if the dead woman's luggage turned out to have fancy locking arrangements.

Sabrina pocketed the tool roll and stood close to the door. She slid the torque wrench into the bottom of the key slot and with the other hand she inserted the pick, prong upwards, sliding it all the way to the back of the lock. She slowly withdrew it again, getting the feel of resistance from the springs pressing down on the pins.

Now she turned the wrench a fraction to the right and put the pick back in the lock, pushing it in all the way, not letting it touch the pins. Then she began pulling it out, applying steady upward force to the pins. The correct pressure had to be only a shade greater than the minimum needed to overcome the force of each spring. She stroked the pick over the farthest of the five pins, increasing the pressure on the wrench until the pin stuck. She brought the pick forward to the next pin and did the same. She repeated the manoeuvre with the third pin.

There was a sound along the corridor, a creak like boot leather. Or like an old door shrinking in the night air. Or like a million possible things. Sabrina remained frozen by the door, counting to a hundred before she moved again.

The next pin would not stay up when she probed it. This was not unusual: the pins at the front of a lock were often bevelled at the edges from simple wear. Sabrina kept the torque pressure fixed and began sliding the pick back and forward over the remaining two pins, scrubbing, as professionals called it. As the pick moved over the pins Sabrina gradually increased the upward pressure of the prong. Suddenly both pins slid up-wards and stuck. She turned the wrench another fraction and the door slid open, tearing softly away from the adhesive tape.

Sabrina pulled out the picking tools and pocketed them as she stepped into the room. She made sure the door was locked behind her, then she closed the heavy curtains and put on the overhead light.

There was always an eeriness about a room a person had planned to return to, but never did. Clothes had been laid out for the evening, bottles and jars were lined up in the bathroom, shoes stood in a row in the bottom of an open closet.

Sabrina assumed the police had touched nothing. It was also safe to assume they knew where everything was. She took out the Polaroid camera and photographed the room from several angles. She took close-ups of the distribution of items on the dressing table, the bathroom ledge and the closet shelves.

When she had leaned the pictures in a row along the top of the washbasin to dry, she pulled on the latex gloves and set to work.

Any search, to be effective, had to be strictly methodical, and no improbability had to be rejected. Sabrina had trained with an FBI Search Unit, people so skilled and so downright suspicious of human deviancy that nothing could be hidden from them. She began at the front of the room, by the door, and worked backwards to an imagined three-dimensional grid pattern.

In the course of an hour she learned several things about Emily Selby. For a start, she had had a mild but distinct case of obsessional neurosis. Her shoes in the closet were not only lined up neatly, they were positioned with their toes a precise distance from the back of the closet. Prior to noticing this, Sabrina had found a small cut-off piece of a plastic ruler carefully wrapped in tissue. It was 10 millimetres long, the precise distance of each well-polished toe from the wooden back panel of the closet.

Emily had also been an enthusiastic botanist, and in her notebook she had prepared a detailed itinerary for herself around Kew Gardens, which she had planned to visit on Friday.

Most fascinating of all, for Sabrina, was the fact Emily had been writing a traveller's guide to Israel. Two hundred pages of the hand-written manuscript were in her suitcase, together with working notes and a letter of encouragement from her publisher.

For ten minutes Sabrina speed-read the pages, looking for further insights on Emily. She picked up interesting facts about places like Ashdod, Gedera, Giv'atayim, Migdal and Nazareth, but none of it was likely to throw light on why the bookish, seemingly repressed political analyst had been murdered.

Sabrina was drawn back to the closet. Something there was wrong, the smallest thing perhaps . . .

She stood back and looked at the row of clothes, the jackets, skirts and slacks on their hangers, the lower edges aligned, the spacing between hangers just so, a monument to obsessive compulsion. Manically precise, a little masterpiece of symmetry. But yes, something was wrong. A beige jacket, squared and creaseless on its hanger, hung a fraction low on the near side. What was more, when Sabrina bent and peered at it, she saw a clear centimetre of loose thread at the hem of the jacket, just where it hung low.

She touched the hem and felt something hard. She took out the jacket and fingered the object. It was a key. It had been sewn into the hem.

Carefully, stitch by stitch, she unpicked the hem enough to fish out the key. It was made of brass with a toughened plastic top, the kind used to open high-security lockers and strong-boxes. Sabrina slipped it into her pocket.

By 2.15 she believed she had made a thorough search of the room. She stood by the door, letting her eyes do a slow pan, left to right, up and down. No area had been missed. She walked slowly round the place again, looked in the closets, drawers, bathroom cabinets and under the bed.

Still on her knees she paused and looked under the bed again. She saw something, paper, folded and tucked under a canvas strap supporting the mattress near the foot of the bed. Only one folded edge was showing, but she knew she should have seen it first time.

'For that,' she told herself, reaching for the paper, 'you get one drink instead of two.'

It was a sheet of computer printout paper with perforated sides, folded in four. She opened it and spread it flat on the carpet. There was a vertical row of printed names, with an address opposite each. At first sight the names appeared to be all male, and all German. At the bottom were a couple of pen-cilled lines in tidy handwriting she recognized from the manu-script: *Journal note: list completed 2/15/96, passed to ES, 2/24/96.*

Sabrina looked at the names again. They meant nothing to her. She folded the list and put it in her pocket. As an additional act of penance for missing the paper the first time, she made one more trawl of the room, swift but detailed. She found noth-ing new.

Finally she put everything back as it was, using the Polaroids to guide her. She put out the light, opened the curtains and left, locking the door behind her.

Ten minutes later, back in her room with a drink and the list beside her, she called Philpott on her mobile, using the scrambled satellite line. It was after ten o'clock in New York, but he was still at his desk.

'I assumed you'd like a progress bulletin on the Emily Selby case,' Sabrina said. 'I got into her room and picked up a couple of things.'

'Specifically?'

'A key and a list of names. Men, all German I think.'

'Do you have the list there?'

'Yes.'

'Read out a few of the names.'

'They're not in alphabetical order – looking at the addresses, I'd guess they're graded in order of their proximity to Berlin. Here goes. Gunther Blascher, Walter Höllerer, Johann Boumann, Andreas Wolff, Friedrich Schadow, Albrecht Schröder, Kurt Ditscher, Karl Schinkel –'

'That'll do. Fax it to my secure number.'

'Do the names mean anything?'

'We'll discuss it when you get back.' A phone was ringing. 'I'll talk to you soon. Just get that list to me.'

'Very good, sir.'

Sabrina thumbed the red button and put down the phone. She looked at her watch. There was hardly any night left. For a while she stood there, wondering if she should get in the tub or go straight to bed.

Tub, she decided. And no bed. At a pinch, a long hot soak could do the work of six hours' sleep. She could get herself dressed and ready for the day at a comfortable pace, take an early breakfast, read the morning paper and still be out on the street by 7.30.

She ran a hot bath and undressed as it filled. As she climbed in and sank up to her neck, the heat seeped smoothly into her muscles. She closed her eyes and her mind drifted. She thought of home, the reassurance and comfort of her own apartment in New York, her favourite weekend restaurant . . .

Abruptly she thought of lunch. Today. Her eyes opened. She had forgotten. Lunch with gooey-eyed Inspector Lowther.

'*Merde*,' she groaned, in a perfect replica of her mother's voice.

FIVE

At 9.10 a.m. on Monday, C.W. Whitlock downloaded the final piece of information to expand the details of the list Philpott had given him on Friday morning. The job had been painstaking, frustrating and exhausting. Worse than that, the expenditure of a whole weekend on the work had put a strain on Whitlock's private life. Following a hurried and stressful cancellation of a Saturday-night dinner party, his wife was no longer communicating.

After the fourth attempt to reach her that morning he put down the telephone and saw the final lines of text scroll up on the computer screen. He sat back and yawned. Feeling old, he decided, was a matter of how much hope you abandoned. For twenty-four hours he had felt rundown and sinking, aware of no clear end. Seeing the long job finished did not quite lift his spirits, but there was a measure of relief. Relief, in turn, fired a tiny hope: things between himself and Carmen might work out with a minimum of fighting. 'And a pig will go flapping over the UN complex any minute,' he said aloud.

Whitlock was a man people tended to like on sight, a native Kenyan with skin a girl once called light umber, and gold-brown eyes his mother swore would break many hearts. His skin colour was part of a legacy from his grandfather, a white British Army officer, whose genes had also conferred a strong jaw and a firm mouth, which C.W. softened with a moustache.

He leaned forward, tapped the PRINT button and checked the clock. He was up against the deadline. Too often, it seemed, he was handed jobs with no slack in the schedule. He picked up the internal telephone and dialled 3 for Security.

'Calvin? Has Mr Philpott arrived yet?'

'He signed in five minutes ago.'

42

'Thanks.'

'Sorry to dash your hopes.'

'That's all right, Calvin. The day he does turn up late, I'll buy you lunch.' He put down the phone. 'This,' he sighed, 'is no life for a sensitive boy.'

He was Oxford-educated, a former soldier with wide experience as an officer in the Kenya Intelligence Corps. He had been recruited into UNACO by Philpott himself, and was now the longest serving member of Task Force Three. On two occasions Philpott had openly acknowledged that Whitlock was the most versatile and well-informed of his active agents – a distinction, Whitlock believed, that invited abuse.

As the last piece of information came off the printer he signalled Interpol's National Central Bureau in Berlin and switched momentarily to voice contact. He thanked the duty information controller for his help and expressed the hope that he could return the favour.

Two minutes later he walked into the washroom with the accumulated data in a manila folder under his arm. Mike Graham was there, standing by the basins, bending to see himself in the mirror as he combed his hair. His reflection nodded at Whitlock, who looked grim.

'Morning, C.W. Nice to see a guy who can start the week with a grin.'

Whitlock put down his folder and rolled back his shirtsleeves. He washed his hands and face, re-tied his tie and buffed his toecaps at the polisher. He came back to the basins and leaned close to the mirror, pulling up one eyelid, then the other.

'I can't decide if I'm anaemic, or if clinical depression has crept in.'

'I hear you've been on all weekend.'

'The Selby case. I did a workup on a list of German citizens, most of them hard to nail. Not a criminal record among them, so I had to trespass on a lot of legitimate secrecy.'

'Nobody does it better.'

'Go ahead,' Whitlock sighed, 'patronize me. I thrive on that.'

Mike put on his jacket as he went to the door. 'Meeting in five minutes,' he said. 'Don't be late.'

'I'm moving as fast as I can . . .'

Three sides of UNACO's briefing room were panelled in dark shiny wood. The fourth was a ceiling-to-floor window looking out on the East River. The centrepiece of the room was a long polished table with three chairs at each side and one at the end near the window. On the table were notepads, pencils, glasses and two water pitchers. A long ebony sideboard against the right-hand wall had a steel tray with coffee, tea and a Thermos jug of chilled Coke.

Philpott was already there when Mike Graham and C.W. Whitlock walked in. He stood by the window reading a fax. Lucy Dow sat at the end of the table nearest the door. Lucy was a tall, solemn-faced young woman, an authority on Arab affairs with three years experience in Lebanon as a field operative. Sabrina was there too, pouring coffee.

'Welcome home,' Mike said. 'How was England?'

'Strenuous.'

'Did you remember my Bath Olivers?' Whitlock said. 'Or did they get forgotten in the whirl of events?'

Sabrina pointed to a Fortnum and Mason's bag on the sideboard. 'Six packets. Enough to turn up the flame of nostalgia till it hurts.'

'Bless you.' Whitlock pecked Sabrina's cheek. 'Those biscuits are all I really miss about my student days.'

'You must have really lived it up,' Mike said. 'What did you do – crumble them into a chillum and smoke them?'

'Right.' Philpott looked up from his fax and pointed at the table. 'Sit down, will you? I've a busy day so we must keep this brief.'

Whitlock and Mike brought coffee to the table and sat opposite each other as they always did. Sabrina sat somewhere different every time. She did that in case anyone imagined there was significance in the way the only permanent female member of the unit sat in relation to the other two operatives and to the chief. Today she sat at the top of the table on the same side as Whitlock, adjacent to Philpott.

44

'You're all familiar with the superficial details of the Emily Selby shooting,' Philpott said, opening a folder in front of him. 'Lucy is here this morning to add anything that might help in formulating at least the nucleus of a procedure. I can add to what you all know about the case by telling you that early on Saturday, a call was received here at the UN from Colonel Wolrich of Security Liaison, working out of the US Embassy in London. He talked about the case with the Deputy Secretary General of the Security Council. As a result of their discussion, the Selby inquiry has been made our business.'

'So my weekend wasn't a complete waste,' Whitlock said.

'Why did they pass it straight to UNACO?' Lucy asked.

'Well, there's the hard evidence the gunman was a trained assassin, and a high-profile one at that. There's the fact that he travelled West to kill an American who happened to be a Jew, and who happened to be working for the government, right inside the White House. That bare-bones synopsis alone makes this our kind of case. We have a strong enough indication of international crime, with the attendant danger of escalation, to warrant UNACO intervention.'

'I can vouch for the killer's prominent profile,' Lucy said, crossing and uncrossing her long legs as she spoke. 'They were very proud of Yaqub Hisham in the Lebanon.'

'Ever meet him?' Sabrina said.

'He wasn't a social animal, but yes, I was in the same big tent as him one time, along with maybe fifty others, while I was doing a hill-gypsy routine for cover. He was nothing unusual as terrorists go, except he was maybe luckier than most, or more foolhardy. Until he got too hot a target for the Israelis, he was really the main man. Scourge of the Jews, they called him. When things warmed up and Mossad started closing in, it was a top Arab surgeon that volunteered to change Yaqub's face. A big freebie, carried out in one of the finest hospitals in Egypt.'

'Was it business as usual after the face-change?' Philpott said.

Lucy shook her head. 'Mossad got leaked a picture of him. From Yaqub's point of view it was a waste of time. He ended up with a face he thought wasn't nearly as pretty as his real one, and the way things turned out he might as well have hung

45

on to the old face. He had to get back into hiding. That's why he went to Morocco. Hard for the avenging Israelis to get at him there.'

Philpott looked at Mike. 'Fill us in on what you learned.'

Mike gave them a summary on the Arab's unexceptional stay in London, up to the time he killed Emily Selby and then shot himself. 'Lucy could tell us more, but the things we most need to know are his reason for killing Emily Selby, and the source of the gun he used. So far, those things remain a mystery.'

'Sabrina?'

Sabrina explained how she got into Emily Selby's hotel room, and what she found during her search. 'For a tourist Emily carried a lot of stuff, but the key and the list were the only items out of the ordinary. The key wouldn't be half so interesting if it hadn't been stitched into her jacket.'

'What impressions did you get about the woman herself?' Philpott asked.

'Tidy and well organized, though perhaps to a pathological extent.' Sabrina explained about the piece of ruler she had found, and about clothes stored by colour, bottles in the bathroom regimented by size. 'The kind of clothes she wore indicated she had good fashion sense, but she was also reticent, modest probably, because she had what I call an extravagance-shut-off. She had limits and barriers, she showed flair but with enough of a conservative streak to stop herself from being flamboyant.'

'Overall impression?' Philpott said.

'That she was intelligent, gifted and inquisitive, with a tragedy at the centre of her life, supported by the evidence of her compulsive neurosis,' Sabrina said. 'Compulsive rituals, notably in the behaviour patterns of intelligent people, indicate that they use rigid and complicated routines to divert their minds from areas of pain.'

C.W. was nodding. So was Lucy.

'Emily Selby's history supports that interpretation,' Sabrina went on. 'Her employment record, which I read as soon as I got here this morning, shows she was widowed three years ago. She suffered a compound tragedy, because her husband and father died at the same time and in the same place.'

Philpott tapped the photocopy in front of him. 'Lake Cayuga, Ithaca, New York State,' he said. 'A fishing accident. Verdict of drowning on both men. We will look into the details. Now, Sabrina, did you find anything at all to link Emily Selby with Erika Stramm, the woman with her in the picture?'

'I'm assuming the pencilled initials ES at the bottom of the list stand for Erika Stramm. But that's all I have. I'm still working on a connection.'

Philpott looked at Whitlock. 'Tell us how you fared with the list.'

Whitlock had his folder open, the sheets of information spread out before him. 'It's a list of thirty German names and addresses, and all the names are male,' he said. 'I sifted the criminal records first, but there was nothing. Whatever else they are, these are law-abiding citizens. Then I had to go the slow route, with the help of Interpol. Everybody was very helpful, and eventually I got expansion – as much as is known – on every name on the list.'

'What's their connection?' Mike said.

'Nothing worthy of the name. They don't appear to be related by blood or commercial ties. They're apparently prospering in various quiet ways, but that's all they seem to have in common. Well, except for one factor. We know that fifteen of the men on the list were adopted. They were war orphans.'

'And the others?' Philpott said.

'No childhood records extant. Destroyed by enemy action. The bombing of Dresden and Berlin and countless other communities wiped out millions of official histories. It simultaneously provided a blank slate for the creation of others.' C.W. spread his hands. 'About two-thirds of the population records collated in Germany during the immediate post-war years are just not reliable, from an investigative standpoint.'

'What's the men's professional range?' Sabrina asked.

'Everything from bookbinding and carpet-tile manufacture to medicine and law – there are two doctors and two lawyers – the rest are one-offs. Interpol tried a few test searches with the records of marriages but no links showed up.'

Mike asked if they were all about the same age.

'It's tight, between fifty-nine and sixty-five years old.'

'I think there might be something in the fact there are so many orphans,' Sabrina said. She saw Mike shake his head. 'At least I won't close my mind to the possibility,' she added, giving it an edge.

'And in the meantime,' Philpott said, 'I won't make any wild guesses about the significance of this list. However...' He pushed forward a copy of the list and pointed to a name halfway down the page. 'I'm concerned that this man's name appears on it.'

The others turned their heads to peer at the list.

'His name is Andreas Wolff. He's an Austrian computer systems engineer and program designer.'

'I can see his face now,' Mike said.

The others looked at him.

'Youthful middle-aged, short salt-and-pepper haircut, steel-framed glasses and a great smile.'

Philpott nodded slowly. 'What are you trying to tell us, Michael?'

'His picture's on the boxes of a very expensive series of computer games. They're on sale all over the place.'

'Mike spends a lot of time in toy shops,' Sabrina said.

'This guy is a king of contemporary games design. He specializes in hybrids: dungeons and dragons, arcade stuff and straight crime detection rolled into one. It must be a great formula, the games sell fast and they ain't cheap.'

'Andreas Wolff is certainly well known for his recreational software,' Philpott said dryly. 'However, in security and law-enforcement circles, which is to say *serious* circles, he's also an eminent individual. He created the software that protects all the data carried by ICON.'

ICON – the International Criminal Observation Network – was the main criminal intelligence service in the West. Criminal records, fingerprint files, *modus operandi* profiles and databases, plus details of hundreds of current and impending police operations were carried and interchanged on the ICON network. With appropriate clearance and the necessary keyboard skills, an operator could call up the details of virtually any crime, any criminal or any current police record in a matter of seconds.

'The man on the list is definitely the same Andreas Wolff?' Sabrina said.

'The address is the same,' Philpott said, 'and I see from C.W.'s information that the age is right, too. Wolff is fifty-eight. I repeat, I won't make wild guesses about the significance of the list, but it's worrying that Wolff's name comes up in a *mysterious* context at a time like this.'

'Like what?' Sabrina said.

'Well, as you know, the complexities of ICON have multiplied in the past year. What you don't know is that as more law-enforcement agencies have committed their data to the network, Andreas Wolff has become indispensable. ICON's continued existence depends on his expertise.'

'You mean,' Mike said, 'that half the world's police and national security organizations have been silly enough to put all their eggs in one basket? How come?'

'It's not an ideal state of affairs,' Philpott said, 'and nobody planned it that way. Wolff has become so closely linked to the system, and to determining its rate of development, that he's pulled ahead of others in the field. No one else understands his programming routines or his security protocols.'

'So if anything were to happen to Wolff,' Whitlock said, 'archive security could stagnate and the files would soon be vulnerable.'

'That's precisely what I'm saying. The potential gain from hacking into ICON is vast. It's inestimable. And it pains me to tell you that the possibility of getting inside ICON is the driving force behind a lot of developments in electronic crime.'

'Do hackers stand a serious chance?' Lucy said.

'Oh, yes, they have a chance and they've taken it. ICON's security has already been breached.'

Lucy looked startled. So did Sabrina.

'Twice in three weeks,' Philpott said. 'Each time it was open for only a microsecond before alternative encryption routines cut in, but the warning is clear enough. The current generation of safeguards is being eroded, and we're not over-stocked with alternatives.'

'Who's doing it?' Lucy said.

'Lord knows who. I shouldn't think it's any one group. It suits criminal organizations anywhere in the world to have a hole knocked in law enforcement. Hackers try all the time, and they're fed big financial inducements to keep trying.'

'So what's being done?' Mike said.

'For the moment, Andreas Wolff provides emergency ICON security by changing the custodian routines at twelve-hour intervals. He will do this until his new generation of self-enhancing safeguards are test-run and installed.'

'So if Wolff leaves the picture for any reason,' Sabrina said, 'the whole of ICON security collapses?'

'It could be that extreme,' Philpott said. 'We could shut down ICON temporarily in an emergency, but the disruption would be catastrophic. It would be nearly as bad as having the system broken into. The new security arrangements will change every-thing. ICON will in effect become auto-secure. But until then we remain at serious risk. Without Wolff's support, records and operational strategies could be uncloaked long enough to bring this organization's security to its knees.'

Philpott stopped abruptly and looked at his watch.

'Right.' He stood. 'That's it. I have to go. Compare notes. Make sure you all know the same amount about the case. The facts as they stand present us with a paradox, but in theory the way forward is simple. Find out what links the names on that list and you will have a line on why Emily Selby was killed. When you know that, you'll know what you're up against. Lucy, thanks for your input.'

Halfway to the door he stopped. 'I may change my mind later, but in the meantime I think Sabrina should dig up the whole story on Emily Selby, with special reference to her association with Erika Stramm.'

'Shouldn't we maybe get somebody to interview Stramm right away?' Whitlock said.

'No. I want us to know something about the relationship before she feeds us her version. Mike, I want you to get to work on that key Sabrina found. C.W., keep trying for a linking factor between the names on the list.'

Philpott strode to the door and pulled it open. 'In order to proceed we need a picture, something with shape and features we can identify. Do your best for me on this one.'

Mike and C.W. muttered assurances. Sabrina nodded.

'I deserve it, after all,' Philpott said, and left.

SIX

'Now, tell me honestly, what did you think? Were you bored? Or did you enjoy the visit as much as you told the guide you did?'

Karl Sonnemann, one week off his sixty-fourth birthday, stood smiling like a boy on the street outside Goethe's birthplace in Frankfurt. His hands rested on the shoulders of Charlotte Gustl, a slender, shapely Münster girl with hair the colour of butter. Charlotte was twenty-two, one of Karl's literature students at the Johann Wolfgang von Goethe University. As of last night she was technically his mistress, too.

'I truly, truly loved the place,' Charlotte said. 'I'm sure I shall dream about it.'

'I did feel that a visit to the birthplace might touch a chord in you,' Karl said.

'Seeing that little room where he slept. Where he had his dreams, oh . . .' Charlotte clasped her hands under her chin. 'I could feel, or I imagined I could feel, the surge of the forces that empowered him. This has given me a new perspective on Goethe, Professor.'

'Karl,' he said, beaming at her. 'I told you, call me Karl.'

'Very well.' She coloured a little as he slid his arm through hers. 'I seem to have moved forward *years* in the space of twenty-four hours.'

As they walked towards the taxi rank he squeezed her arm, thinking how alike they all were, the girls he picked to be his special blossoms for a term or two. How much alike in the way they looked, in what they said, in how they gave their bodies to him, season after season . . .

How much alike, yet he never tired of them, and he found each one breathtakingly new. When he turned fifty a friend had winked at him and asked him how long now, how long before he would have to defer to his years and abandon his little hobby. At the time, Karl had said he would never cease, not until he died, and he said it wishing it were true. Now he felt it might indeed be true; he would simply never stop. The girls showed no more resistance as time passed, he still managed to charm them and, just as important, he could identify the ones he had charmed the most, and so take advantage.

'I thought we would have a leisurely lunch at Alexander's,' he said, 'and then go back to the university, where my only tutorial of the day is with a Fräulein Charlotte Gustl, if I'm not mistaken.'

She chuckled. It was a moist throaty sound, a variation of the sounds she made against his ear in the night, under crisp sheets at the Excelsior Hotel. For a moment Karl found himself overcome by the swiftness of one sound conjuring up another, and by the sharp, tactile memory of her warmth and closeness . . .

'There's that young man again,' Charlotte said.

'Which one?'

'The one I said was watching you at the birthplace.'

Karl turned. The young man was looking in a shop window a few metres away. Karl had noticed him as they went into Goethe's house, standing by the edge of the pavement, looking aimless, or trying to. For a terrible moment Karl considered the possibility that the young man, for all his fair-haired, clear-eyed wholesomeness, was a detective. What if Ursula, after so many years, had begun to suspect, and had set this snooper to find out for sure?

Karl turned away, smiling at the wildness of his imagination. 'I think he has taken your fancy, that young man. You seem to be tracing his movements.'

'Oh! That's not true!' Charlotte looked genuinely offended. 'How could you think such a thing?'

She stopped talking abruptly and stared over Karl's shoulder. He turned and saw the young man had stepped over beside them. His face was very serious and purposeful. He glanced beyond them to the taxi rank, then looked directly at Karl.

'You are Professor Sonnemann, is that correct?'

'Why do you ask?' Karl said stiffly.

'Well, I was sure, actually,' the young man said, blinking rapidly, gesturing with one hand, the other buried in his jacket pocket. 'But mistakes cannot be rectified afterwards, as they say in the supermarkets.'

'What do you want with us?'

'You *are* Professor Sonnemann? Professor Karl Sonnemann?'

'Yes, yes,' Karl snapped. 'So what of it?'

'I have a message,' the young man said.

His face became very grave. He took his hand from his pocket. He was holding a long, straight butcher's trussing needle.

'This is for Yitzhak Brenner.'

He thrust the needle deep into the side of Karl's neck. Charlotte screamed. Karl felt nothing. He was only aware that suddenly his control of himself was gone. Charlotte pulled her arm free of Karl's and ran to the taxi rank.

The young man did not follow. He stood staring into Karl's shocked face. The eyes were already glassy. His whole frame trembled as arterial blood left his body in a surge, draining him of life. He let out a rasping breath, his mouth foaming as blood surged from his neck down over his fine woollen overcoat.

Charlotte was at the rank, howling and pleading. Karl sank to his knees, coughing blood. His face looked waxen and artificial.

Two taxi drivers were coming, both of them running. The young man wiped his fingers on the shoulder of Karl's coat. He turned, pressed his elbows to his sides and started to run. He ducked round a corner and disappeared into a throng of pedestrians.

One taxi driver tried to follow him. The other knelt by Karl. He was on his back on the pavement, completely still, the big needle jutting from his throat.

SEVEN

The following morning Sabrina Carver took an early flight to Washington DC. It was her intention to interview, as casually as possible, the known friends and associates of Emily Selby, with a view to gaining the kind of insight the records didn't show. Ahead of her visit UNACO administration made an appointment for her at the White House, where she hoped to talk to Emily's former colleagues under the guise of a police investigator. Her laminated ID card, exquisitely printed in muted, solemn colours, identified her as an officer of the United States National Central Bureau of the International Criminal Police Commission. It was the stiff-necked official way of declaring she was an agent of Interpol.

At White House Reception she was met by a brisk young woman who showed her to a visitors' waiting room. There, after a few minutes, she was joined by the Information Officer's number-two assistant, Kevin Riley. He was a firm man, entrenched in his procedures.

'White House security regulations demand that you stay in this room at all times during your visit,' he told Sabrina. 'If you leave the room for any reason whatsoever, you must be accompanied by a member of White House Security. Of course, we will do all we can to accommodate you within the rules governing your visit here.'

'Thank you.'

'Since your people emphasized you're not here on official investigative business, we've let people make up their own minds whether they want to be interviewed or not. Three colleagues of Mrs Selby have shown a willingness to talk to you. The first should be along shortly. Naturally, we want to do all we can to clear Emily's name of any shadow.'

The first to arrive was Janice Cleary, a short, overweight woman in her forties. Janice wore the kind of perfume that surrounded her with a cloying miasma. She wheezed as she sat down and took a moment to rearrange her voluminous clothing. When she spoke, her voice had a high, childish register.

'I was probably Emily's closest friend, professionally,' she told Sabrina. 'Four years ago we worked on the Herzog project together. I think our friendship cemented around that time.'

'What was the Herzog project?'

'It was named after the President of Israel at that time, Chaim Herzog. He was looking for a solid basis for an Arab–Israeli peace settlement, and the feeling here was that he could use a shade more support from the USA, which wasn't officially all that cosy with Israel at the time. Emily and me, we did what we could to high-profile non-political areas of common ground between the two nations.'

'How did you do that, exactly?'

'We used press and radio outlets to boost awareness of cultural exchange programmes, we got an information booklet together showing how alike many of the American and Israeli down-home aspirations were. The aim, overall, was to pass on the message, to both nations, that, political differences aside, we were really natural friends. Emily really put her heart into that programme and, as I said, we became real close.'

'Tell me about Emily as a person,' Sabrina said. 'Did she socialize much? Go to parties, the theatre, concerts?'

'Not after Desmond died,' Janice said. 'Not too much before that either, I don't think . . .'

'She took it badly, her husband dying?'

'Well, wouldn't you?'

'Was she a long time getting over it?'

'She never got over it.'

'She told you that.'

'No need. I could tell. The change in her. She became with-drawn. Reclusive. She developed little daily rituals of work that involved only herself, which is easy to do in this line. It's how you get to be a specialist, and Emily was our shiniest specialist of all. On the ball, always.'

Sabrina was sure Janice had never been as close to Emily Selby as she thought; crass people often mistake politeness for friendliness. They talked for a few more minutes, long enough for Sabrina to be sure that whatever the extent of Emily's social life, Janice Cleary knew nothing about it. Sabrina thanked her and apologized for taking her away from work.

A minute after Janice left, a young man came in. He was tall, with a narrow mouth that looked incapable of smiling. He looked at Sabrina cautiously from pale sunken eyes. He was Joe Dexter. For five years, he said, he had been a research assistant working for three senior political analysts, and Emily Selby had been one of them.

He talked for ten minutes about Emily, without once needing to be prompted. He described her working methods, her talent for organization, her patience with other people, her unending devotion to her job. He thought the world of her, he said.

As he continued to talk, Sabrina realized he meant that literally: he thought the world of Emily Selby, and although it appeared Emily had regarded him as no more than a valued assistant, he had obviously been obsessed with her. But he had said nothing, he had never betrayed to Emily any sign of his emotional response to her. It would have been unprofessional to do that, he said.

Just like me and Mike, Sabrina thought, startling herself. She had confronted a buried truth, not for the first time, but, as always, she was inclined to shy away. She bowed her head over her notepad and closed her eyes for a moment.

Just like me and Mike.

Nothing had ever been declared, or demonstrated. Usually, it was the opposite of affection that prevailed. They were rivals on the same team, antagonists in a single cause. At times there was a strength of antipathy that felt like hatred, at least on her side. Yet she knew she kept the lid on a richness of feeling that would have engulfed him, smothered him. And she suspected, without having examined the suspicion, that he kept something suppressed, too.

Joe Dexter fell silent, and Sabrina thanked him for his time. He left without another word.

She gazed at her notebook. Again, she had been told nothing that threw any real light on Emily Selby. She accepted that she might be going back to New York empty-handed. It would be best to get used to the idea now and work on her defence against Philpott's displeasure.

And then the telephone beside her rang. A woman introduced herself as Dilys Craig. She was a former colleague of Emily's, she said, and she would love to talk to Sabrina about her, but right now she was tied up.

'It's an unexpected job, something I can't get out of,' she said. 'How about we meet outside later today? For coffee, say?'

'That would be fine,' Sabrina said, 'if it's no trouble. Where will I meet you?'

'Harvey and Hannah's,' Dilys said. 'Go down Pennsylvania Avenue till you come to the Willard Hotel complex, look for the Occidental Grill, and it's right alongside. Four-thirty. Does that suit?'

'Perfectly,' Sabrina said.

At 4.32 Dilys Craig walked into the coffee shop, looking stunning in a checked Escada jacket and grey pencil skirt. She came straight to the table where Sabrina sat. She was tall with large hazel eyes and skin smoothed to perfection by cosmetics. Her hair was cut short and had been tinted a shade somewhere between chestnut and auburn. She was not young, tiny crow's-feet were visible at the corners of her eyes and mouth, but she had impressive poise and energy.

'I got you coffee,' Sabrina said, pointing to the cup opposite hers. 'The woman seemed to know what you like.'

'She's a doll,' Dilys said, sitting down, crossing elegant sheened legs. 'Nice to meet you, Sabrina.' She took a sip of coffee. 'Shall we get right to it?'

'Sure.'

'Well, let me tell you right off, I was as close to being friendly with Emily as you could get. But that wasn't very close. She was good at keeping the world at a distance.' Dilys took out a matt black cigarette case. 'Mind if I smoke?'

'I don't mind, no, but I thought –'

'It's banned in here? Right. That makes me enjoy it all the more. I can smoke so long as there are no other customers.' She lit up, and sighed. 'This all seems so unreal, I still can't quite believe that she's gone. But I obviously want to help your investigation in any way I can.'

'I'm trying to get background on Emily's off-duty life,' Sabrina said. 'Did you ever meet her socially?'

'Oh, yes, often. That was when Desmond was around, of course. He lived in Ithaca teaching at Cornell during the week of course, but would come down to Washington on week-ends. Or Emily would go up there. Anyway, they used to go to functions here in DC and so did I, usually with whoever I was seeing at the time, so we met outside office hours on a fairly regular basis.'

'Did you meet any of her friends, anyone not associated with her work here?'

'No,' Dilys shook her head. 'I don't think they had friends, not in the sense of relationships with people they saw regularly, nothing like that. They had each other, you see, and that seemed to be enough. And of course there was Emily's father, whom Desmond lived with on the campus at Cornell. I know she was deeply fond of her father.'

'Did she ever mention a woman called Erika?'

'Erika Stramm?' Dilys smiled, catching the look of surprise cross Sabrina's face. 'She was her cousin.'

'Cousin?'

'Well, second cousin, actually.'

Sabrina wondered how the resources of UNACO hadn't managed to determine that Emily and Erika were blood relations.

'Emily's father was born Johannes Stramm,' Dilys said. 'But he changed his name in the concentration camp where he spent three years of the war. He did it to lose his identity and save his life. When he came to America he kept the assumed name. He was known here as Johannes Lustig, so Lustig was Emily's maiden name. Erika is his cousin's daughter. I knew about Erika, sure. So did some of the White House administration. It wasn't really a black mark, having a semi-violent lefty for a relative – not if you were someone as universally respected as Emily. It

59

certainly isn't the kind of fact that gets entered on a person's record these days. Too tackily McCarthy-ish, you know?'

Sabrina noted with interest Erika Stramm's established reputation as an active leftist terrorist. 'Do you know anything about the people Emily associated with after her husband died?'

Dilys shrugged elegantly with one shoulder. 'She was very close about that. I had the feeling her circle of acquaintances shrank to near nothing. That happens a lot to widows.'

'I guess so. Tell me more about her as a person.'

Dilys sucked on the cigarette and peered at the tiny Gucci watch on her wrist. 'One thing that needs saying about Emily is, she was selfless. We've all heard of it. Selflessness. But Emily was the only person I actually met who had it. If two sets of interests were at issue, she would always disregard her own.'

'I get the impression she was something of a saint.'

'Jeez, no.' Dilys made a face. 'Who said she was a saint, for heaven's sake?'

'Nobody did. But what I've been told about her adds up to a picture of an unusually good person.'

'She had some of the characteristics, I suppose, but she didn't have the sickly bits that would qualify her for sainthood. What she was, I suppose, was a good scout. She was withdrawn but she was never remote, she was always there for you, and she would really put herself out. She was shy, too, but she never tried to play it like she was mysterious. Do you see what I mean?'

'I think so.'

Sabrina watched the woman behind the counter make a cappuccino with a head on it an inch high. It was fluffy but firm at the same time. She wished she could do that. Whatever she did wrong, the head always came out nice and creamy, but also flat as a pancake.

'Dilys, do you have any theory about why she was killed?'

'I was getting around to asking you that.'

'We only know how. We haven't a clue why.'

'Well. Given the way she was – good-hearted, generous, also a woman who kept pretty much to herself . . .' Dilys did her one-shoulder shrug. 'I'd say it was either a bad mistake on the part of the killer, or it had something to do with her cousin.'

'Erika Stramm.'

'Right.'

'Do you know if they saw much of each other?'

'In recent times they corresponded a lot. And it was serious business.'

'What kind of business?'

'I don't know. But Joe Dexter – you spoke to him, right? – he used to be the mailman.'

'What do you mean?'

'Joe has a kind of quiet life. He lives alone, doesn't know enough about human nature to tussle with it, so he gets his fulfilment being a sysop.'

'I should know what that is.'

'System operator,' Dilys said. 'On a dial-up bulletin board service. He sits by his board most evenings. The board is a computer with a whole clutch of information that people can download or add to, and sections where members can have written discussions with each other. The sysop's the bulletin board manager.'

'How does someone communicate with the board?'

'It's reached with a phone and a modem. The thing is, Joe can receive e-mail on his bulletin board from anywhere in the world, via the Internet. So he received e-mail for Emily from Erika, and Emily would send stuff through Joe to Erika's electronic mailbox, wherever it is.'

'She talked to you about that?'

'No, and I didn't ask her,' Dilys said. 'But if you want to see the irregularities in a pattern all you have to do is stare long enough, right? About six, seven months ago, I began to think Joe was no longer just researching for Emily. So I watched. There were definitely new and much more frequent transactions between them. That was the change in the pattern.'

'What did you do?'

'I cornered Joe and pumped him. He admitted he carried mail back and forward, but he had no idea what it was. The messages were coded, and he never tried to jemmy the code.'

'I can believe it.'

'Sure. He had too much respect for Emily to do anything like that. I think he was in love with her.'

'Do you think he suspected he was doing something wrong?'

'No, not at all. He believed what he was doing was confidential, just plain private. He didn't even think he had been secretive the way he handled the e-mail traffic. How he looked at it was, he had just been discreet.'

Dilys drained her cup and stood up. 'Listen,' she said, nodding in the direction of two customers who had taken a table nearby, 'I'll get us more coffee, but do you mind if we go out on the little veranda there to drink it?'

'You need a smoke?'

'Have pity. I'm an addict.'

'No problem.'

They took their fresh coffee to a small table at the end of the veranda, beside a canvas sheet tied between two uprights to make a windbreak.

Dilys said, 'When I stop to think about this, it makes me laugh.' She cupped her hand around the lighter and puffed several times, sending up a big flame on the last drag. She sat back and exhaled slowly. 'The ironies. As you get older they accumulate like luggage. Every day, at some point, I will do this. I will go out in the fresh air, so I can have an opportunity to fill my lungs with smoke.'

Sabrina tasted her coffee, waiting for Dilys to volunteer whatever she still wanted to say about Emily Selby.

'Have you ever been married, Sabrina?'

'Never.'

'I have. Twice. And divorced twice. Each break-up was a wrench, even though I was at the point of hatred in one case and disgust in the other. I was a long time recovering, both times. I thought of that when I tried to imagine what Emily went through, with her husband actually *dead*, the man who happened to be what she loved most in the world. God . . .'

'Her father, too.'

'She talked to me about it.'

'About her father?'

62

'About the two men dying.' Dilys drew on the cigarette and blew smoke out over the veranda. 'She also asked me not to say anything to anybody.' Dilys looked straight at Sabrina. 'Maybe it's important now that I do.'

Sabrina waited.

'I think she talked to me because she had to spill it to somebody. It seemed like a straightforward tragedy. Her husband Desmond and her father were out fishing on Lake Cayuga, which is inside the campus at Cornell, and within view of the house Desmond and Emily's father lived in. Emily was taking a week's vacation up there at the time. On the afternoon it happened, she came back from the university library with a stack of references for a book she was working on, and from the sitting-room window she could see the empty boat out on the lake. Her first thought, she told me, was that it had drifted. Des and Dad, she assumed, were having a couple of quiet ones at the tavern, like they sometimes did at that time of day.

'But it dawned on Emily there were no signs in the house that the men had come back from the trip. She looked everywhere. Finally, when she got frightened and was frantic with worry, she called the police. They mounted a search straight away and they found the bodies around sunset.'

'It happens,' Sabrina said. 'I had a school friend died the same way.'

'Me too, a cousin. The boat capsized, he was in heavy fishing clothes and couldn't swim as far as the shore.'

'But the accident wasn't what Emily asked you to keep quiet about, was it?'

'No.' Dilys flipped away her cigarette and lit another. 'After it happened Emily's neighbours, her colleagues, the authorities at Cornell and the police were all saying the same thing. It was what we just said – it was the kind of accident that's always happening. But Emily didn't believe it was an accident at all.'

'Did she have any reason?'

'The pathologist who did the autopsies gave her one. His evidence was skimmed at the inquest. There was pressure on the system, cases were backed up, so it was more like a rubber-stamping than a hearing. Cause of death, drowning. No evidence

63

was brought to show that the deaths could have been anything but a mishap. But the pathologist tried to object, he had misgivings and he wanted to air them. No dice. Emily heard him complain to a police officer that the inquest had been rushed, and she went to see him.'

Dilys broke off and pointed to her cup. 'Look, I know I'm a sad old thing, but the truth is I'm also addicted to caffeine. If you wouldn't mind hanging on . . .'

She made to get up but Sabrina insisted it was her turn. She went inside and asked for two more coffees. Before she returned to the veranda she went to the rest room and put through a call to UNACO on her mobile. Philpott's secretary came on. Sabrina gave her the names and rough date of the Selby–Stramm boating accident, and asked her to get a printout of the autopsy report.

She walked slowly back with the brimming cups and sat down opposite Dilys.

'OK,' she said. 'Tell me.'

Dilys explained that Emily had gone to the hospital where the pathologist worked as a teaching consultant. At first he had been reluctant to speak to her, because in his view, as an accredited Medical Examiner for the State of New York, he would be committing a breach of ethics if he expressed a controversial opinion of any case to an interested party.

'But she had no trouble wearing him down,' Dilys said. 'He was miffed at the way the court steam-rollered him when he tried to raise a few points. His sense of justice was injured and his pride was, too. So in the end he told Emily about his uncertainties.'

There was no doubt, the pathologist had said, that both Emily's husband and her father had died of drowning. But he was not at all sure they had simply fallen out of their boat when it capsized.

'Both bodies showed signs of trauma,' Dilys said, 'things like bruising on the neck, a gash on Desmond's forehead and one on the old man's scalp. There were grazes, contusions around the eyes and even a sign of hip dislocation in Desmond's case. The pathologist said the marks and injuries were not the kind he would associate with an accident of that sort. These looked like the signs of assault and serious struggle with an assailant.'

'What did Emily do about that?'

'She told me she tried to get the case re-opened, but the authorities brushed her off. For a while the pathologist tried to help her. He made representations to the police. He prepared a long statement explaining that in addition to the unusual marks on the bodies, the men also showed strange internal signs, the kind of thing that just didn't chime with what was supposed to have happened to them. But he was up against a wall, same as Emily, and a month after he started lending her his support, he was diagnosed as having some kind of cancer. She called it by initials, NLH, something like that.'

'NHL,' Sabrina said. 'Non-Hodgkin's lymphoma.'

'Whatever. He died soon after. So Emily's one and only ally was gone. She was bitter then, but she went quiet and I never found out any more. After the pathologist died, though, I don't think she tried to get the case re-opened.'

'Do you think she knew of a reason why somebody would kill her husband and father?'

'I'm sure she had suspicions,' Dilys said. 'I mean, she found the suggestion of foul play easy to accept, didn't she? The one thing she mentioned to me on that angle was about her husband's death. She said she believed he died because he got in the way of a person or persons sent to kill her father.'

'She actually said that?'

'Once only. Afterwards, she seemed to regret it, and she wouldn't discuss it any more.'

They sat in silence for a minute, drinking their coffee. Finally Dilys looked at the clock and said she had to rush.

'I've got a date, and at my time of life I take such an event very seriously. I go to extravagant lengths to look right. I'm at the stage where it takes me an hour just to prepare the ground.'

'Don't sell yourself short,' Sabrina said. 'You look great.'

'If I looked even a tenth as good as you, honey, I'd let up on myself.'

They made their way back through the coffee shop. At the door Sabrina held out her hand.

'Thanks for your time, Dilys.'

'It was a pleasure. Have I been any help?'

'A great help. I've got a clearer picture of Emily now, and you gave me some avenues to explore.'

'Well, that's something, huh?'

'It's more than I expected,' Sabrina told her.

EIGHT

At approximately the time Sabrina Carver was leaving the White House, Peter Leder was finishing dinner at Alfons, in Blisse Strasse in the Wilmersdorf district of Berlin. It was almost 10.20 in the evening, and Leder always tried to be in bed by eleven. He decided he had had enough pudding and put down his spoon.

'That was excellent,' he said. 'This is the only restaurant I know where they put vanilla in the zabaglione.'

In 1969, at the age of thirty-four, Peter had undergone an emergency gastrectomy operation following the rupture of a duodenal ulcer. He almost died of the haemorrhage, but the operation was a success and after a long period of recuperation he was restored to health.

After the operation Peter's stomach was smaller than a tennis ball. He had to eat very small meals for the rest of his life. If he ate too much at one time the results were distressing, and by the time he was forty he had learned never to swallow another morsel, or drink another drop, once the pressure in his gut told him he had touched his limit.

'This has not meant I can't enjoy my food and my wine,' he said now, after explaining to his dinner companion why he had such tiny portions, and why he took so long to eat them. 'I simply have to be prudent, and rely on the patience of those unfortunate enough to be dining with me.'

His guest, Stefan Fliegel, said he had hardly noticed anything unusual. It was obvious that could not be true, since the host had gagged, spluttered and hiccuped his way through the entire meal. But Fliegel knew that Peter Leder was susceptible to boot-licking. It had helped engineer this meeting, and Fliegel saw no reason to abandon the tactic.

'My only regret,' Leder said, 'is that my condition has aged me in a number of ways. Doctors have explained that it is a nutritive defect, a failure of the body to take in nourishment at the rate I need it. My reliance on food supplements, while sustaining me, has meant my tissues have aged ahead of their time.'

'You don't look any older than your years,' Fliegel said smoothly. 'I happen to know you're sixty-one, which is a year younger than I am.'

'There you are, then!' Fliegel said, fluttering his napkin. 'Look at the difference in us.'

'I was about to say, Herr Leder, that I observed no apparent age difference at all.'

The truth was that Stefan Fliegel could have been mistaken for Peter Leder's son. Leder looked twenty years older than his age, while Fliegel, who spent a portion of every year bronzing himself at the Italian lakes, looked like a man of fifty. Fliegel was also good-looking and moderately athletic in his build. Leder was stooped and pot-bellied; he had blotchy skin, his face was deeply lined, and his teeth were discoloured by years of drinking iron tonic.

'Ahem.' Leder dabbed his mouth with his napkin, heralding a change of subject. 'I see no need to delay telling you this any further – I have decided that your application for funding should be approved.'

'Oh . . .' Fliegel sat back, mouth slightly open.

'The fact that I asked you to dinner was no indication of my approval, as I warned you when I issued the invitation.'

'I understand that, Herr Leder,' Fliegel beamed.

'I have frequently entertained men to dinner on occasions when I have had to decline their applications. I simply feel that the dinner table is an excellent place to conclude an item of business, one way or the other.'

'I'm very grateful you've seen fit to help our foundation, sir.'

'Well now, any properly-run organization aimed at improving the quality of life and outlook for disadvantaged young Germans is bound to have the support of myself and my directors.'

'It is through the foresight and generosity of people such as yourself that we are able to carry on our work.'

Fliegel was proud of the way he could match Leder's stuffy manner of speech. He also sat forward when Leder sat forward, and folded his hands when Leder did. Mirroring, he had learned, was a way to lower the other fellow's guard.

'Your record of accomplishment is most impressive,' Leder said. 'I was interested to note you contribute a sizeable proportion of your time as well as a percentage of your income to the work.'

'Indeed.' Fliegel nodded, lowering his eyes with rehearsed modesty. 'There is a large measure of vocation in what we do. I would feel my week had been wasted if I didn't contribute at least ten hours to the work of the foundation.'

The waiter had been hovering. Now he came forward as Fliegel sat back and reached for his wine glass. It was not the same waiter as before. This one was taller. He had a face with the serene gravity of a graveyard angel's, Fliegel thought, and he was attractively lean and wiry. This was the kind of young man who could break Fliegel's heart, given half a chance. Fliegel smiled at him.

'Did you enjoy the meal, sir?'

Fliegel nodded. The waiter watched as he drank a little wine and put down the glass.

'Will there be anything else?'

'Well . . .'

Fliegel would have liked a cognac. But for the moment he was confused, diverted. For one thing, Leder was obviously offended that the waiter was ignoring him; for another, the head waiter was standing in the middle of the restaurant staring at them, frowning as if something was wrong. Fliegel was aware, too, that this waiter didn't quite have the aura for the job. In fact, he was distinctly un-waiterly in his lack of deference, and in the bold way he stared.

'Nothing more then, sir?' The blue eyes were fixed on Fliegel's, disturbing him. 'Perhaps it's time to make final settlement,' the waiter said.

That jarred Fliegel. 'I'm sorry?'

The head waiter was approaching, weaving carefully between the tables. The waiter looked over his shoulder, saw the man and nodded, smiling.

'*Oberkellner*,' he muttered, nodding again.

The head waiter glared at him. He kept coming, bumping a woman's shoulder and stopping to apologize.

'Yes, the settlement, I think,' the waiter said, looking at Fliegel again.

'I don't know what you mean.'

The waiter reached inside his jacket and brought out a pistol. To Fliegel the world suddenly became unreal. This was not happening. It was a recollection, or he imagined it, or . . .

He heard his pulse thump in his ears and felt himself rise out of the chair as the waiter pointed the gun at his face. Fliegel had an intuition of magnetism, of somehow compelling the barrel of the gun to follow his movements. He felt his foot catch on the chair leg and grasped the table to keep his balance.

'Settlement for Nathan Barash,' the waiter said.

Fliegel heard the gun make a tiny metallic sound, then there was a rushing redness and noise like hollow boxes falling, then there was nothing.

A man two tables away had been combing his fingers through his hair when the gun went off. Now, bewildered by the noise and the screaming of women, the man looked at his hand where something had landed, warm and wet. He stared, uncomprehending, at the lumpy emulsion of blood and brain sticking to his fingertips.

'Stop that man!' the head waiter yelled.

Peter Leder stared at the body of Stefan Fliegel, sprawled back in the chair, one eye and half his forehead gone. The noise of the shot still rang in Leder's ears, but he heard glass breaking and looked up. The waiter, still brandishing the pistol, had jumped clean through the restaurant window. He was running across the lanes of traffic, away from the restaurant, into the dark.

NINE

Mike spent the morning in the UNACO technical library scanning the records of keys and locks. After two hours of blind alleys he turned to *Security Overviews*, a classified listing of 10,000 key-and-lock combinations in use by American banks and security institutions. The entry he wanted was on the third from last page:

Lock series BL 921773 to BL 921872:
Sanders Lowe Inc. for Luckham Depositories

One hundred keys and locks of the same series, probably all in the same place. Emily Selby's key was number BL 921786. It was a one-off no-copy device, high tungsten, with advanced precision in the cutting and grooving. It was a key which must have cost as much as a good strong-box. Mike decided it would be best to look for the matching lock at one of Luckham's top three security operations.

To track down the lock he had to go to the communications suite, fire up a computer and enter a code word. His word was *licet*, Latin for 'it is allowed'. After a second a menu appeared on screen. He clicked the box next to the entry *CSC*.

A number of facilities at UNACO took no account of the law. The CSC – Company Scrutiny Corpus – was one of them. It was a substantial collection of data that violated several important laws and business regulations covering privacy and the rights of groups and individuals. In addition, the greater part of the information had been obtained by illegal means.

But CSC was a priceless tool. The search for the lock to accommodate Emily Selby's key could have taken days, and would have cost hundreds of dollars in bribes; using CSC, Mike completed the search in eight minutes.

He began by calling up a full list of depositories owned by Luckham, then began the search with the most secure depository. He found a listing of all lock numbers on the boxes, even a recently updated list of depositors. The lock numbers were not of the BL series so he moved to the next depository down the list, 400 dollars a month cheaper than the one above, and there he found the entry he wanted:

> **Sanders Lowe** Lock numbers BL 921773 to BL 921872, fitted in Coverley Titanic-grade fire-resistant deed boxes, fossil-cell filled cavity, 5 milli-metre sheet steel, cold bent. Boxes in rows of ten, ten rows high, protected out of hours by 8 laseroptic alarms.

The depository was on the eighth floor of the Okasaki Bank building at Mount Vernon in Washington, DC. Mike noted the address, spent five minutes on the internal phone explaining to C.W. Whitlock what he planned to do, then shut down the computer and went straight to Kitting and Outfitting.

'I need to be smoothed and enriched,' he told Theresa, the stony-faced woman in charge of wardrobe.

'Which means?'

'Dark silk floral Dior tie?' he suggested. 'Mid-blue Turnbull and Asser cotton shirt – and how about the petrol-blue Armani suit?'

'The one you got gazpacho on.' Theresa's voice was tight.

He blinked at her innocently. 'I did? Are you sure about that?'

'There were witnesses.'

'Well, there you go, how soon we forget things. Is there a problem?'

'For a dry-cleaner, gazpacho is always a problem. Remove the stain completely, you leave a cleaning mark behind. Take out the stain so you don't leave a mark, the smell of garlic stays. What's a person to do?'

'Theresa, I'm in a hurry here. Is the suit available or what?'

'In Armani you've a choice of navy or light grey. Petrol blue is still on the critical list.'

He chose the navy. While it was being freshened with the

steamer he took off his jeans and sweatshirt and put on a robe. Coming out of the changing cubicle he collided with a haggard-looking repair man in overalls and a wool cap. He smiled at Mike and nodded.

'Hi,' Mike said, turning away.

'You don't know me,' the man said flatly. 'These people are good, aren't they?'

Mike turned and looked at him again. 'I'm sorry?'

'Less than a month ago, when I overdid the jollity at Nancy Blair's farewell party, you helped me home and put me to bed. You were a real pal. Today I'm someone you walk past with a *hi*. What's the truth here, Mike? Do you really not recognize me, or did I do something that makes you want to be a stranger?'

Mike looked really closely. 'You're Jackie Lloyd?'

'None other.'

'They did a great job on you. The false nose works, but I don't think it's too realistic.'

'Oh, funny, *funny*.' Lloyd put his fingers under the artificial sagging on his cheeks. 'I thought I'd keep the jowls and the red-rimmed eyes for a while, use them to play the pity card with my ex-wife. I could show her the alimony is killing me.'

'I truly didn't know you,' Mike said. 'We do strange things for a living, Jackie.'

'Aw, come on, it's no worse than living off immoral earnings.' Lloyd pointed towards the sound of the steamer. 'I've got to explain the oil on the boots and overalls. Theresa is going to do terrible things to me. I'll see you around, Mike.'

'Take care, Jackie.'

Mike went through an adjoining door to the domain of Imogen Kelly.

'Why, Mr Graham.' Imogen was the hairdresser and make-up person. She grinned at him. 'You got here just in time, by the look of things. At first glance I thought a sheepdog had come to see me.'

Imogen had entered the UN as a mail clerk, but had been enticed away by UNACO when word of her natural talent for hair and cosmetics got around. As far as her friends and her former colleagues downstairs were concerned, Imogen worked in a tiny department handling specialized semi-classified mail. In fact she had the run of a superbly equipped salon where she passed her days repairing, improving or altering the appearance of UNACO agents.

'I need to look like a front-edge businessman,' Mike told her. 'East Coast rather than West. I need it to happen in as short a time as you can manage.'

Theresa told him to sit down in the barber's chair, which looked more like an airline pilot's seat. She switched on a number of overhead lamps, creating shadowless illumination around his head and face.

'Here.' She threw a copy of GQ into his lap. 'Pick an Adonis. I'll tell you if it can be done, or if you're just being silly.'

He leafed through the glossy pages and settled on a young man with longish hair waved smoothly on either side of a soft centre parting.

'Is it possible to get that look without it blowing all over my face at the first puff of wind?'

'Sure.' Imogen threw a white sheet over him and tucked it into the collar of his robe. 'I'll adjust the shape and the length a little, then I'll wash it. Then, before I blow it dry, I'll douse you with this new stuff.' She held up a black plastic bottle. 'It gives your hair thermal protection, so I can work fast and really blast it with the dryer to give you the kind of burned-on shape a bomb won't shift.'

The makeover took fifteen minutes, and at the end of it Mike's hair looked very much like the man's in the picture.

'Marvellous.' He turned his head from side to side in front of the mirror. 'I didn't know you could get results like this so fast.'

'There's a downside I didn't mention,' Imogen said. She took away the sheet and brushed the back of his neck, 'After three days it all falls out. But you can't have everything, right? Make the most of it.'

At five minutes past three, looking every inch a Wall Street high-roller, with a black Gucci briefcase jammed between his ankles, Mike belted himself in beside the pilot of a UN heli-courier. It was raining as they took off, but the pilot promised Mike they would be flying into better weather.

'That's a blessing,' Mike shouted above the noise of the rotor. 'If I get a mark on this jacket, I don't think I can go back to the UN ever again.'

It was breezy and dry as Mike stood in front of the Okasaki Bank in Mount Vernon, Washington, one hour before closing time. He patted his wallet, feeling the potent bulk of his new identity, then marched in through the smoked-glass door. The elevator took him to the eighth floor.

The first barrier he encountered was a wall of armoured glass panels mounted into a shiny steel framework. He stood before it, looking for a door. A voice spoke somewhere above eye-level.

'Good afternoon, sir. How can we help you?'

'I want to talk to somebody about renting a safe-deposit box.'

'Certainly. Please come in and take a seat.'

A panel slid aside and he stepped into a room with walls covered in a dark green, heavily textured cloth. There was a narrow vertical strip of window at one end with two low leather chairs nearby, fronted by a small table. As he sat down the panel slid back into place and another one opened. A middle-aged man with a suit nearly as good as Mike's came in. He had the clipped, grey-templed grooming of a federal judge. He smiled carefully as he approached.

'I'm Dan Conway.' He held out his hand as Mike stood. 'I hope we can be of service, Mr ah . . .'

'Lewis. Brett Lewis.'

Conway put a leather folder on the table and sat down. He opened it and Mike saw an application blank. The kind of thing he wanted to bypass. Written applications meant delay.

'Could you give me some idea of the kind of facility you require, Mr Lewis? It saves time at the start if we discover you should be at one of our other branches.'

That was another tiny hazard. Mike had to be the right customer for the facilities on offer at this branch.

'Document storage,' he said. 'That and some small valuables.'

'Nothing bigger than fourteen by eleven inches, by seven deep?'

'Oh no. In fact that sounds an ideal size. I have to tell you, there's some urgency about this. I have documents relating to a sensitive and eventually high-profile buyout that has to stay absolutely secret for the time being. The papers have been prepared by hand, there are no copies and they need to be held in a place I know is perfectly safe.'

'Well, first of all,' Conway said, 'let me give you the details of what we offer, and what we expect in exchange from our clients.'

Total anonymity was guaranteed, he said, and Mike would have liked to laugh. Back at UNACO they had the names of every depositor at every one of Luckham's branches. Security was also guaranteed, first by the unequalled rigidity and fire-resistance of the storage medium, secondly by the intricate locking system, and third, by a series of laseroptic alarms linked to automatic door locks and to alarms in three police stations. There was also extensive insurance cover.

'What we need from you, Mr Lewis, is a bank's guarantee that you are good for the seven-hundred dollars monthly rental. We also need three good business references, and your permission to check that you have no criminal record or criminal affiliations – you appreciate this last is a formality which is insisted upon by our insurers.'

'Well, fine, but there's a snag in there,' Mike said, and he saw Conway's eyes harden a fraction. 'I need your protection now, I mean right now, this very day. Early this evening I have to fly to Asia on business, and I must know these –' he patted the briefcase, 'are completely safe in my absence.'

Conway cleared his throat delicately. 'It would take exceptional measures to secure a box for you today, sir.'

'But is it possible?'

'I can't say I would hold out much hope.'

'Can I short-circuit this?' Mike said. 'I believe you have a regularly adjusted and updated record of safe bets, isn't that so? A confidential list, two hundred men and women in commerce who can be trusted no matter what. Am I right?'

This was shaky. Depending on how Conway stood on confidentiality, he might deny the existence of the list.

'Well, now.' Conway cleared his throat again. 'The list you

76

refer to is intended to be a record of guarantors and referees whose opinion of others we would accept without question. Are you saying that you wish to cite someone on the list as a character referee?'

'Yes, I do. But I also want to point out that I'm on the list myself. Or so I believe.'

'Frankly, Mr Lewis, I don't see how you could know such a thing.'

'Please accept that no one deliberately told me,' Mike said. 'In business, at the level of sensitivity where I operate, important secrets occasionally become transparent by sheer accident.'

Conway got to his feet. 'If you will excuse me for a few minutes, Mr Lewis . . .' He turned to go, then turned back. 'Could you give me the name of the other person, the one you wish to cite as referee?'

'Kenneth Ross.'

Conway noted the name and went away. Mike waited, imagining what was happening. Conway would go to a secure computer. He would open the special database of 200 names, initiate a search, and lo, under the name of Brett Lewis, there would be a picture of Mike. Attached to it would be a glittering business pedigree; appropriate electronic signatures would appear on a short status profile declaring him to be a man of solid-gold probity.

The search of Kenneth Ross's name would bring up a picture of Alan Flint, a character actor whose talent for faces was in regular demand at UNACO. The fictitious Ross, like Lewis, would have a shining business lineage, hybridized from several genuine histories. The work had still been underway as Mike left the UN Secretariat building.

When Mr Conway called the number on the secret file to check Brett Lewis's credentials – a formality, but Mike would bet he'd do it anyway – the Kenneth Ross who would come on the line would be C.W. Whitlock himself, ready and able to spin a line that would charm the keys off a jailer.

Conway was back in five minutes. His respectful manner now had a much clearer streak of deference.

'Mr Lewis,' he breathed, 'I'm sorry to have kept you. I am

happy to tell you that Luckham would be glad to offer you whatever facilities they can, whenever you need them.'

Ten minutes later Mike was alone in a small humidified vault with the ten-by-ten battery of deed boxes. He had been rented number 8, after scribbling his signature on a commitment to rent it for a minimum period of one month. His privacy in the chamber, Conway had assured him, was total. Mike believed that.

As soon as the door was shut he took a pen torch from his pocket and walked along the rows of boxes, shining the torch obliquely on each escutcheon plate, making the engraved numbers stand out.

Emily Selby's number was on box 29. He slid the box from its nest, put it on the table and unlocked it. He raised the lid slowly, as if something was coiled in there, ready to jump.

He had come with no preconception, but there was less in the box than he had expected. Furthermore, it looked like the kind of stuff that would be found in a shoebox on the top shelf of a closet, not in a high-security deed box. There were old holiday snapshots of Emily and her husband, an early picture of her father and mother with their names engraved on the gilt frame, several small books of children's stories with the name Emily Lustig written in a childish hand on the flyleaf of each; there were birth and marriage documents, one or two defunct insurance policies, and a sealed white envelope. Mike opened it.

Inside was a photograph of ten people, men and women, sitting in two solemn-faced rows, stiff-backed, under a banner embroidered with the initials *JZ*, and underneath the initials the legend *Gründed 1994*. The only other item in the envelope was a cheap notebook with one scribbled entry: *17a Scharweber Strasse, Berlin*.

Mike removed most of the articles, apart from the framed picture and the children's books, and put them in his briefcase. The notebook and the group photograph he put in his inside jacket pocket. There was nothing like being thorough, but he knew the only significant items were the picture and the address in the notebook.

He locked Emily's box and slid it back into its nest. He took down his own box, opened it, and put in a bundle of newspapers. He had brought the papers for padding, so the briefcase would look the same going out as it did coming in – not that anyone here would suspect a man like Brett Lewis of doing anything underhanded.

As he left the depository Mr Conway appeared from behind his glass panel and walked with him to the elevator.

'I hope we continue to be of service to you, Mr Lewis.'

Mike smiled and nodded.

'I think I can safely say,' Conway beamed, 'your property could not be safer anywhere.'

'Thanks for your help,' Mike said as the doors opened. 'Good day, Mr Conway.'

As the elevator plummeted, he reflected that one place safer than Luckham's he could think of, straight away, was his locker back at UNACO. Nobody, so far as he knew, would ever dare open it without authorization, and the contents, if trivial, were still completely private.

TEN

Philpott had left messages for Sabrina, Mike and C.W. to gather for a meeting at three o'clock. By 2.55 they were all in the UNACO briefing room. C.W. and Mike sat opposite each other. Again Sabrina had taken the seat adjacent to Philpott's, but this time on the opposite side of the table. Philpott leaned by the window, leafing through computer printouts. As Sabrina sat down he looked at the clock.

'So let's begin.' He came and sat at the table. 'This case is taking on an air of urgency, of which more in a few minutes. First we'll update. Sabrina, tell us what you've gleaned on Emily Selby.'

Sabrina summarized what she had learned from talking to Emily's three former colleagues, especially Dilys Craig.

'The death on July 20th, 1993, of Emily's husband and her father, who were her only family, affected her severely. She had cause to believe that the two men died in suspicious circumstances.'

Sabrina read an extract of the autopsy report, which indicated both men had suffered trauma not usually associated with drowning cases.

'Moving on from that matter for the moment,' Sabrina said, 'I can now tell you I've found a connection between Emily Selby and Erika Stramm.'

She explained how the women were related, and added that in recent times they appeared to have been in regular correspondence.

'What's known about Emily's husband?' Philpott said.

'I dug through the press files and professional directories for information on both men.' Sabrina took out another sheet. 'Nothing exceptional on Desmond Selby. He was forty-three, an assistant professor of Eastern Studies at Cornell. He and Emily met in Baghdad when they went there on separate research projects. Selby was Jewish, but like his wife he had no known affiliations to Jewish organizations here or abroad. By all accounts, Desmond Selby was a fine academic and a model citizen. For what it's worth, Emily believed he was killed because he just happened to be where her father was at the time the executioner or executioners showed up.'

'The old man?' Philpott said.

Sabrina found the notes. 'He was born Johannes Georg Hofmannsthal Stramm,' she said, 'born in 1923 in Munich, educated there and in Berlin. In 1941, when he was eighteen, he was ousted by the Nazis, along with several others, from the college where he had been studying. He wasn't allowed to work and so he tried several times, unsuccessfully, to leave Germany. He was caught in a round-up of Jews in 1942 and was transported to the concentration camp at Buchenwald. He changed identities with a dead inmate, Johannes Lustig, and by various means he managed to survive. When the camp was liberated he applied for permission to travel to the USA and was accepted. He eventually took American citizenship and distinguished himself as a scholar.

'Johannes Lustig was a supporter of the Zionist cause and was present among the spectators when David Ben-Gurion announced the birth of the state of Israel in 1948. He had a doctorate in Hebraic Studies, another in pure philosophy, and he held a professorship of European History at Cornell; he wrote four books about the Russian pogroms and a number of pamphlets on the Holocaust.'

'Was he any kind of agitator?'

'I've no evidence of that,' Sabrina said. 'He wrote angry letters to the press from time to time, and one or two of his pamphlets came down hard on what he saw as fascist tendencies in certain aspects of US domestic policy. But that was it.'

Notes were made.

'Your turn, Mike,' Philpott said.

Mike gave them a summary of his break-in at the depository. 'Emily placed high value on simple things,' he said. 'The strong-box was full of items with no commercial value. I have to say it was kind of touching.'

He passed copies of the notebook entry and the group photograph to Sabrina and C.W.

'The address has been checked,' Philpott said. 'It's in the Kreuzberg district of Berlin, a racially tense area with a fair bit of crime and sundry inner-city unpleasantness. The address is a high-security apartment, one of those places with no windows, metal-clad doors, alarms and a couple of surveillance cameras. It's owned by Herschell and Grosz, a large firm of property renters and developers. They won't say who the tenant is.'

'Any bets it's Erika Stramm?' Whitlock said.

'Well, she has no listed home address,' Philpott said, 'all we have is an e-mail location.'

More notes were taken, then Sabrina, Mike and C.W. sat back and looked at Philpott, who obviously had something important to say. Several times in the past few minutes he had centred his tie and shot his cuffs. It was a sign: substantial news was imminent.

'These are details of two recent murders in Germany.' Philpott handed out information sheets. 'Karl Sonnemann, sixty-three, a university professor, was killed in Frankfurt. Stefan Fliegel, sixty-two, a businessman, died in Berlin. The names of both these men appear on the list Sabrina found in Emily Selby's hotel room. So, whatever else that document might be, it's a hit-list, and the killings have begun.'

'Do we have a line on the killer or killers?' Mike said.

'In both cases the perpetrator was described as a young man, no older than twenty-five, approximately six feet two inches tall, fair hair, blue eyes . . .'

'Finding him will be a cinch, then,' Mike said. 'A guy like that will really stand out in Germany.'

'He may not be a German,' Philpott said. 'A witness who was with Professor Sonnemann said the young man spoke German with a peculiar accent. She couldn't be any more specific about it.'

'What's being done to shield Andreas Wolff?' Whitlock said. 'I presume you are making his safety a priority?'

82

'He has been given an armed guard,' Philpott said, 'and there is round-the-clock surveillance on his Tiergarten apartment.'

Sabrina asked if anything was being done to safeguard the others on the list.

'Not at present,' Philpott said. 'The decision not to alert them may be seen as callous, but for the present we are anxious to know what connects these men, and our efforts in that direction might be harmed if we approached them.'

Sabrina said no more on the point. She wasn't paid to argue.

'We still have no depth in this picture,' Philpott said. 'I want you to go to Morocco, Sabrina. Find out about the man who killed Emily Selby, get hold of everything there is to know. Chances are he didn't act on his own initiative, so if he was put up to it we want to know who did the putting up.'

'Are we sure Morocco's where he came from?' Sabrina said. 'Most recently, I mean?'

'Mossad local intelligence in Rabat have checked out his movements and they're sure he was resident in Tetuán. You'll have a briefing docket before you leave and details of the approximate area of habitation will be in there, with a map.'

'Fine.'

Philpott turned to Mike. 'I want you to get inside that secure apartment in Berlin and find out what Erika Stramm is up to.'

'Shouldn't we maybe do this the other way around?' Mike said. 'Me go to Morocco, Sabrina take Germany.'

'Are you displaying chivalrous concern?' Philpott said.

'Morocco *can* be very dicey,' Mike said. 'I've some experience there and –'

'Thanks for your concern, Mike, but I think I'll manage,' Sabrina said coldly.

'My decision to assign Sabrina to Morocco,' Philpott said, 'is based on the belief that, as a woman, she won't be perceived as a threat. More fools them, I might add. By not encountering as much resistance as a man would, she will potentially be the most efficient.'

Mike shrugged.

'Besides,' Philpott went on, 'she won't be going alone. Lucy

83

Dow will be there, in position, ready to act as cover, diversion, or guide.'

'Why the two of them?' Mike said.

'Lucy is there anyway, keeping a weather eye on a *Sendero Luminoso* splinter group hiding out in the area. Lucy knows the territory and customs, she can help Sabrina find her way around. She may even come in handy for back-up.' Philpott paused. 'Do you have a problem with that, Mike?'

'None at all,' Mike snapped.

'So.' Philpott turned to Sabrina. 'You will present yourself at the Briefing Suite at 17.30 hours today and they will provide what you need. In Morocco I want you to travel light, look like a typical tourist.'

Philpott stood, picked up his papers and tamped them on the desk. 'That's it. Time to disperse and perform good works. I'll be waiting for you to report back. Remember, the clock is now running. You must take all necessary steps to evaluate the problem, contain it and neutralize it.'

'Easy for you to say,' Mike murmured as he walked away from the table.

He waited outside the briefing room for Sabrina.

'Hey,' he said as she came out, 'no hard feelings. I just thought the job in Berlin would be more your style, that's all.'

'I'll take my chances with what I've been assigned,' Sabrina said. 'The way I always do.'

'I didn't think you wouldn't. I was trying to be helpful.'

'There's no need. In fact, I'd take it kindly if you'd smother the impulse to help me any time it comes up.'

'Why?' Sabrina started to walk away and Mike followed her. 'Why do you say that?'

'Because some offers of help affect me the same way that setbacks do.'

As she hurried away from him Mike noticed red spots had appeared on her cheeks. It was a sign she was angry. He often made that happen. It was, he decided, one of his more depressing talents.

Back in the briefing room Philpott talked to C.W. Whitlock about the two men who had died. In spite of extensive background searches by the German police, not a thread of a connection could be found between the victims.

'All they appear to have in common is their killer, and the fact that they are both on the list.'

Philpott's years at Scotland Yard had ingrained an old cops' motto that a lack of evidence was usually the fault of the investigator – until it could be proved there was another cause.

'Two men on a mystery list get mysteriously murdered. There's a link all right, and if we don't find it soon there'll be more dead Germans on our plate.'

'More information is emerging,' Whitlock said. 'The danger is that we may start seeing connections that don't mean anything, similarities that aren't connections at all. We now know that during the past fifteen years, nine of the men on the list have taken holidays in South America. Eleven are known to have Swiss bank accounts. Then there's the fact that so many of them are orphans, and several of the others now appear to have been adopted. The gaps and inconsistencies in the German records system don't help, but I'll make the most of what we turn up. Rely on that.'

'I already do,' Philpott said.

Whitlock knew he would be expected to see connections where others saw none. Philpott believed C.W. had a peculiarly analytical brain which suited him to that kind of task. Whitlock believed Philpott missed the point. He was not especially gifted in the analytical department, but he *was* extremely patient – to the extent that he would dwell on a problem for days if necessary, familiarizing himself with it, piece by minuscule piece until familiarity equalled transparency and it was solved. Patience was the secret of many kinds of success, but patience was one of the inborn tools people didn't use much any more. Which, Whitlock thought, was just too bad for people.

'What's known about the victims?' he asked Philpott.

'The usual bland stuff. Sonnemann, the professor, had a long, distinguished career as an academic. Only known weak point was for young women, which is almost grounds for canonization these days. The other one, Fliegel, was nearly as respectable, except his sexual enthusiasm was for males. Neither man was ever in trouble with the law. They lived in different parts of Germany and there is no traceable reason to believe they knew each other, or had ever met.'

'Will I be sent copies of the police reports?'

'You should have them within the hour.'

'As soon as I have the paperwork I'll get out the runes and the tarot pack and see what comes up.'

Philpott went off to a meeting to discuss the failing credibility of the International Court of Justice. Whitlock crossed the corridor to the UNACO Command Centre and looked into the office of the duty Newsline Monitor. No one was around. For a while he watched the bulletins flash up on the screens, then decided he should be a man and face at least one of his terrors.

He picked up a phone and dialled the number of his wife's mobile. Carmen answered at once.

'It's me,' he said.

'What is it?'

'About last night, and the night before, for that matter . . .'

'Sorry?'

'When I tried to apologize, and you turned it into something else both times –'

'I'm working, C.W. Is there any point to this call?'

He wondered if she was ever this way with colleagues. Carmen was a consultant paediatrician, established in a good private practice, and putting in a conscience-cleansing ten hours a week in the Emergency Room of a city hospital – 'the kind listed in blue pages, not yellow pages,' C.W. would point out to friends, proud of Carmen's work among poorer people.

'Well?' she said. 'What exactly do you want?'

'To say I really am sorry, I suppose.'

'Saying sorry doesn't cut it.'

'So what do you want from me?'

'What's the good of you doing anything if I've to tell you to do it first?'

Now he wondered if maybe she was this hard with patients too. Poor kids.

'Carmen, make one thing clear.'

'What?'

86

'Are you going to let up on me before I'm too old to enjoy making up?'

'Now you're being flippant.'

'Yes, you're right,' he said, feeling his temper rise. 'And what kind of woman does that make you, sharing your life with somebody as flippant and superficial as I am?'

He threw down the receiver.

'Trouble?' a voice said behind him.

He turned and saw Caroline, the duty Line Monitor for the afternoon.

'I have a habit of walking into knives,' C.W. told her. 'Then I try to lay the blame for my carelessness on the knives themselves, if you follow me.'

'Oh, sure,' Caroline put down her fresh cup of coffee. 'It doesn't sound very original, as dumb streaks go.'

She swiped a smart card across a slot in the drawer under the computer console. The drawer slid open. She took out a big brown envelope.

'This came for you about ten minutes ago.'

C.W. took it. He pulled back the flap and looked inside. It was from the Berlin police, preliminary investigative reports on the murders of Karl Sonnemann and Stefan Fliegel.

'Work,' he said, glad of the distraction.

'Work is the only practical consolation for being born, someone great once said. Miguel de Unamuno, if I'm not mistaken,' said Caroline.

'Thank you, Caroline, you do a lot to push back the boundaries of my ignorance.'

Whitlock stuck the envelope under his arm and left. As he walked along the passage he repeated the words in his head: *Work is the only practical consolation for being born.*

There were times, times like now, when a line like that seemed perfectly apt.

ELEVEN

As Sabrina stepped off the plane at Tangier she felt she was
breathing steam. The sun blazed from a cloudless sky, but ten
minutes earlier it had rained, and now great pools of water
on the tarmac were evaporating, making the air heavy with
moisture.

She had deliberately dressed down for the trip, wearing a
brown check shirt, soft brown chinos and loafers. Her hair was
tied back in a dark gold ribbon and she wore no make-up. Even
so, she attracted the attention of a red-faced businessman who
fell in behind her at immigration control. She felt his fingertips
make light contact with her hip.

'I don't know if you've been here before,' he said, 'but these
guys will try to use any excuse at all to make you submit to a
body-search. They're apes, believe me. Just be careful how you
answer their questions.'

The immigration officers looked perfectly civilized to Sabrina.
The only ape-like creature in sight was the one breathing on
her, the whisky on his breath emphasized by the damp air. He
had the bug-eyed, snaggle-toothed look, Sabrina thought, of the
one and only child molester she had ever seen. On the other
hand, the heat and the fact she had a slight headache could be
tilting her judgement.

'I'll watch it,' she told the man.

'It's not that they want to humiliate you,' he went on, winking at her. 'They don't make much money, so they go after
any bonuses they can pick up, like handling an American
woman.'

'I hear what you say.'

'Here on business, are you?' He was now standing beside her,
even though the sign at the door emphasized they should stay

in single file. 'I don't get the impression you've come here searching for fun.'

'It's business,' Sabrina said, not looking at him.

'Harvey Bristow's my name.'

'Fine.'

'So who are you?'

Sabrina saw a vacant desk and the officer behind it beckoning to her. She strode across the tiled floor and handed over her passport, aware that Bristow was plodding after her.

'Remember what I told you,' he muttered, too close to her ear.

The immigration officer smiled at Sabrina. He was tall and dapper and cool in his light cotton uniform. He opened her passport, looked hard at her face, smiled again and stamped a blank page. He handed back the passport, still smiling.

Sabrina thanked him and legged it across the concourse, looking for the baggage carousel. Two things happened almost at once. She heard the pest running to catch up, and a familiar Japanese voice rang out from a Hertz desk to her right.

'*Kogatasha o karitai no desu ga.*'

She turned and saw Nat Takahashi of the UN Economic and Social Council. He was a short, lean, very brisk man in his late thirties. In spite of the heat he was wearing a dark wool business suit and his customary white shirt and dark-blue tie. He looked pleased that the clerk at the desk understood Japanese.

'*Isshuukan karitai no desu ga . . .*'

Sabrina's Japanese wasn't strong, but she believed he was saying he wanted to hire a small car for a week.

'The carousels are over there,' Bristow said, panting with the effort to catch up to her. This time he put his hand on her shoulder. 'Come on, I'll give you a hand with your bags.'

'Nat!' Sabrina called out.

Takahashi turned, frowning, looking for the source of the sound. He saw her and beamed.

'Hey! Sabrina! You following me or what?'

She made eye signals, telegraphing displeasure at the sweaty presence with his hand on her shoulder.

'Stay right there.' Nat had caught on. 'I'll just finish this item of business.'

Bristow looked put out. 'The guy is a friend of yours?'

'He sure is.'

Together they watched Nat take back his credit card, his hire documents and a set of car keys. He put everything carefully in his pockets, then he turned and walked to where Sabrina stood. He was not smiling now. His face was impassive, the eyes fixed on Bristow.

'Is this gentleman bothering you?'

'Hey now, hang on.' Bristow let out a nervous chuckle. 'I was just talking to the lady here . . .'

'Take a hike.'

Bristow looked stunned. He swallowed. 'There's no call to go taking that tone, now –'

'You deaf, or what?' Nat's harsh New York delivery clashed with his oriental looks and conservative dress. Bristow could have been told that this was a Japanese gangster and he would have believed it. 'This lady does not need your attentions, OK?'

'Jesus, what did I do here?'

'Just turn and go about your business,' Nat told him. 'Otherwise you could be going back to base with your windpipe in your pocket.'

Bristow snatched up his hand baggage and stamped away, face redder than ever, his mouth churning. Sabrina looked at Nat wide-eyed.

'I only wanted an excuse to shake him off.'

'Well . . .' Nat shrugged. 'If you're going to do a job, why not do it thoroughly?'

He took her arm and led the way to the carousel.

'I know there's no sense asking you why you're here, Sabrina, because you'll only hand me a pack of lies, but you can tell me if this is your first time in Tangier.'

'It is. But my destination's Tetuán.'

'Good. I'm heading for a town called Martil, which lies a few miles beyond the place you're going. Let's get our bags, then I can give you a lift to your hotel.'

90

'That's great.'

'Don't be too sure. I love showing off my local knowledge, and even if you yawn a lot it won't stop me. By the time we get to Tetuán you might wish you'd stuck with the bleary guy.'

In a little red Peugeot with the windows wound down, Nat Takahashi drove through Tangier with the kind of reckless unconcern Sabrina had seen only once before, in Saigon, where they drove with what seemed to be a total dependence on Providence. Every few yards Nat would bang on the horn, making people scatter.

'To civilized people forced to spend time in this part of the world,' he told Sabrina, 'the horn is known as the Arab footbrake. Once you get the hang of the technique, it has a certain charming logic.'

So that Sabrina could see a few of the sights of Tangier, Nat drove out of the city by a meandering route, taking them across a network of streets lined with restaurants, bars and nightclubs.

'This used to be a really international city,' he said. 'Exciting. Dangerous. You had smugglers, spies, all kinds of exiles. It was a heady kind of place.'

'Were you here in those days?'

'I wasn't even born in those days. But I've heard the stories, talked to some of the veterans. If you want a taste of the exotic seediness they had in the thirties, try spending some time in the old town. It's a maze of alleys and narrow little streets and shady doorways. I do it from time to time. It's fascinating.'

Sabrina tried to imagine the reactions of the Arabs in the old town to a smart-suited Japanese nosing round their territory.

'What brings you here, Nat?'

'The usual.' He stopped talking to concentrate as he eased the car round a corner on to the long stretch of Rue de la Liberté from Place de France. 'I have to make plans to initiate UN activities in Morocco, things related to development, trade, economic mobilization, economic use of resources – even population control. Anything, in fact, that fits with the policies we chase under the authority of the General Assembly.'

'I'm impressed.'

'I've been doing it so long it feels like I do nothing. I haven't faced a real challenge in years. I should join UNACO and get my responses tightened up.'

Like most UN officials and employees, Nat knew of UNACO's existence and its aims, but he had no clear idea who were the agents and who were the administrative staff. He didn't really know, either, what a UNACO agent might be called upon to do. Occasionally an agent would die in circumstances never specified, and the others at the UN would become aware, for a while, that there were people in their midst who did incredibly dangerous things in the line of duty.

'You'd probably get bored anywhere you worked,' Sabrina said, getting off the topic of UNACO. 'Check out your ancestry and you'll find you're descended from warriors. Samurai. People like that never feel the challenges of modern life are worthwhile.'

'I'm descended from accountants of one kind and another,' Nat said. 'No warriors anywhere in my history. Even during the war, my grandfather was an army pay clerk in Kobe.' Nat leaned forward, his forehead nearly touching the windshield. 'There you are, Sabrina. Take a look at it. The Grand Socco – the great market.'

Long rows and clusters of stalls were tended by women – Nat said they were farmers' wives – in wide-brimmed pompom hats, selling fruit and vegetables of every kind.

'Marvellous,' Sabrina said, meaning it. 'Simply marvellous.'

The mingle of voices and rich aromas entering the car worked on her like a drug. One of her first priorities, anywhere she went, was to catch what she imagined to be the essence of a place, to savour it and take it into herself, until she felt she was involved and no longer a simple observer. It had been that way with her since childhood, and now, with a pang as strong as any she had ever felt, she knew that the spirit of Morocco was reaching her. She would never say anything so corny out loud, but she knew that it was true. She was suddenly aware that Nat was watching her, taking in her rapturous expression.

'I like this place,' she told him.

'I hoped you would. Personally, I adore it.'

He slowed the car, so she could see a gnarled old artisan beating a copper bowl into shape, using only a stone and a cloth-covered hammer to fashion the elegant curves of the vessel's sides. At Nat's window a child put in her head and smiled at him. He smiled back.

'Enchanting,' Sabrina said.

'Right.' Nat ruffled the child's hair and eased the car forward. 'But you should be careful not to get too hooked on all this. It gets into your blood.' Nat looked at Sabrina and his face was serious. 'I'll tell you something. I couldn't go on doing my job if I didn't get my regular fixes of Morocco.' He laughed. 'There. It's out. My unspoken passion. Now you can blackmail the hell out of me.'

They left Tangier on a wide dusty road, heading south-east to Tetuán, 57 kilometres away. Nat gunned the car forward, winding up his window against the dust.

'I promise I won't try to pry into your business,' he said, 'but tell me this, do you plan to have dealings with people in Tetuán who could loosely – or tightly – be classed as, um, not entirely law-abiding?'

Sabrina nodded. 'It's very likely,' she said.

'Well, my second promise is I won't underestimate your ability to look after yourself. But be careful. The old criminal element here was never restrained in the way it defended itself, but, even so, there were rules and barriers. But now things have changed.'

'What, recently, you mean?'

'In the past year or so.'

'Care to tell me about it?'

'It's to do with a new kind of contamination,' Nat said. 'Extremism used to be breaking somebody's arm to steal five dollars off him. Nowadays extremism is killing as many people as you can, not because you want anything from them, or because they've harmed you, but because killing them draws attention to your political posture.'

'You said contamination.'

'Right. Politics has contaminated the criminal impulse. And

the results are catastrophic. Political causes, so-called, attract people with violent instincts. Cheap political messages give their brutality a focus. It becomes noble, too. Blowing up a main street full of innocent human beings is now termed an act of political extremism, when in fact we know it's nothing more than the behaviour of moral midgets with psychopathic compulsions.'

'How do you reckon this could touch me?' Sabrina said, although she guessed she was slightly ahead of Nat.

'Anything goes,' he said. 'Two years ago, you might have got a sock on the nose for snooping around the wrong places in Tetuán. Today they'd just as soon kill you. The restraints are gone. Blame political contamination.'

'I'll stay on my guard.'

'Do more than that,' Nat said. He took his eyes off the road for a second to stare at Sabrina. 'Let no circumstance put you at a physical disadvantage, no matter how slight or unimportant it might seem. Watch your back. The rule with certain factions is, when in doubt, eliminate. Life is cheap and too many people know it.'

When they arrived in Tetuán Nat drove straight to the district of Bab Ceuta. They got out of the car and looked out over a Muslim cemetery to the old Jewish quarter beyond.

'It's absolutely beautiful,' Sabrina said.

'Yes it is, and this is just the time of day to see this part of town. Look at it, soak up the beauty, and try to make yourself remember that, for the likes of us, it's seething with danger. Never let the loveliness of the place lull you.'

If Philpott ever resigned, Sabrina thought, they could do worse than move Nat Takahashi into the job. He had the technique for labouring a point, he could be something of an old woman, and he knew how to drill a warning into a person's skull. Sabrina wondered if he really believed she could look after herself. Few men did, it seemed.

'Where are you staying?' Nat said.

'A place called the National. It's got one star. Do you know it?'

'Sure. It's over that way.' He swung his arm to the left. 'On the Rue Mohammed Ben Larbi Torres. It's an old hotel, it's quiet and it has a really peaceful internal courtyard.'

'And is it a safe place?'

'I'd say so. But try not to assume anywhere is safe.' He touched her arm. 'Come on, I'll drive you to the hotel.'

TWELVE

'This news has made me sad, Viktor.'

The big American underlined his sorrow by putting a hand to his fat chest, close to the region of his heart. With his other hand he pushed back his grey Stetson. He let out a long sigh.

'Stefan Fliegel and Karl Sonnemann were good people. Their passing will leave a gap.'

Viktor's mouth tightened for a moment. 'An adequate reprisal would go some way to repairing the damage.'

'But you don't know who did it, do you?'

'We will find out. In any case, we know the general source of the attacks, if not the attacker.'

The American was Harold Gibson of Waxahachie, Texas, newly arrived at Tegel airport, Berlin. His companion was Viktor Kretzer, a German architect, who was completely bald and wore a brown wig which emphasized the fact. Kretzer had come to the airport to greet Gibson and to bring him news of the two deaths. They sat together in the airport coffee lounge, sipping Kenyan blend, looking balefully at travellers heading for check-in.

'It was *JZ*, of course?' Gibson said.

'It's their avowed intention to eliminate us all, and that's what they have begun to do. One thing we have learned about the Jews: they are as serious about their threats as they are about their money.'

'Do the others know the position? Nobody's in the dark and off guard?'

'Everyone has been alerted and they are all taking precautions. But we need more than that.' Kretzer touched his wig. 'It is bad tactics to remain passive in the teeth of specific aggression. We must hit back.'

'Well, we've taken steps already, as you know. They've been hit hard, right at their heart . . .'

'That stopped nothing. It pales to no more than a gesture in the light of what has happened.'

'Oh, come now, I'd say it was more than that.'

'The death of the Selby woman was meant to stop an unwanted investigation, as well as being aimed at buckling the will of *JZ* in general. She died before either Stefan or Karl. In that regard it clearly failed. In fact, if what I hear is true, it stopped short of backfiring into disaster. No attempt was made on the second woman, who is by far the more serious irritant. Your man killed himself before reaching that part of his programme.'

Kretzer had spoken impatiently and now appeared to realize that. 'Forgive me, Harold. I have taken this badly.'

'As well you might, old friend.' Gibson fingered a silver ornament on the clasp of his briefcase. 'Do you have plans for retaliation, or is it too soon to ask that?'

'We need a target that occasionally stops moving.'

'Well, any way we can be of help, just say the word. This has to be straightened out.'

'I think the help you bring us today,' Kretzer said, 'will go some way to establishing a solution. The business of eliminating Red Sea pedestrians has always been costly. Your moral and financial support are twin buttresses, I never tire of saying so. Without them we would not have achieved as much as we have. But now we have to change our focus, we must redirect our resources and find a way to destroy *JZ* at its core.'

'I never imagined,' Gibson said, 'when we arranged a certain boating accident, that knowledge of the *Jugend* would pass into the hands of the daughter, and the other . . .'

'Small wonder that I get depressed,' Kretzer said. 'Think of the lives we lead, think of the endless furtiveness, never openly acknowledging each other, always communicating by routes that would make a juggler dizzy – it tells on the spirit. And now, at a time when we should be feeling some pleasure in our achievements, we are instead fearful for our lives, because we are being picked off one by one –'

'Ssh . . .'

'I'm sorry, my friend. I am despondent. In such a state I should keep my mouth shut.'

'Just hold a few good thoughts,' Gibson said. 'In the fifty years of your existence, you've carried out the work the Führer passed on. Be proud. Leave despondency for the kind who deserve it.'

'You're right, of course,' Kretzer said. 'We should count our blessings.'

'And try to remember that *JZ* is small and narrow. They're fragile at bottom. They've just been lucky, that's all.' Gibson patted Kretzer's hand. 'Now I've got to go, I have to be at the bank at eleven sharp. Everything should be waiting ready for my signature. Where will we meet?'

Kretzer smiled thinly. 'Today, I thought we would meet at the International Congress Centre.'

'I think I know the way.'

'Between the Messedamm and the S-Bahn. You can get there on the Avus motorway, there is plenty of parking space.'

'As I recall, it's a big development, Viktor.'

'Yes, so I have decided on a precise spot for us to meet. Shall we say twelve-thirty?'

'Where?'

'Outside the Jewish Community House. It's a double irony, Harold. The place was designed by architects I particularly despise.'

They stood and Kretzer handed Gibson a set of Mercedes keys. 'It's in the west-side car park. Drive carefully.'

They parted at the door to the concourse. Gibson went straight to the parking area, navigated the neat system of paths to the west section and stood by the first row of cars. He pressed the button on the ignition key. Halfway along the second row the lights of a blue Mercedes saloon flashed.

He squeezed his bulk between two cars, strode to the Mercedes and put his bags in the boot. He got in, started up, and fumbled in his pocket for his cassette. He found it and popped it into the player.

As he pulled out to the airport perimeter road Andy Williams began singing 'Home Lovin' Man'. Gibson turned up the volume.

This was his favourite album of all time, he never went any-where without it. He had told his wife till she was probably sick of hearing him say it, they could keep the simpering crooners they called singers nowadays. This was proper ballad singing by a man with a man's voice, singing about a man's emotions. And the music had a tune.

He reached the bank at three minutes to eleven. The sub-manager recognized him and beckoned him to a side room. Without a word Gibson was seated at a table and given a pen. He signed three identical withdrawal documents, declined a cup of coffee, and stood again to receive a black leather attaché case, brought by the sub-manager from the secure area at the rear of the banking hall.

'A pleasure, as always, Herr Gibson,' the sub-manager said.

'Nice to see you again.'

Gibson slapped the little man's shoulder and left.

The car was parked across the street. He skipped through the traffic, panting with the effort, and got in. As he pulled the seatbelt across his chest he saw a young man at the corner watching him.

Or it looked as if he was watching.

Gibson sat still for a minute. The watcher had gone now, vanished round the corner. But he *had* been watching, Gibson was sure of it now. Maybe he should make different arrange-ments for receiving the cash next time.

Gibson fumbled the ignition key into the lock. He did not see there was something extra on the dashboard now, a small metal prong attached to a stick-on circuit board the size of a shirt button.

He turned the key. The surge of ignition put micro-power through the tiny device on the dashboard. It transmitted a signal a distance of 90 centimetres to a receiver in a plastic bottle under the front passenger seat. In response to the signal, the receiver was configured to produce a spark. The spark ignited 2 litres of aircraft fuel, also in the bottle. The chain of events, from transmission of the signal to ignition of the fuel, took a two-hundredth of a second.

The car exploded. Windows and glass doors along the street

shattered. Burning debris and showering flames set fire to two shops and a telephone kiosk. For five minutes the heat from the burning car was too intense to allow any approach.

When firemen were finally able to get close and douse the wreck with foam, a charred body was seen arched backwards across the driver's seat. Beside it lay the blackened remains of an attaché case.

THIRTEEN

Sabrina had been warned she should go to the tourist office at Avenue Mohammed V, where a few dollars would buy her the services of a guide to show her round the old town.

'You will become lost if you go alone,' the man at the hotel reception warned her. He was a tall stooping Indian, with a look of bottomless grievance, as if some wrong had been done to him for which there was no remedy. He held up a finger as Sabrina moved away from the desk. 'Even if you do not become lost,' he said, 'you may see only a small proportion of what might have been revealed to you with the help of a guide.' He made that possibility sound like a tragedy.

Sabrina promised him she would be fine on her own, and left the hotel. At the end of the road she hailed a battered replica of a Yellow Cab and showed the driver the scribbled address she had for Lucy Dow. The man screwed up his eyes at the paper, as if it caused him pain.

'Is small place,' he said, holding up his hands, the palms an inch apart. 'I drive you near, is all.'

'Do what you can,' Sabrina told him.

It took twenty minutes through narrower and narrower streets, until finally they were in a passageway only a couple of metres wider than the car. The driver stopped and pointed up ahead to a narrow gap between two tall buildings.

'Is place,' he said, and held out his hand for the fare.

When he drove off Sabrina walked slowly towards the alley. She had expected a populated spot, but this place was deserted. The stillness was weird. It was the kind of silence that made her imagine dozens of people holding their breath. The houses around looked empty, but she could imagine people were there, tucked back into the shadows, watching.

'I'm only paranoid because the whole world is out to get me. . .'

At the mouth of the alley she stopped and looked at her piece of paper again. The single word KABILA was pencilled above the street address. She looked up and saw it again, painted on a piece of lath pointing along the alley.

She moved into the gloom, smelling dampness and cats. On her right, 10 metres along, there was a solitary doorway. She went in and saw thin beams of daylight from high up, dappling a splintered staircase.

'Nice little *pied-à-terre*, Lucy.'

She climbed the stairs, feeling them move with her weight. At the top was a room with no door. A heavy curtain was slung across the gap. She pushed it aside. The room beyond was clean and bright. The floor was tiled and shiny, with a rug at the centre. And Lucy was there, sitting in a winged cane armchair facing the window.

'Surprise, surprise!'

Sabrina took three steps into the room and knew everything was wrong. Lucy continued to stare out of the window. No living person was ever that still.

'Oh God, oh God, my poor Lucy . . .'

They had not known each other well, but they had got on. That was closeness enough to put a pang through Sabrina's heart. She stepped close to the chair. Lucy's hands were tied in front of her. Her throat had been opened. Flies clustered on the edge of the wound and across the caked blood in her lap.

Sabrina looked around the room. If there had been anything there belonging to Lucy it had been taken. Her body was all they had left.

Sabrina looked at the filmed, half-lidded eyes. Lucy had died some hours ago. Already the tan of her skin was turning deeper brown at the hairline; the sweetish smell of early decay hung in the room. She put a hand on Lucy's shoulder briefly, as a farewell gesture, then slipped out of the room. If whoever had done this was coming back, she didn't want to be there when they did.

Sabrina went quickly back down to the alley. She walked to the far end and found a quiet, private space. She fished out her mobile and tapped three digits. C.W. Whitlock came on the line. She told him what had happened in a calm voice that didn't betray her churning emotions.

'Go back to your hotel and have a strong drink,' he told her. 'The proper authorities will be alerted. They'll deal with it.'

'Do you think this had anything to do with Yaqub Hisham and my investigation? This would be a fairly strong signal that they don't want anyone poking around.'

'No. This was the boys from Peru, I'd say. She believed they were on to her. She also believed she could handle it. She obviously got it wrong.'

'Are they holed up in this area?'

'Never you mind, Sabrina. This isn't your turf. It's a matter for Task Force Six.'

'Sure.'

'Sabrina? You listening?'

'It's all right, I got the message. You can't blame me for feeling enraged.'

'Don't you mean vengeful? That particular itch will be scratched. We'll bring them to justice, I promise. Now listen, Sabrina, wait for back-up if the situation heats up too much. I would rather have you slow and alive, than quick and dead. Take care out there, OK?'

'If I don't, it won't be for want of warnings.'

'Keep in touch.'

'Right.'

It had happened before and – *God help me*, she thought – it would happen again. At the hotel she bathed, changed her clothes and put Lucy Dow firmly from her mind. Then she set out to find Yaqub Hisham's cronies on her own.

She took the map that had been provided with the briefing docket. Her destination, the place where Mossad believed Emily Selby's killer had lived, was called Rouelle Nador. She memorized the name and pictured the words in her head, ready and waiting for a match. But after two hours of tramping the narrow streets, retracing her steps at several points, she admitted that she was lost.

Part of the problem was that only some of the streets had names, so there was no logical way to progress from one to the other, in spite of what the map appeared to suggest. Another snag was that some names were duplicated, because little signs with pointers had been tacked up to help tourists find certain locations, and in many cases the pointers had fallen off and now only the names remained, misleading anybody trying to use names as a guide.

On top of that, she was making people curious about her. Once again she had tried to dress down, in a dark bronze-and-mustard ankle-length skirt and a matching peasant top, but she was American and she was blonde and that undid most of the effort. People were watching as she passed, and they were muttering.

Towards noon Sabrina considered giving up and going back to the hotel to rethink her tactics. She had assumed that Lucy would take her to within spitting distance of the place she wanted to go. Bereft of that guidance, she had trudged through streets crammed with mosques and townhouses – some of them highly elegant – and had bowed her head to pass through countless arches and follow the alleys beyond. Around the walled perimeter of the old town were dozens of gates, some of them locked, most of them imposingly built from oak with iron and copper banding. They seemed not to lead outside of the old town, but into other shadowy areas not shown on her map. As an experience, that part of Tetuán was unforgettable. But trying to find an address was hell.

She asked no one the way. An American woman visiting that area with a destination in mind would go beyond being a curiosity and become an object of suspicion. She simply kept wandering, sure that by now she looked lost and faintly dazed without having to strain for the effect.

Outside a café she stopped, took a deep breath of the coffee aroma and dropped into a chair. The street was no more than 3 metres wide and an overhanging balcony cast an oblong of shade where she sat. The scent of coffee was delicious but she ordered iced tea. For the moment it was sheer pleasure just to sit there dabbing her face and neck with a handkerchief, feeling a gentle draught from a passageway opposite.

She looked up as the tea was brought. Over the waiter's shoulder she saw a sign: *Rouelle Nador*.

'Goddamn it!'

'Mam'selle?' The waiter looked startled.

'That looks wonderful,' she said, switching on a bright smile. She picked up the tall glass in its silver holder. 'Really wonderful.'

The waiter went away, confused.

Sabrina took her time over the tea, watching the pedestrian traffic to and from Rouelle Nador. It was a long street, narrower than most of the others and very drab. Raucous Arab music blared from a couple of upstairs windows, and that was unusual. Most of the music playing from shops and from the open doorways of houses was subdued and melodious, western in tone with a distinct French bias.

The people going down Rouelle Nador and those coming out were unmistakably a ghetto breed, she decided. They had the look of the community's bad guys. They displayed a sullen, automatic dislike of the scene around them, just like the thugs of the *esquadrones muertes*, the death-squad men she had seen hanging around the beach bars of La Libertad in El Salvador.

There was no sense in trying to kid herself; the people around Rouelle Nador made her nervous. She took a deep breath and silently admitted it. She knew why it was happening, too: she associated these characters with what had happened to Lucy Dow.

Abruptly, like a dose of the right medicine at precisely the right moment, she had a sudden recollection of Mike Graham offering to take this job and let her go to Germany.

That shifted her focus. She straightened her shoulders, threw back her head and drained the glass. She put a handful of Moroccan francs on the table, got up and made her way into Rouelle Nador.

There were no shops or cafés, no mosques or elegant houses. None of the odours escaping on to the street inspired exotic sensations. Mostly it was staleness and decay she smelled, with the occasional whiff of hashish. Definitely a ghetto, a concentration of self-segregated nastiness at the centre of other people's domestic lives.

A man standing in a doorway stared at her as she went past. He was dressed in flip-flops, cut-off jeans and a green Day-Glo undershirt. His eyes followed her and as she turned to stare back at him he stopped chewing the matchstick jutting from the side of his mouth.

'Do you speak English?' she said.

He hesitated, then nodded.

'I'm trying to find the family or the friends of Yaqub Hisham,' she said.

The man shook his head.

'You don't know him?'

He shook his head again and resumed chewing the match.

Sabrina walked on. She counted to ten, then turned and looked back. He had gone from the doorway. Word would now be travelling. She wiggled her shoulders to dispel a sudden tingling along her back. She began walking again.

After a minute she heard someone running behind her, the sound getting rapidly closer. The feet sounded light, not at all threatening, and when she turned she saw a small boy no more than five or six years old.

'Missy go that place,' he said breathlessly, pointing. 'Go Maruf-al-Hakim.'

'Whoa, there.' Sabrina knelt by the boy and put her hand on his skinny shoulder. 'Say it again, slowly.'

He frowned at her, not understanding. She realized he had been told exactly what to say. He didn't speak English.

'I go there?' Sabrina pointed to a door on the corner of two alleys, dead ahead. 'That place?'

The boy nodded rapidly. 'Missy go that place. Go Maruf-al-Hakim.'

'Maruf-al-Hakim.'

He nodded again. Sabrina fumbled in her pocket for change to give him, but he turned and ran back the way he had come.

Sabrina went to the door and knocked. Where so much was unknown it was best to improvise her story, because a fresh *ad hoc* lie worked better than the stale, all-purpose variety. With no certainty of what she would find, she had no concrete plan to execute after she delivered her opener. But she was ready for the worst.

The door opened a crack. A girl of fifteen or sixteen put her face in the opening.

'Can I speak to Maruf-al-Hakim?'

The girl shut the door. It opened again a moment later, wide this time. A man stood there, tall and bearded, barrel-chested, dressed in US Army fatigue pants and a dirty green polo shirt. He was barefoot.

'Are you Maruf-al-Hakim?'

'That is my name.'

No toothbrush, Sabrina would swear, had ever been near the mouth that lurked behind the fringes of Maruf-al-Hakim's moustache. She recalled Philpott's description of teeth like that: *If one of them was white he'd have a snooker set.*

'Could I talk to you about Yaqub Hisham?' Sabrina said.

Maruf shrugged. 'Who are you?'

'My name is Mary Smith. Is Yaqub a friend of yours?'

'We are brothers.'

'Oh, I see –'

'We are all brothers.'

She saw a poster on the wall behind him. It depicted a bunch of incredibly healthy-looking Arabs brandishing guns above their heads, the sun blazing behind them as they marched forward with a scarlet-lettered Arabic slogan at their feet.

'That's your brotherhood?' Sabrina said, pointing.

'What business do you have with us?' Maruf demanded. He folded his arms, suggesting a stand-off.

'I know about Yaqub's business in London,' she said.

Maruf shook his head firmly. 'Not possible. Yaqub is in Palestine.'

'No, he was in London all right. He didn't use his real name. He was calling himself Kamul Haidar.'

Maruf's eyes went down to slits. He tilted his head one way then the other. 'I ask again, what is your business here?'

'I need to know why Yaqub went to London.'

She was sure these people knew Yaqub Hisham was dead. If they ran true to type, they would have plans for her already.

Which was fine. She wanted that. She wanted their full belligerent attention, for that way she would get to know things. Quickly.

'I see,' Maruf said.

The hair around his mouth was so dense it was hard to see how he was responding, but as he stepped back now he seemed to smile.

'You will take mint tea with us.'

'Thank you, but I don't feel it's proper to enter a stranger's house without a chaperone.' She watched him scowl. They just *hated* a woman to show any determination. 'Can I invite you perhaps to join me for tea or a soft drink at a café?'

Maruf appeared to think about it. 'One moment,' he said, and disappeared, pushing the door almost shut.

Sabrina waited, watching the gap in the door. She thought she heard music. Then she heard footsteps and turned sharply because they were behind her suddenly. She felt pain and saw a flash of bright, blinding light as something hard struck the side of her head. She fell back into churning darkness.

She came round with a stink like rotting fish in her nostrils. The pain in her head was so bad she was sure her skull was fractured. When she tried to touch her head something kept her hand from moving.

It was a long time before she opened her eyes. When she did the faint light penetrated like knives, sending a shaft of pain across the back of her head. She shut her eyes, waited a while, then slowly opened them again. This time the pain was only a throb.

She was lying in a filthy little room with broken floorboards and cracked, pock-marked plaster on the walls. It was intensely hot. Beams of light poked through gaps in the boards across the window, illuminating floating particles of dust. When she moved her head even a fraction it hurt, so she took several minutes to understand her position in the room.

It came to her a piece at a time. She was on the floor. She was half sitting, her shoulders against a wall. The smell came from a cracked waste-pipe beside her. Her wrists were held in handcuffs, which were looped through the waste-pipe, which was under a sink.

She was desperately thirsty.

After a few more minutes her training asserted itself. She had to accept her situation calmly. Emotional calm was the only route to a productive frame of mind. She had to put herself in a state of alertness where she could make the most of the slightest advantage.

So she faced facts. Her situation was serious. Probably grave. This was the case because she had failed to take adequate precautions. However, regret for past actions was inappropriate. It was a squandering of spirit. She must concentrate on setting matters right.

If she was left like this for too long she would die of dehydration. If she called out somebody might come, but whoever came could possibly kill her. On the other hand, only another human presence would provide the opportunity to reverse her position.

Sabrina tried out her larynx. As she had suspected, it was so dry she could only croak.

She began moving her legs and flexing her calf muscles. That would stimulate the movement of blood and enliven her lymphatic system, which would in turn create a little moisture in her mouth. With a moist throat she could swallow and, after that, perhaps she would be able to call for help.

FOURTEEN

The telephone on Philpott's desk rang as he was preparing to leave the office. He finished buttoning his overcoat and picked up the receiver.

'Philpott.'

He heard the electronic burble as the scrambler circuit cut in.

'Glad I caught you,' Mike Graham said.

'Only just. I have a Trusteeship Council reception this evening.'

'Oh, dear.'

'One of the penalties of high office, Michael. Where are you?'

'Berlin. The apartment on Husemannstrasse. I got here two hours ago. I'm just calling to touch base.'

'Fine. Can I just mention – something interesting happened this morning, not far from where you are. An American citizen was barbecued in his hire car minutes after he completed a transaction at a nearby bank.'

'I was going to tell you that,' Mike said. 'The man was Harold Gibson of Waxahachie. He was oil-rich and real-estate-rich, and five years ago he inherited six thousand acres of prime land around Lake Texoma, about sixty miles north of Dallas. This was a seriously wealthy man.'

'But it didn't make him fireproof. How do you know so much about him?'

'It's an interesting coincidence. I researched him two years ago, after the Fossil Rim killing. Actually interviewed him, too.'

The murder of a black police officer at the wildlife centre at Glenrose, south of Fort Worth, had been faked to look like an animal attack. Mexican grey wolves were blamed but careful investigation by C.W. Whitlock, and follow-up work by Mike Graham, proved that the killing was carried out by white

110

supremacists and was linked to a number of other murders in the vicinity of Dallas–Fort Worth over a six-year period. No one was ever charged with the Fossil Rim killing.

'One of the police officers on the case had bad feelings about Gibson and his chums, and the bad feelings worked their way back to UNACO.'

'What did you find out?' Philpott said.

'Well, it was a while ago, but I remember Gibson was a worshipper of all things fascist. He made no secret about it. I introduced myself as a journalist doing a series on rich men of principle. He was flattered to pieces. Told me about his possessions, his business coups, his skill at making things happen. He also told me about the promotional effort he put into republishing Henry Ford's *Dearborn Independent* articles about the International Jew.'

'Saints above,' Philpott groaned, 'have you ever read that stuff?'

'No, sir, I never felt inclined. Always thought it would depress me.'

'I'll tell you something really depressing. Adolf Hitler acknowledged that the Ford articles were an influence on the arguments he put forward in *Mein Kampf.*'

'I'll bet Harold Gibson knew that. He thought Hitler was the hottest visionary since John the Baptist. He had a little framed picture of Adolf on the wall in his den.'

'Intriguing.'

'On the last news bulletin I heard,' Mike said, 'they reported that forensic examiners found the incinerated remains of two hundred thousand dollars lying on the car seat next to Gibson's body.'

'I think the matter could merit some attention. Before you ring off, there's one piece of sad news from this end.' He told Mike about Lucy Dow. 'It's part and parcel of our business, of course, but it's no less unfortunate for that.' Philpott looked at his watch. 'I must go, Michael. Thank you for calling. Get back to me as soon as you have anything on the Stramm woman.'

Philpott's evening was frenetic. Over a period of five hours he spoke to a lot of people and gave his attention to numerous issues. At 11 p.m. he was back in his office, going through classified status files on the computer.

'Don't tell me,' C.W. Whitlock said from the doorway. 'You couldn't stand the idea of wasting hours and hours doing nothing but lying unconscious in your bed.'

Philpott turned. 'You too?'

'That's right.'

Philpott looked at him levelly. 'Domestic trouble, is it?'

'More than I need.' Whitlock came in and closed the door.

'Is it because of your work?'

'Part of it is.' Whitlock poured himself a cup of coffee.

'Well, it's customary for someone standing where I do to say it's no business of mine, and of course it isn't. But I'll interfere to the extent of expressing one opinion. In our trade, a man who can live with an unstable domestic background is better at his work than one who enjoys a life of wedded bliss.' Philpott smiled. 'It's a peculiarity that gets stimulated by the nature of our work, I think.'

Whitlock was nodding. 'It's the same in the police.'

'That's where I first noticed it.'

Whitlock's discomfort was showing. To change the subject, he asked if Philpott was doing anything he could help with. Philpott explained he was researching a Texan right-winger called Harold Gibson.

'I had a rummage through the status files and turned up a couple of interesting things. Two months ago, at a garden party in the Dallas Arboretum and Botanical Gardens, a field agent of the FBI overheard Harold Gibson tell a lady guest that he counted himself blessed, because he had shaken the hands of several men who had shaken the hand of Adolf Hitler. It also appears that twice a year, since 1989, Harold made trips to Berlin. That's about as much as I've found.'

'I could have a flip through the bigot book if you like,' Whitlock said. 'There may be something in there.'

'A very sound idea.' Philpott vacated the chair by the computer. 'Be my guest.'

Whitlock's bigot book was an assemblage of data on fanatics, dogmatists and racists, randomly gathered, fed to the computer and organized into categories. The information was encoded by software that Whitlock had helped to design, and there was agreement within UNACO that only he should be able to access the files.

The computer began to click softly and purr as it conducted searches and file-collections based around the name Harold Gibson.

'I get the feeling the man's well represented,' Whitlock said. He glanced over his shoulder. Philpott was behind his desk, drumming his fingers softly on the blotter. 'I can do this on my own if you want to go home.'

'No – I'll need to make a decision shortly,' Philpott said. 'It will involve you.'

A photograph appeared on the computer screen. Philpott saw it and came to the table. It was a shot of a middle-aged man with a grey crew-cut and an ornament on a cord around his neck in place of a necktie. He was fat and he was laughing heartily.

'Is that him?'

'Harold Gibson, sixty years old, resident of Waxahachie, chairman and managing director of Munro, Davis and Gibson, realtors, of North Main Street, Fort Worth.' Whitlock ran his finger down the column of close-printed details. 'Here we go. In 1960 he was listed among the members of the US Nazi Party, founded by George Lincoln Rockwell. In '62 he was present in London as a member of Rockwell's entourage when Rockwell was ordered to leave Britain after attempting to disseminate Nazi propaganda. In August '67, following Rockwell's assassination by a sniper, Gibson was a principal mourner at the funeral and later gave an address to followers, in which he praised the dead Nazi and pledged himself to carry on what he called the noble fight.'

'Did he have a sheet?'

'Nothing criminal. A couple of cautions for inflammatory behaviour at rallies, and a civil action for obstruction when he did a protest sit-in on the proposed site of a synagogue.'

'Anything on fund-raising?'

Whitlock scrolled the text. 'Indeed, indeed. Together with Don

Chadwick and Emerett Pearce, listed here as entrepreneurs of Fort Davis and Brownsville respectively, he formed the Lone Star Patriots.'

Whitlock was silent for a moment, scrolling the dense text. 'Well now. The Lone Star Patriots isn't quite the localized hick-racist outfit it sounds. They're shown to have links with long-term Swiss-based eugenics research, aimed at proving the intellectual inferiority of the non-Caucasian races. Three Washington sub-committees have studied evidence implicating the Patriots in financing the protection of Nazi fugitives in South America. There is strong evidence that their propaganda teams have infiltrated university campuses and the boardrooms of major corporations. They are also known to provide funding for three extreme right-wing senatorial hopefuls. Three years ago Gibson personally put up half the defence money at the trial of a Nazi war criminal in Kraków.'

'I don't think we need to know any more.' Philpott sat down again. 'The man whose works you've been describing died less than twenty-four hours ago in Berlin. He appears to have died as a result of possible bomb-planting, and he perished in the company of a lot of money. Do you sense a connection there to matters that have taken our attention lately? Or at least a possibility of one?'

'It warrants digging into.'

'So you think we should go to Texas?'

Whitlock stared.

'The European and North African aspects of the case are in competent hands,' Philpott said, 'or so I'll assume until I hear anything to the contrary. The possibility of an American side merits attention.'

'So when you say *we* . . .'

'You and me.' Philpott studied Whitlock's face. 'You think perhaps I'm not up to field work?'

'I didn't say that.'

'I've been considering this move since I left the reception this evening, but at that point my first instinct was to send Geoff Prentice. But I learn he's laid up in the Punjab with a touch of Delhi-belly. A second choice would have been Timothy Osborne, but new intrigues in Bosnia are exercising a powerful draw on him right now.' Philpott shrugged. 'So then I thought, why not go myself? I'm an old cop, after all, an old conniver, and frankly I spend too much time behind this desk. The change will do me good. My secretaries can earn their keep for a change and front for me while we're away.'

'The trip could all be a big mistake, of course,' Whitlock said. 'But I suppose wild goose chases are OK now and then.'

'Of course.' Philpott's eyelid dropped a fraction, as near as he ever came to winking. 'Time away from New York could work wonders for your domestic situation.' He stood and stretched carefully. 'If I don't sleep soon, I'm going to collapse.'

'Don't for pity's sake do that.' Whitlock had been with Philpott when he suffered a myocardial infarction, two years before. 'I'm under enough stress already.'

'So the decision is taken?' Philpott got his coat. 'We go to Texas and we do some prospecting.'

'Whatever you say.'

'I thought you might have put up some resistance.'

'At another time, in different circumstances, maybe.' Whitlock switched off the computer and came to the door. 'Right now it seems like a good plan. Besides, I couldn't really trust anyone else to keep an eye on you.'

FIFTEEN

Dusty beams of light had moved from high on the wall on Sabrina's right to low on the wall to her left. She had long since lost the power to shout. For a while she must have slept, though she could not be sure. It had grown hotter in the room but, ominously, she no longer felt thirsty. The handcuffs had chafed away the skin on both her wrists, and she was aware that her hip and buttock had gone completely numb where they touched the floor.

She tried to move now, and found that her body seemed too heavy to shift.

I've lost my strength.

Water was the answer. Even in near-death situations, a few ounces of water could revive a human being and trigger the faculties.

Water.

She looked up at the cracked and grimed sink above her head. It looked as if it hadn't held water in years, it was a derelict like the rest of the place. Sabrina had realized, after the first hour of consciousness, that this was not the place where she had spoken to Maruf-al-Hakim. That had been a house and gave off a smell of habitation. This place smelled of decay. It was a neglected hovel.

She had heard no human sound here. Not even distant voices, or the shuffle of feet on a street. Once a rat had scuttled across the floor, but that was it; that was all the living nearness she had experienced.

Her knees were skinned, and so was the top of her left foot – the sandal thongs on that foot were scuffed, too. She had been dragged, roughly; some of the pain in her head felt displaced from the point where she had been hit. She could picture herself being unceremoniously dragged along a stinking alley and dumped in here to die.

Except they didn't want her to die. Not yet, or they would have killed her by now. They wanted her weak and despairing before they questioned her – with torture, she would bet – so they could find out what she knew about Yaqub Hisham's death.

The scenario wasn't new, although it was the first time for Sabrina. She had never been treated like this in the past, never made so weak. Before, people had simply tried to kill her. It was a dispiriting thought that she had been jumped upon by more men trying to kill her than by men trying to make love to her.

She began to sink into a delirious slumber, then she heard a sound and felt her skin prickle. A chain rattled and a bolt slid. The door swung open.

A man came in. It was not Maruf. This one was shorter and thinner. As he came nearer Sabrina saw that although he was not old, his lack of teeth and his wispy hair gave him a seedy, crabbed look. She stared at him and mustered her loathing. In her position any chance for survival relied, among other things, on a clean wellspring of focused hatred.

The man carried an enamel jug and a plastic tumbler.

'You wish water?'

'Please,' she croaked.

He knelt beside her and poured water into the tumbler. It was fresh and she smelled its coldness. He put the tumbler to her lips and the small cool wave washed over her tongue. Her throat seemed to swell when she tried to swallow and the man drew back the tumbler. He knew what to expect. Sabrina coughed weakly, then he put the tumbler to her mouth again and she was able to take another sip. As the water went down it felt hard and sharp.

The man withdrew the tumbler and looked at her. 'You must wait a few minutes,' he said. 'Then you can drink more.' His English was accented, but perfectly distinct.

'Why is this happening to me?'

'Do not talk.'

'But I'm afraid.' She managed a tremor in her lip. 'Please tell me what's happening.'

117

'I do not know anything.' He looked at her dispassionately. 'I am following instructions. Orders. You understand?'

'But please . . .' She took a deep shaky breath and produced a semblance of tears. 'I haven't done any harm. Can't you tell me anything?'

'I can tell you my guess.'

Sabrina stared at him, looking pitiful.

'I can guess that before tomorrow is over,' he said, 'you will be found in the rubbish at the Guersa el Kebir market, with no hands and no head.'

She shuddered. 'Can I have more water, please?'

'Drink it slowly, then.'

When the cup touched her lip she sucked in water and swilled it around her mouth.

Focus, she thought.

She let the water pass over her throat in tiny trickles, while with her lips she pretended to sip.

Focus.

When she had swallowed all the water in her mouth she deliberately coughed against the rim of the cup, pretending she was choking.

'Please . . .' She whimpered as the cup was withdrawn. 'Please, let me have one hand free, I can't swallow properly when you hold the cup.'

The Arab grunted but made no move.

'Just for a moment,' Sabrina whined. 'I'm so very thirsty.'

He grunted again and stood up. He fumbled in the pocket of his voluminous trousers and pulled out a bunch of keys on a chain anchored to his belt. He found a small shiny key and squatted beside Sabrina. The smell of his breath and his sweaty clothes assailed her. He undid the right bracelet then locked it round the waste-pipe.

Sabrina flexed her fingers, feeling them tingle as blood surged to her fingertips. She made a sad, grateful face.

Focus.

She held the man's eyes with hers as he handed her the cup.

He is between you and your freedom.

'Thanks.'

118

She put the cup to her lips and revolved her wrist sharply forward, throwing the water in his eyes. As his hand came up to his face she caught his thumb, jerked it back and down, breaking it.

He screamed.

Still twisting the thumb, Sabrina lowered her head and butted him twice on the nose. He fell against her, howling, blood running from his nostrils. Sabrina wrapped her legs round his waist.

'Cut the noise,' she said close to his ear.

He howled louder. She tightened the grip of her legs, pinching his kidneys. As he began to roar she thrust her head forward again, splitting his lips.

He stopped howling and began to gasp. Still holding him with her legs, Sabrina slid her hand quickly from his thumb to half-way along his hand. She took a tight grip, compressed her strength in her shoulder and twisted his wrist past its limit, tearing the flexor tendons.

The man passed out.

She pushed him on to his back, got his keys and freed her left hand. She removed the cuffs from the waste-pipe, rolled him on his face, cuffed his hands behind him and rolled him on to his back again. Blood still trickled from his nose.

She stood up, stretching her legs carefully, flexing them, then she slowly raised her arms and stretched them above her head.

She stood in the middle of the floor, fingering the bump on her head as she slowly rotated her pelvis, feeling the bones of her spine line up. She shuffled round the room a few times until her circulation stabilized, then she drank more water.

It was getting dark, the sunlight turning deep gold. She peered through the slats at the window and saw a path leading away from the building, up past a stand of dusty trees that screened the place from the road. Fifty metres beyond the trees she could see the front end of an old Citroën 2CV.

She turned her attention to the man. He was still unconscious and breathing erratically. Blood oozed from his nose and down over his cheek, making a pool on the floor at the side of his head. She picked up the jug and threw the remaining water in his face.

119

He came round coughing and spitting, jerking his head from side to side. Sabrina watched as the pain reasserted itself. His eyes opened wide.

'How're you feeling, pal?'

'Let me up!' he hissed at her.

'Maybe.'

'I will kill you!'

'Not shackled like that, you won't.'

He shouted something in Arabic.

'Was that an insult?'

'My hand is injured! You must let me up! The pain is unbearable!'

Sabrina knelt and rolled him on his side. 'Curl your knees, that'll stop you rolling over again.'

His relief was visible. Even so, Sabrina thought, the pain must still be severe, judging from the way his hand had swollen and the thumb hung down.

'Tell me your name,' she said, bunching her skirt, cushioning her knees from the floorboards.

'I am called Sayed.'

'Well Sayed, I want to know all about Yaqub Hisham.'

'I do not know the name.'

Sabrina reached out and jerked his arm. He roared with pain.

'A brief word about me, Sayed.' She waited until his noise died to a groan. 'I'm not the kind of woman you're familiar with. I'm not subservient. I don't find your maleness daunting. More to the point, I'm vindictive, irritable, pushy and given to excessive violence.' She leaned close for emphasis. 'Just so you understand the scale of things, I'll warn you I haven't started to hurt you yet.'

She sat back on her heels. 'Now. One more time. Tell me about Yaqub Hisham.'

Sayed coughed, blowing a puff of dust across the floor. 'He was a freedom fighter.'

'A terrorist. I know that. Why did he go to England? Who was he working for?'

'I am only a messenger, I do not know these things.'

'Do you swear that?'

'I swear.'

Sabrina took hold of his elbow and jiggled his arm up and down. He howled again and this time a tear ran along his cheek.

'Do you still swear?'

'He . . . he was here, in Tetuán. He had to hide, you see. Then a man came looking for him. An American.'

'What was the American's name?'

'I don't know. I swear it,' Sayed added hastily. 'I never heard his name. But he had a letter of introduction from a senior officer of Hezbollah.'

'Now tell me how you know that.'

'I am a member of a freedom movement which Yaqub Hisham supported.'

'He trained you, did he?'

'Yes.' Sayed paused and took a painful breath. 'He was our teacher, and also our cousin. We are a movement amassed from his family.'

'Amassed? How many?'

'Thirty, perhaps more. We are small, but our determination is great.' For a moment he looked defiant, turning his head to look up at Sabrina. 'The strength of our will overcomes any oppression.'

'Whatever gets you through the day, Sayed. Go ahead with the story. What did the American want with Yaqub?'

'He wished to give him a professional commission. In England. Yaqub had strong doubts, but he needed money.'

'And what was the commission?'

'I swear, I do not know the details.'

Sabrina looked at him. 'Sayed, that's not completely true, is it?' She moved his arm the smallest fraction. 'Is it?'

'The commission was to eliminate certain members of an organization.'

Sabrina waited. 'Well?'

'I have told you.'

'*What* organization?'

'The name was difficult, I do not –'

He cut off and clamped his mouth shut as Sabrina reached for his arm. She saw he was determined to stay quiet on this one. Using both hands she pushed him sharply on to his back, making him groan. She held his head steady with one hand, leaning her weight on his forehead. She pushed the forefinger of the other hand in under his eyelid. He whimpered and tried to twist away.

'Bank on what I tell you, Sayed. If I don't get a believable answer in the next five seconds, I will pull your eye out.' She pressed hard against the eyeball, making him gasp with pain. 'If that isn't enough, then I'll take out the other eye. Now again, what's the name of the organization Yaqub was gunning for?'

'It . . . it is an emerging Jewish group, based in Germany. They are called *Juli Zwanzig*. It means July twentieth.'

Sabrina remembered the photograph from the strong-box, the initials *JZ* on the banner. She withdrew her finger from his eye and sat back. He blinked furiously.

'Yaqub was given a – what is it called? – a paper with events he had to observe.'

'A timetable.'

'Timetable, yes. And first he had to go to London, and there he would stay for a time, and he would use credentials supplied by the American.'

'So that's when Yaqub became Kamul Haidar?'

'He had passport, visa, all necessary identifications. He was supplied with a gun, special model, easy to smuggle.' Sayed raised his head from the floor. 'Can I turn on my side? My hand hurts like fire.'

Sabrina rolled him on to his side and stood up.

'One more question. How many people was Yaqub supposed to kill?'

'I swear by Allah, I do not know.'

'Two? More than two?'

'Yaqub was not told. The American would only say that leading members of *Juli Zwanzig* were to be his target. He would learn more when he reached England.' Sayed rolled his eyes sideways, trying to see Sabrina's face. 'He believed the visit to Europe was bad luck.'

'He was right on that one.' Sabrina rattled through the bunch of keys she had taken from Sayed and found one for a Citroën. 'I'll be leaving now.'

'But you must release me!'

'I don't *must* do anything. Just you lie still and try to feel lucky I didn't kill you.' She stood up. 'One piece of advice before I go, Sayed. Next time you eat a skunk, try peeling it first.'

As she hurried out through the outer room a man coming in from outside nearly collided with her. He stared, leaped back and pulled a curved knife from his belt.

'Don't do this,' Sabrina said, crouching, spreading her arms, getting the car key positioned in her fist like a spike. 'Just back off.'

The man lunged with the knife. Sabrina jumped aside then leaped forward as the knife swung past her face. She jerked out her fist and felt the key penetrate his cheek. He screamed. She drew her fist back. As he swung the knife again she jabbed the key into the space between his collarbones, splitting the cartilage between his larynx and his windpipe. He dropped the knife and fell back, clutching his neck. Sabrina kicked open the door and ran for the car.

She was back at the National by nine o'clock. The drive across dusty roads filmed her skin with fine sand the colour of terra-cotta. At reception the old Indian told her a visitor was waiting. He did not look as if he approved.

She went to the tiny bar and found Nat Takahashi sitting in the corner reading a copy of the local evening paper. When he saw her he looked shocked.

'What happened? Did a bus hit you, or what?'

'Just everyday UNACO business. We don't mind getting our hands and all our other bits dirty. What brings you here, Nat?'

'I thought I'd buy you dinner before you went back.'

'You're an angel,' she said. 'I can't think of anything nicer.'

'But promise me you'll clean yourself up first. I have a reputation to look after.'

'Twenty minutes,' she promised, going to the stairs. 'You won't believe the change.'

Nat sat down to finish reading a late news item, printed in

red on the back page, about two Peruvians being fished dead from a well in the Medina quarter that afternoon.

Upstairs Sabrina entered her room, thinking how good it would be to talk to Nat about what had happened since the last time she saw him. But that was out of the question. Rules were rules, her lips were sealed.

'He wouldn't believe a word of it, anyway,' she said, heading for the bathroom.

SIXTEEN

By 7.00 a.m., one hour after Sabrina had boarded her early flight out of Tangier, Mike Graham was in the bushes on the fringe of a public park in the Kreuzberg district of Berlin. He was positioned directly opposite a squat, black-walled block of high-security apartments at Scharweber Strasse. The front door of number 17a was angled fractionally towards his vantage point, and the view was unobstructed.

The official start of spring was only a few days off, but it was a cold morning nevertheless, and since dawn it had been raining. Mike wore the latest in lightweight, one-piece, low-reflectance thermal suits, and he had brought a flask of coffee, but by 8.30 he felt distinctly chilled.

Beside him in the bushes, mounted on top of a garden cane stuck in the ground, was a high-frequency sound assimilator with its viewfinder fixed on the lock panel at number 17a. He had prepared for this morning's work with a drive-by the previous day; a quick look had told him the door lock was sonic, with a deadlock back-up. In addition to the assimilator, he had brought a selection of deadlock skeletons plus a keyform profiler, with two blanks and a selection of carbon steel files, in case the deadlock was cleverer than it looked.

At 9.10 a woman wearing a fashionable variation of a duffel coat came out of the apartment, pulling up her hood before Mike got his monocular to his eye. She closed the door, turned and pointed her sonic key at the panel. Mike pressed the button on top of the assimilator and heard it peep softly to confirm it had collected the signal.

The woman pocketed the key, turned and went down the steps. All Mike saw of her face was a firm mouth with bright lipstick, before she turned at the foot of the steps and walked away from him. He pulled the assimilator off the cane and put it in his pocket.

He waited and watched. On a basis of averages, it was safe to assume the flat was now empty, but waiting did no harm, except to his hands and feet, which appeared to have been isolated from his circulation.

At ten o'clock he crossed the road and went up the steps to number 17a. It was raining heavily now and no one was about. He looked right and left, keeping his chin tucked in and leading with the top of his head so the camera above the door wouldn't identify him. He brought out the assimilator, pointed it at the lock panel on the door and pushed the TRANSMIT button. The machine emitted a crisp beep, a duplicate of the sound the woman had used to lock the door. He was pleased she hadn't troubled to use the deadlock key. A light push and the door opened.

He slipped inside and shut the door behind him. For a minute he stood still, eyes shut, conditioning them to the dark. In secure premises without windows the lights were often wired to alarm systems. If an intruder switched them on, a signal was sent to the local police station. It was best to move around in the dark, using a torch any time a strong light was needed.

When he opened his eyes he saw a dim red night light above the front door. He could see across the hall and part of the way into the room opposite, which looked like the sitting room. He went in there and switched on his little MagLite torch.

The place was furnished with heavy modern pieces, mostly finished in black lacquer, the upholstery covered in black and dark-blue canvas. Above the fake fireplace was a painting in a frame with a dim picture light above it. He stepped forward and looked. The painting was not good, but it was a true enough likeness for him to identify the subject as Erika Stramm.

A sideboard along the wall opposite the door had a cupboard at one end and drawers at the other. He put the torch between his teeth and slid open the bottom drawer. It was crammed with books, perhaps a hundred of them, all paperbacks, all new, all in English, and only two titles: *Armageddon in the East* and *The Abuses of Power*, both by Erika Stramm. The drawer above held

126

a drawing board, professional-looking drawing instruments and several dozen sheets of self-adhesive lettering.

The top drawer looked more interesting. The torch beam picked out a stack of notebooks at the back, all well thumbed, held together with a rubber band. He put them on top of the sideboard for further examination. He also took out a ledger and a ring-binder full of invoices.

As he probed the back of the drawer, carefully sliding a sheaf of papers past a stapler and a bottle of ink, he failed to hear a man come out of a bedroom adjoining the sitting room. He approached Mike slowly from behind, raising a walking stick in the air above his head.

The stick came down and Mike dropped to his knees and rolled sideways. The move was instinctive, triggered every time he heard the *whoosh* of a blunt object moving fast. The walking stick crashed on the top of the sideboard. Simultaneously Mike kicked the feet from his assailant, knocking him on his back.

'*Kak eto nazy –*'

There was a scrambling, a thud as a heavy chair went over, and suddenly a terrible weight landed on Mike's chest. Hands gripped his neck, trying to strangle him. He smelled good cologne and a trace of stale brandy.

'Take it easy . . .'

They wrestled in the dark, rolling across the floor until the open door stopped them. Mike's head cracked on the other man's cheek, making him howl and let go. Mike jumped to his feet, feeling his leg grabbed. He kicked out with the other foot. While it was still travelling his static foot was jerked forward and he landed on his back. His head struck something hard and for a moment his senses swam.

He was aware the other man was up on his knees now and punching. Mike forced himself up, taking the blows, feeling the impact on his face and ribs. With an effort he drove himself to his feet, grabbed the man's hair and with the other hand jabbed him in the gut. The man folded, groaning.

Mike turned, looking for the door. He saw it but never took the first step towards it. A bunched fist hit the back of his skull and put him on his knees. He was hoisted, punched again,

127

dumped into a chair and felt himself being tied there. There was no longer any strength in his arms to resist.

The light came on. Mike raised his head slowly and saw the man he had fought. He was big, very big, with a shaved head and a nose that must have been broken at least three times. He wore a blue athletic singlet and tracksuit bottoms. He was standing by the settee, looking at Mike as if he would like to hit him again.

'Hi,' Mike said.

The man turned and walked out of the room. A moment later, Mike heard a telephone being lifted and a number tapped in.

The dove-grey Lear jet taxied off the apron and waited to line up with the runway take-off lights. Malcolm Philpott and C.W. Whitlock were the only passengers on board.

'I find executive flights soothing,' Philpott said. He squirmed his shoulders against the sculpted padding of the seat. 'Lots of leg-room, every convenience within reach . . .' He pointed at the panel beside them. 'Video, reading light – a really *good* reading light – window shades, music, even a direct line to the pilot. When you eat it's individual attention, as enriching an experience as you'll have in any restaurant.'

'You like being pampered,' Whitlock said.

'Of course I do.'

'It's good of you to let me share your just desserts.'

They were flying to Dallas–Fort Worth International airport, one of the busiest in the world, where Philpott was sure their arrival would pass unnoticed.

'It would have been nice if we'd been able to stay at the same hotel,' Philpott said. 'But the scenario hardly permits that.'

Whitlock took a slip of paper from his pocket and read it. 'I'm boarded somewhere off the LBJ Freeway. How far does that put me from you?'

'Not far. I'm at the Fairmont on North Ackard Street – the number's at the bottom of your bit of paper.'

'And you're Mr Beamish.'

'That's correct, Mr Tait.'

There was a sudden roar, blanking out every other sound.

128

The plane surged forward and bumped across the runway seams, each one shaking the cabin, and then the speed increased and they were sailing down the runway. After only a few seconds they were airborne and the noise in the cabin settled to a hum.

'I'm still nervous about doing this ahead of any word from Sabrina or Mike,' Whitlock said. 'It's like going on stage without any lines.'

'Improvisation is supposed to be one of our talents.'

'Sure. But we don't know the score with these people, do we? An improvisation has to fit or it's not worth doing.'

'We'll soon know the score. Whatever Mike and Sabrina uncover, whether it's connected or unconnected with Harold Gibson's cohorts, we can adjust our approach accordingly. Meanwhile, we will be wasting no time getting the first-hand low-down on the Texas connection.'

'Assuming there is one.'

'I'm sure there's one,' Philpott said. 'And if there isn't, I have to tell you it won't matter. Last night I thought over the whole nasty, sprawling picture you painted from the notes in the bigot book. It's time something positive was done about the Patriots, wouldn't you say?'

'If you mean do I think passive surveillance is no way to curtail the activities of thugs, well yes, I think a new tack would be in order.'

'And there's just enough of the agitator left in me to fight them with their own weapon.'

'Which is?'

'Bullying. Dressed to look like something else, of course. *But.*' Philpott slapped the armrest. 'I don't want to muddle our thinking at this stage. My gut feeling is, there's a connection between Gibson's crowd, Emily Selby's murder and Emily's German hit-list. If the connection is there, we need to discover its nature and its dimensions. *And*, as I already pointed out, there may well be some advantage in getting to Texas in time for Gibson's funeral.'

Whitlock smiled. 'You're really set on doing serious harm to these people, aren't you?'

'What makes you think that?'

'The speed. The way you got up and running. You hardly stopped to plan this trip.'

'I'll admit to a certain grim enthusiasm for the project.' Philpott looked out of the window, seeing the matrix of New York City below them. 'I have the conviction, too, that this is a job for men who are not entirely conditioned to a politically structured way of doing things.'

Seven years as a detective chief superintendent, and another six as joint chief of Scotland Yard's Special Branch, had given Philpott a firm point of view on the operational limitations of government security services. The G-men were better at gathering and analysing intelligence, and better at presenting their results. But they lacked a policeman's understanding of criminals and a soldier's iron discipline in putting his duty above every other consideration. Cops and soldiers were better at keeping in mind the rigorous requirements of the law, especially in the way evidence had to be gathered. They were unequalled, also, at handing out punishment of their own devising when the authorities' hands were tied.

'The idea of Nazism is a particular pain for me,' Philpott said. 'I lost members of my family in the Blitz, and later I grew up through a period when my country had to recover from the most appalling setbacks – industrial, social, domestic. People had to rebuild their lives against a backdrop of unrelieved dreariness and hardship. That was all down to the Nazis. Then when I was older I visited Belsen and Auschwitz-Birkenau and I learned about the true scale and scope of what they did.' He looked at Whitlock. 'Any day I do something to damage a Nazi-sympathizer has got to be a day well spent.'

They landed at Dallas–Fort Worth at noon. Philpott took a cab straight to his hotel. Whitlock rented a Ford sedan at the Hertz desk and drove out to the Comfort Inn on West Kingsley.

When he had checked in he changed into a sports shirt and lightweight slacks and took a drink out to the balcony. There was a heated pool and for a while he sat in the hazy sunlight watching people swim. The drink and the warm air relaxed him. He had another drink, and by the time it was gone he was ready to call Carmen.

He tapped button 4 on his mobile, her office number. After two rings the answering machine told him she would not be in the office until tomorrow. He tried calling home, but she wasn't there either. He was still trying to decide what to do next when the telephone in his room warbled. He went in and picked it up.

'Tait speaking,' he said.

'You liar.'

Whitlock waited, then once again he identified himself as Tait.

'And I said that's a lie.' The man at the other end laughed. 'How're you doing, C. W.?'

Suddenly Whitlock recognized the voice. 'Grundy? Is that Russ Grundy?'

'Yep.'

Grundy was a senior UNACO multi-tasker, an agent with a range of skills and hardware at his disposal that enabled him to provide short-notice auxiliary services for Task Force personnel in the field. Grundy's services included night-time surveillance photography, *ad hoc* telecommunications, wire-tapping, hi-tech burglary and sabotage. Like UNACO's four other multi-taskers, Russ Grundy was permanently in the field. Over the years he and Whitlock had collaborated on dozens of assignments.

'How did you know I was here?' Whitlock said.

'The eyes of Texas are upon you. I saw you and Mr Philpott at the airport.'

'And we thought nobody would notice.'

'There's always somebody, C. W. What are you doing in Dallas?'

'I was going to ask you that.'

'I'm shadowing a money-laundering outfit on behalf of the Fraud Commission at the Security Council. It's international stuff – yen turning into dollars, dollars being transformed to pounds and marks . . .'

'Interesting,' Whitlock said.

'Well, no, actually. It's dull. These guys are so predictable. And right now they're lying low, or they think they are, so nothing is happening. Are you going to tell me now why you're here?'

131

'I'm afraid I can't tell you, Russ. It's up to the boss to do that. If he wants to.'

'Well, why not suggest to him we all three have a drink together tonight,' Grundy said. 'I know a couple of really discreet spots. Then Philpott can tell me what you're doing, if he wants to, and I can remind him I always enjoy getting roped into a tasty caper. That way, my stay in Dallas might turn out interesting after all.'

'Consider it done. I'll call the old man now. How do I get back to you?'

'Try waving from the balcony. I'm sitting by the pool.'

SEVENTEEN

'I take it your friend doesn't speak English,' Mike said, addressing the woman in the duffel coat. He assumed she had come back in response to the phone call.

'He only has a few words.' Her German accent was very slight. 'But he does tend to assume other people speak Russian. I, on the other hand, probably speak English better than you do.'

She was standing in the sitting-room doorway, removing the coat. She was a handsome woman with small, firmly defined features. Her lipstick looked even brighter in artificial light.

'You'll be Erika Stramm,' Mike said.

Pain sliced through his jaw when he moved it. He checked his teeth with his tongue. They were all there. He tried to smile.

'You have me at a disadvantage,' she said.

'It doesn't feel that way.'

'I gather your restraints were necessary.' She came into the room and walked once round the chair, stopping in front of Mike. 'You don't look like a fascist.'

'That's because I'm not one. My name is Desmond Miles. I'm a US citizen and I'm in the same business you are.'

'What business is that?'

'Journalism. I'm a political stringer for three West Coast papers.'

'You're not a journalist.' Erika pointed to the assimilator where it lay on the sideboard with his other belongings. 'Journalists don't know about things like that.'

'You seem to.'

'I'm different.' She smiled coldly. 'Why did you break into my apartment?'

'I wanted to find out about you.'

'You'll have to enlarge on that.' Erika glanced at the other

133

man. 'If you don't, I'll set Gregor on you again. He's from Sverdlovsk, you know. They're savages, if they have to be.'

'I came here,' Mike said, 'because I needed to know about your connection to an outfit that calls itself *JZ*.' He watched her face but she didn't waver. 'It's very important. I think it could be a matter of life or death.'

'Whose death?'

'Yours,' Mike said.

'I don't know what you're talking about.'

'You never heard of *JZ*?'

'Never. It sounds like another lame made-up yarn.'

'You never heard of Emily Selby?'

Erika's smile shrank. 'What about her?'

'You admit you know her?'

'Look . . .' Suddenly she was edgy. 'Say what you have to say. Stop all this screwing around.'

'Emily Selby is dead. Did you know that?'

She stared at him. 'You're a liar!'

He had wondered how much truth leaked through the published facts. Hardly any, it seemed. The English papers reported that an American visitor had been shot. No name was given. By the following day diplomatic pressure had put the story into two inches on an inside page, and into limbo the day after that.

'Emily was shot dead several days ago in London,' Mike said. 'The gunman was Arabic. He killed himself shortly after.'

An interesting thing happened then. For no apparent reason Erika looked across the room; it was only for a moment, but to do it she turned her head at right angles to the spot where she stood. It was an awkward thing to do, yet it appeared involuntary. Mike guessed she was looking at something related to what he had told her. He looked too, but he saw only a compact hi-fi speaker, fixed to the wall, and a plain black chair beneath it.

'It would be easy to check this,' Erika said.

'Go ahead.'

She marched out of the room. Gregor stayed where he was, scowling at Mike. From another room there was the sound of a modem making a connection. After a couple of minutes Erika came back. She looked ill.

'Emily is dead,' she said quietly. 'I hadn't heard a thing about it.' She looked at Mike. 'You said he was an Arab?'

'Apparently.'

'How did you make the connection between me and Emily?'

'Sources. I can't divulge.'

'I could make you divulge,' Erika said, but she sounded too dispirited to try. 'Why did you ask about the initials thing?'

'JZ. There was a picture of a group of people in front of a banner with JZ on it. It was in Emily's bag.'

'How could you know that?' she demanded.

'I just know. How did you come to know her?'

'We were friends, she and I.'

Erika massaged her temples. She muttered something in Russian to Gregor. He stood away from the couch, gave Mike a hard look, then left the room.

'So you came here looking for a story,' Erika said.

'Your story. I want to know about you, your connections, your possible connection to the fact Emily was murdered.'

Erika stood staring at the floor for a minute. She looked up at Mike. 'I could have you minced in a garbage truck within the hour. By tonight you'd be gull food.'

'I believe you.'

She came to the chair and stood before him. 'There could have been many worse ways for me to learn of Emily's death.' She began untying the rope that held Mike's arms. 'I don't forgive you for the break-in, I simply don't feel vindictive now.' Her hands paused. 'Take warning, please – that is not like me. I don't forgive you for the matter-of-life-and-death bullshit, either.'

'That could be true,' Mike said.

'Whether it is or not, you don't care. The story is your only concern. I checked your credentials. You have the pedigree of a seasoned vulture.'

For a moment he was puzzled, then it clicked. The modem. She had done an Internet check on his listing. UNACO kept it updated and always in the appropriate place, complete with a photograph. His medical credentials were up there too, so was his accreditation as a lawyer, his status as an inspector with

135

the Department of the Treasury and four other finely detailed aliases.

'There.' Erika uncoiled the rope and let him stand up. 'Count yourself incredibly lucky, Mr Miles.' She picked up his torch, the key kit and the sound assimilator. 'I've purged my door's frequency code from your little machine, but I haven't damaged it. I respect nice technology, even when it's used against me.'

'Thanks.'

Erika walked with Mike to the door. 'There is no story here. Not the one you were hoping to find.'

'You could still be in danger,' he said as she opened the door. 'I know you don't believe I'm concerned, but I promise you I get very troubled when Arabs with guns arrive on the scene.'

'Whatever the truth of Emily's murder, it doesn't have anything to do with me. I'm sure of that.' Erika was trying to sound detached, but she still looked pale and shaken. 'Good luck with your next story, and take serious warning: if you ever interfere in my affairs again, you won't get off so lightly. In fact, you won't get off at all.'

Mike went down the steps. At the side of the road he looked back. She was still there. He waved and began walking.

When he had covered half a kilometre he crossed the road and went into the park again. Keeping to the far side of the trees and bushes he walked back towards Scharweber Strasse. He located the cane where he had left it sticking in the ground and re-mounted the assimilator, positioning its viewfinder on the lock plate of the door at number 17a. Then he sat down to wait.

At 5.00 a.m. Central time, C. W. Whitlock rose, showered and shaved, then got dressed. Breakfast came to his room at 5.45.

When he had eaten he set up his Macintosh PowerBook on a writing table by the balcony window. He plugged the cord from the internal communications card into the telephone socket on the wall. When he had dialled the UN server number and tapped in the UNACO password for Mailbox Access, the screen showed him a picture of a padlocked box. He put in his personal access code and the lid of the box opened. An information balloon appeared and told him there were two messages. He opened the first one. A facsimile of a note on FBI notepaper came up on the screen. It was from Special Agent Tim Webster, confirming that business and social links between Harold Gibson, Don Chadwick and Emerett Pearce were being exhaustively researched as a matter of priority; all relevant information would be posted to that address no later than forty-eight hours from the date and time of the note.

The second note was from ICON Administration in Zürich, Switzerland. It was addressed to All Agencies Concerned:

A third breach of ICON data protection has been reported. Clocked records show that a break-in occurred at 4.17 p.m. Mid-European time on 21st March, 1996. The files were uncloaked for only a microsecond before alternative encryption routines cut in. It is clear that although the unprotected period is small, it is possible for an intruder to make substantial transfers of data with the aid of ultra-speed electronic-capture apparatus recently developed and soon to be marketed by Preceptor Systems of California.

It is estimated that Andreas Wolff will complete testing of the new generation of safeguard modules for ICON within a few days, a week at most. When the new safeguards are in place, the system will be secure for the foreseeable future.

Whitlock picked up his mobile, switched on the scrambler circuit and called Philpott at the Fairmont. He came on the line at once.

'You sound fresh for the time of day,' Whitlock said.

'Texas air. It's full of fizz. I could never live out here full time. I'd burn myself out in a year. What's up?'

Whitlock read him the note from Zürich.

'We do have a responsibility there,' Philpott said. 'I can't begin to imagine the ramifications if ICON falls down. Can you get a signal to Mike?'

'If he's operational his phone will be off. I could leave something for him in the skyhigh mailbox. He checks it twice a day, when he can get to a terminal.'

'Let him know what's happened. Tell him that when he's

137

finished in Berlin he's to go to Vienna, post haste, and make a personal evaluation of Andreas Wolff's security.'

'Vienna?'

'Wolff's staying there to work on the ICON software. It's a superstitious thing – Vienna is where he devised the secure systems in the first place. The address is on my Rolodex. Call my office and they'll give it to you.'

'Who's laying on Wolff's security?'

'The Austrian police, of all people.' Philpott sighed. 'He's an Austrian national, he's one of their treasures, and what with one thing and another, they insist it's their duty as well as their privilege to look after him. The thing is, they're not too hot on anti-terrorist stuff, although they seem to think they are.'

'We could override them.'

'I know, but we should try diplomacy first. I don't want to tread on any Austrian feet unless there's a clear indication that Wolff is at serious risk. So get Mike on to it. Tell him he has *carte blanche* to sniff around, and if there's any come-back I'll handle it.' He paused. 'Or you will, if I'm otherwise engaged.'

'Very good.'

'Anything else to report?'

'Nothing important. The FBI have prioritized a detailed search on Gibson, Chadwick and Pearce. And I have a headache. I think it was the beer in that place Russ Grundy took us last night.'

'Can't say I feel a thing. Take an aspirin, do all the little things you have to do, then get yourself ready for the big performance.'

Whitlock thought for a moment. 'The funeral,' he said. 'I was up so early, I was thinking it was tomorrow.'

'You haven't forgotten what to do?'

'Of course not.' Whitlock looked at his black tie and Nikon camera hanging on a chairback by the balcony door. 'I've got the props, I've got the motivation. If I need anything else I'll let you know.'

'Jolly good. I'll catch up with you later in the day. Best of luck.'

'Thanks,' Whitlock said. 'Pray I don't get lynched, won't you?'

* * *

It was after one o'clock before the door at 17a Scharweber Strasse opened and Erika Stramm came out. This time Gregor was with her. She locked the door with the sonic key and they moved off, heading northwards on foot.

Mike waited five minutes then stood up, brushed the wet from his thermal suit, snatched the assimilator off the cane and crossed the road with it. This time when he entered the apartment he put on the lights straight away and went directly to the sitting room.

The speaker attached to the wall at the place where Erika had looked was screwed tightly into the plaster and brick. The front grille was not the removable kind and there was no gap between the casing and the wall. He put his hands on either side of the case and tried gently to shake it. The speaker was firm as a rock.

He took out his torch, tipped out the batteries and gave the case an extra hard shake. A stubby ultrasound unit fell out on his palm. He stood back, pointing it in the general direction of the speaker and the chair. After a moment it produced a note, a steady whine. He moved it nearer the speaker and the note rose. Near the back of the chair it dropped. The shift between the metal of the speaker and the wood and cloth of the chair produced exactly the transitional note he expected. There was no blip, no intermediate signal to indicate something unseen.

He dropped to his knees and put the ultrasound unit at floor level. Keeping it pointing forward, he slowly raised it from the floor. When it was level with the seat of the chair there was a blip, a distinct moment of very high pitch. He edged closer and moved the unit upwards in a straight line again. Once more it blipped. A third attempt, inches from the front of the chair, produced the sharpest blip yet. Something unusual was hidden there, somewhere in the area of the padded seat.

He felt the seat, prodded sides and back, felt underneath.

'Ah . . .'

Something slender with hard corners. He slid his fingertips around the underside of the cushion and found a stud fastener. He opened it and the object dropped on to the carpet. It was a computer floppy disk.

The computer set-up was in a small office next to the

bathroom, and the computer had been left switched on. Mike sat down and put in the disk. After a moment a message appeared on the screen: ARCHIVE OPEN.

Erika Stramm was hot for electronic keys. The floppy was for unlocking the files section of the hard disk. He clicked on the archive symbol and it opened on to a row of ten different-coloured labels. One jumped up at him: *JZ: Verfassung und Zielen*.

He opened it. The file was only ten pages long. He closed it again and searched the hard disk for a compression program. He found one, made a drag-copy of the file and compressed it.

He closed the archive, removed the floppy key and tapped in the UN server number. At the prompt he entered the UNACO password for Mailbox Access. The picture of a padlocked box came up and he typed his personal access code. The lid of the box popped open and the information balloon told him he had a message waiting.

He addressed the compressed *JZ* file to C. W. Whitlock and uploaded it. The transfer took less than twenty seconds. Next he downloaded the waiting message. It was from Whitlock. Mike read it, groaned, read it again and memorized the address given at the end.

He scrapped the open message together with the copy of the compressed file that remained on the screen. When he had emptied the electronic trash the computer was just as he had found it. Before he left the apartment he put the floppy disk back inside the chair and switched off the lights.

At the door he paused, feeling a powerful impulse to leave some sign of his visit. As always he resisted, and left.

EIGHTEEN

The Lodge Hill Burial Ground was landscaped like a golf course. Oaks, mature cypresses and willows were grouped at careful intervals across five undulating acres lined with row upon row of headstones in marble, sandstone and granite. Dark red cinder footpaths criss-crossed the lawn-smooth terrain, with broader, shiny blacktop roadways for funeral traffic.

The burial service for Harold Gibson took place on Sector 9 in the south-west of the cemetery, close to a resplendent lone willow planted by his own subscription twenty years before. More than sixty mourners were in attendance, making a dark cluster around the chrome-and-black catafalque on which the coffin sat beside the open grave.

'For man walketh in a vain shadow,' the minister said, reading from a prayer book with purple-edged pages, 'and disquieteth himself in vain. He heapeth up riches and cannot tell who shall gather them. And now, Lord, what is my hope? Truly my hope is even in thee.'

The widow, Ginny, a small plump woman with bright orange-red hair, stood with a handkerchief pressed against her mouth, her black silk coat flapping in the warm breeze. Around her, standing apart from the main gathering of mourners, a group of eight or nine grim-faced men stared at the coffin as if it might tell them something. Behind them a clutch of obvious henchmen stood in tight formation, heads bobbing as they continually looked around them, daring trouble to show itself, thick necks straining against tight white collars.

One member of the group, Don Chadwick, a squat, wide-bodied man with small eyes, nudged the taller man beside him.

'Who's that?'

Emerett Pearce looked cautiously around him. 'Where?'

'There, over there on the right,' Pearce said.

Pearce watched as Malcolm Philpott, wearing a black suit, edged into the group and moved nearer Ginny Gibson.

Pearce stiffened his lips so they wouldn't move when he spoke. 'How should I know who he is?'

'He's not a friend of the family, that's for sure.'

'Keep your voice down.'

The minister was nearing the end of the main part of the service, prior to the body being moved into position for burial. He raised his voice, taking advantage of the fine resonance obtainable at this part of the cemetery, as long as the sound was loud enough.

In a pause the sound of a camera motordrive could be clearly heard. People began to look in the direction of the sound, a hillock some distance behind the spot where the minister stood. C. W. Whitlock was standing there, wearing a sober grey suit and a black necktie. He was taking photographs of the funeral group, panning the camera as he kept his finger jammed on the shutter release.

'He is seriously annoying me,' Don Chadwick finally announced. 'Soon as this is over, I'm going to find out what the hell he thinks he's doing.'

Other people were muttering. Men looked at each other, frowning, shaking their heads. Malcolm Philpott sidled alongside Don Chadwick.

'Mr Chadwick?' he whispered.

Chadwick glared at him.

'Forgive me for butting in like this . . .'

'What is it?'

'My name is Beamish, I'll introduce myself properly after the service. I just wanted to say, I overheard what you said and I understand your concern. I can tell you about that man over there.' He pointed to Whitlock, who was still shooting. 'He is a journalist. He has taken it upon himself to expose what he calls the machinations behind Harold Gibson's death.'

'Yeah?'

'If I were you, I wouldn't approach him in public. A suggestion

142

only, of course, but it's based on my own experience of the man.'

'I see.'

Philpott slipped back into the group behind Chadwick.

The minister had paused to clear his throat. He raised his hand towards the sky before continuing. 'Oh spare me a little, that I may recover my strength, before I go hence and be no more seen.'

The widow emitted a tiny squeak and dabbed her eyes with the handkerchief.

'Glory be to the Father, and to the Son, and to the Holy Ghost. As it was in the beginning, is now, and ever shall be, world without end. Amen.'

The undertaker's men, frock-coated and wearing black leather gloves, stepped forward and expertly manoeuvred shiny struts at the side of the catafalque. The coffin swung slowly and gracefully away from the structure on a slender framework and settled on the lip of the grave. Ginny Gibson howled.

Whitlock stopped taking pictures and slowly unhooked the camera strap from around his neck. He put the camera on his shoulder, stood looking at the group by the graveside for a minute, then turned and walked away up the hill towards the trees bordering the eastern sector of the cemetery.

Chadwick watched him go. He turned and looked at Philpott, who had his eyes closed and his hands clasped as the minister spoke.

'Saviour, thou most worthy judge eternal, suffer us not at our last hour, for any pains of death, to fall from thee.'

The coffin shuddered a second then slowly descended into the grave. Ginny began to sob into her soaked handkerchief. Another woman standing nearby put out a hand to touch her shoulder and had it violently shaken off. Ginny moved to the graveside and watched until the coffin touched bottom. Then she turned to the minister, her face anguished.

'What will I do without him?'

The minister didn't appear to know. He took a handful of earth from a shovel brought by an attendant and threw it into the grave. It hit the coffin with a hollow drumming sound. He read again from his prayer book.

143

'Forasmuch as it hath pleased Almighty God of his great mercy to take unto himself the soul of our dear brother here departed, we therefore commit his body to the ground.'

'Cremated *and* buried,' Don Chadwick whispered, grinning stiffly. 'Harold was always the extravagant one.'

When the service was over the mourners fanned out, heading for their cars. Don Chadwick and Emerett Pearce crossed the cinder path and took a short cut through the trees to the wide central road, where Chadwick's Bentley was parked. The Puerto Rican chauffeur opened the door as they approached. Chadwick let Pearce go first and paused with one foot inside.

'What is it?' Chadwick was looking along the road behind the car. Pearce looked out the back window. 'That's him, isn't it? The guy that spoke to you?'

'Uhuh.' Chadwick waited until Philpott was within earshot then he called to him, 'Could you use a lift?'

Philpott quickened his stride and reached Chadwick out of breath.

'Most kind,' he panted. 'I was hoping I would catch you before you left.'

'Are you going back to the Gibson place?'

'Well, I'm not sure it would be proper.'

'Ginny's holding one of those embarrassing wake affairs, with drinks and finger food.'

'I suppose I could call briefly and pay my respects.'

'She'll appreciate that,' Chadwick said, standing back from the car. 'After you.'

The three of them settled in the back seat. For a couple of minutes they travelled in silence. Philpott made a show of catching his breath, the other two tried to look casual as they stared out of the windows, exchanging occasional glances. Finally, when Philpott appeared to be in control of his breathing, Chadwick pressed a button in the armrest and closed the glass partition behind the driver.

'So, Mister, ah . . .'

'Beamish,' Philpott said, 'Derek Beamish.'

Chadwick introduced Emerett Pearce. When the handshaking

144

was over Chadwick sat back, folding his hands on the hummock of his belly.

'Can I ask you straight away, Mr Beamish, how you come to know who I am.'

'I know you by repute,' Philpott said. 'Your land-dealing strategies have many imitators in Europe. I'm sure you know that.'

Chadwick smiled. 'I'd heard.'

'And of course your monograph on small company structures, *Survival Through Strength*, is a landmark in business writing.'

'It's good of you to say so.' Chadwick had relaxed visibly. 'And what business are you in, Mr Beamish?'

'Oh . . .' Philpott made a dismissive gesture. 'I'm on the boards of a few companies in England and over here. I have a reasonably useful fund of experience, and a range of contacts I gained from my years in politics. I put these at the disposal of the companies I serve.'

'Politics?' Chadwick sounded the word cautiously. 'You mean you were a professional politician?'

'A Member of Parliament, yes.'

Chadwick and Pearce looked impressed.

'Might I ask,' Pearce said, 'what party you were in?'

'Oh, the Conservatives. I've been a Conservative all my life. Although I have to say the party's slide leftward in recent years has saddened me.' Philpott smiled sourly. 'I nearly didn't vote at all, last election.'

'I take it you knew Harold Gibson?'

'Again, by repute. We had interests in common, shall we say. His views on certain social issues touched my own at many points.'

'He was a fine man,' Emerett Pearce said. 'And I don't just say that because he was a business partner of Don's and mine. Harold Gibson had vision, and he had the courage to turn his insights into realities.'

'He will be missed,' Philpott said.

'So.' Chadwick jerked a thumb over his shoulder. 'The guy back there with the camera, who is he?'

Now Philpott looked as if he had been asked something

145

distasteful. 'His name is Jonah Tait,' he said. 'He's a journalist and publisher from New York.'

'What kind of publisher?'

'Books and a magazine or two. Something of a crank, some might say, but he undoubtedly has a following.'

The car turned smoothly into a long rising driveway. The chauffeur dropped the speed and manoeuvred past a group of cars parked irregularly at the front of a large pink-and-white house. Chadwick pressed his button again and the screen moved back.

'Put it over by the trees,' he told the driver. 'I don't want any of these hot-rodders putting marks on the paintwork.'

They got out and followed another group of new arrivals into the house. In a long reception room with a sky-blue carpet, upwards of seventy people were standing in small clusters, murmuring and nodding and helping themselves to food and drink from a table running the length of the room. Waiters moved soundlessly among the guests taking empty glasses and providing replacements.

Philpott approached the widow, who was regally ensconced in a huge chair at the farthest corner of the room, surrounded by several other weepy-eyed women.

'Mrs Gibson.' Philpott approached with folded hands, his eyes sorrowful. 'My name is Derek Beamish, you have no reason to know who I am. I won't intrude any further on your grief than to say how sorry I am for your loss.'

Ginny thanked him in a whisper. She reached out and touched his hand. He closed his other hand over hers, then withdrew and found a drink. Chadwick and Pearce were beside him before he took the second sip.

'You were saying,' Chadwick said, 'about the journalist . . .'

'Jonah Tait.'

'He's doing something on Harold's death?'

'Well.' Philpott frowned. 'I gather he plans to produce a book, no less. An exposé. He wants to use the murder as the basis for an examination of Mr Gibson's way of life, his business practices, his relationships with other businessmen, and his financial connections with certain organizations unsympathetic to the Jews

146

and other irritant minorities. Mr Tait has said his book will offer society a remedy to the likes of Harold Gibson.'

'Remedy.' Pearce seemed to stiffen at that. He leaned forward so he could look straight at Philpott. 'How remedy? What's he advocating?'

'The usual dreary socialist panaceas, inflated with topical hot air.'

'But you believe he's dangerous, even so?'

'Dangerous enough, because, as I say, he has followers. And I wouldn't underestimate his ability to argue or make a point. He is a rather gifted man, in a crowd-pleasing way.'

'You're surely not an admirer of his?' Pearce said.

'Quite the opposite. But it pays to have a balanced evaluation of the enemy. He's currently setting up a campaign. A friend of mine heard him discuss it at a reception in New York only last week.' Philpott looked across the room for a moment. 'I'll be frank with you. Jonah Tait's campaign is partly the reason I came to Texas.'

'Did you know he'd be at the cemetery?' Chadwick said.

'I didn't expect to see him, no, but it didn't surprise me, either.'

'Why did you warn me not to tangle with him?'

'He has a knack of making a legitimate confrontation turn into a racist attack.'

'So what's this campaign?'

'He believes in the heavy advance sell. He'll go back to New York with whatever he can pick up here. When he has manipulated his material to serve his arguments, he'll use it to promote his forthcoming book.'

'Dangerous, indeed,' Pearce said.

For a minute the three men stood tasting their drinks, looking at each other.

Chadwick finally spoke. 'Tell us more about this, Mr Beamish.'

'Whatever I can.'

'And while you're at it, maybe you'll explain why your interest in Tait's project has brought you to Texas.'

'I'll be glad to,' Philpott said. 'But please, call me Derek. It's always Derek to my friends.'

NINETEEN

Whitlock rapped twice on the hotel room door and Philpott let him in.

'You weren't seen?'

'I'm disappointed you have to ask.' Whitlock took off his sunglasses. 'I've been all over the hotel, in and out of shops, I even had a Coke in the bar. No one followed me. How did it go at the wake?'

'Wheels are turning.'

They sat down in easy chairs at opposite sides of the marble-topped coffee table. Whitlock took a sheaf of papers from his pocket and put them down.

'When I got back from the cemetery this afternoon,' Whitlock said, 'there was e-mail waiting. Two items. One was a report from Sabrina via your secretary, who doesn't seem to know where you are.'

'I told my staff they should route any important communiqués directly to you. To make sure they did, I left no address for myself.' Philpott swirled his drink. 'Of course you may choose to read that as an admission that I don't want to handle any more responsibility than I can avoid.'

'As if I'd think that.' Whitlock took out his notebook and opened it at the marker. 'Sabrina has done a good job. In essence, her report tells us that *JZ* stands for *Juli Zwanzig*. I'll get to that in a moment. She also established that an American, probably Harold Gibson, recruited the gunman, Yaqub Hisham, to murder Emily Selby.' Whitlock tapped the papers lying on the table. 'A full printout is in there.'

'So a man who hates Arabs almost as much as he hates blacks and Jews went and hired an Arab to do his killing for him?'

'That seems to be the case, yes.'

148

'Item two?'

'A German computer file from Mike Graham. I've given you a rough translation. Sabrina could have translated it more stylishly but you've got all the facts. He struck gold.'

'Give me a summary.'

'The computer file contains the constitution and objectives of *Juli Zwanzig.*'

'That's July twentieth, right?'

'Very good. The group consists of men and women, all of them Jews, whose objective is to dismantle a highly secret Nazi outfit called *Jugend von Siegfried* – the Siegfried Youth. I checked with records at Central Intelligence, there's no file on any such organization, so we're talking about a *seriously* secret outfit.'

'How young are the Siegfried Youth?'

'Not young at all. Not any more. They were the very last squad of the Hitler Youth, inducted by the Führer himself a few days before Berlin collapsed. Apparently when Hitler addressed the boys in the street at the back of the bunker, he told them they were the embodiment of Siegfried, and years later they adopted the name.'

'And the men on Emily's list are the survivors of the group.'

'Right again. She threw a lot of her life into getting that list together. The men on it are sworn to preserve the memory of Adolf Hitler and to suppress Jews by any and all means. A series of funds and other financial arrangements were used to keep the boys together during the formative years.'

'And they managed to slip through the mid-part of the twentieth century without picking up tracers. That shows remarkable forward planning.'

'There was a lot of smoke-screening,' Whitlock said. 'Several of the mechanics of the old Nazi escape routes were the very people who kept the *Jugend von Siegfried* shielded from any kind of public scrutiny. They were brought up and educated together – again, very secretly, at various locations in Switzerland.'

'They were always kept together?'

'Yes, and their bonding persisted into adult life, as Hitler intended. But on official records there's no hint of that. Like any cross-section of Germans who were kids during the war, some of these men have early records, some have none. Some appear to have been adopted, others apparently grew up with foster parents – but it's all meticulously fabricated bunkum. They stayed together until the time came to leak them into society, mostly into prearranged career paths.'

'Have they lived up to Hitler's hopes?'

'According to the file Mike sent, the Siegfried Youth is nowadays a well-established covert organization which systematically eliminates Jews and Jewish enterprises.'

'And *JZ*, I suppose, is dedicated to wiping out the Siegfried Youth.'

'They certainly are. They're a small amateur band, but they're dedicated.'

'What's the connection with Emily Selby?'

'Her father. Johannes Lustig. The organization was formed at his posthumous prompting. He was a scholar and an ardent Zionist, and he spent eleven years compiling a history of what he called "Hitler's other monsters", the villains we don't hear so much about. During the war there were the *Kultur Büroangestellter*, among others. They were the culture clerks, the SS minions who went around evaluating antiques, pictures, sculpture – anything of value and artistic merit owned by Jews. They would catalogue the stuff then they would confiscate it. They ruined Lustig's own father, a couple of years before he was taken away to Buchenwald.'

'Was the history ever published?'

'Apparently not. Which is a pity, because wider dissemination of the material would have alerted more people to the existence of the *Jugend von Siegfried*, who are apparently hinted at here and there. Lustig himself got the details of the group's beginnings from a diary kept by one of Hitler's aides, a General Albers. He gleaned the rest by combing police records and interviewing retired Swiss nationals who looked after the boys in the early years.'

'So how did Lustig persuade people to set up the *JZ*?'

'In his last will and testament he directed that money be set aside, quote . . .' Whitlock consulted his notebook, '"to create a fellowship in remembrance of those spirits and lives which were

150

dismantled; a fellowship with the central purpose of avenging the wrongs done by the *Jugend von Siegfried*; a fellowship to apply vengeance in full measure and assuage the torment of our beloved dead."'

'What about the group's name? Where does that come from?'

'The twentieth of July was the date when Johannes Lustig and his son-in-law died in Lake Cayuga. Lustig's followers see symbolism in the fact that it was on the same date, in 1944, that the chief of staff to General Fromm, Claus von Stauffenberg, tried to blow up Hitler with a bomb under a map table.'

'That attempt failed.'

'I know, but I suppose the symbol's the thing, the defiance. You'll find a membership list among the papers – Erika Stramm did the recruiting, and she didn't seem to have any trouble getting top people on her team.'

'Do we know who *JZ* uses as executioner?'

'There's no mention of a name.'

Philpott was frowning at his glass. 'I find it hard to believe our computer man, Andreas Wolff, is a member of a latter-day Nazi death-squad.'

'You've met him?'

'Several times. I've also met quite a few racist fanatics. The two impressions don't gel. Wolff is a head-in-the-clouds kind of man, a greying hippie. His professional brilliance is a side issue with him. He is at his happiest using science to firm up his fantasies, his computer games, which all involve adventurer kings and distressed maidens and dragons and all that other mystical nonsense. He is bored by politics, bored by reality in general. Wolff is not bigot material.'

'I'll get Mike to look into it.'

Whitlock rose and Philpott went with him to the door.

'If you hear anything important from Mike, call me,' Philpott said. 'Impress on him how necessary it is that we put a brake on *JZ* before things escalate. He has to find out who the blue-eyed executioner is.'

'Maybe Sabrina could do us some good in Berlin.'

'Maybe she could.' Philpott opened the door. 'Remember to hold the good thought.'

151

'Which one is that?'

'We are here to create havoc.'

'I was maybe ten seconds away from switching off the phone,' Mike Graham said. 'If this is something that can wait until tomorrow, I'd rather it did.'

'It won't take long, Mike.' Whitlock was on his balcony, watching the sun go down. 'I want to update you on a couple of things. Where are you right now?'

'In bed, in the Hotel Zipser. It's the middle of the night here.'

'I'm sorry, I forgot –'

'I was reading,' Mike said. 'Lately I can't sleep. I have to wait until it lands on me all at once.'

'We're in Texas.'

'We?'

'I'm with the old man. Maybe I'll explain later, if I survive this junket. Tell me, have you seen Andreas Wolff yet?'

'Tomorrow, first thing. I used the formal approach and made an appointment. I figured it would be best to start out civilized.'

'Philpott wants you to check something else while you're there.'

Whitlock explained what they had learned about *Juli Zwanzig* from Erika Stramm's computer file, and how Philpott had strong doubts about Wolff's legitimacy as a candidate for assassination. 'I'm sure you'll think of some way to broach it.'

'Anything else?'

'Erika Stramm. Is she pliant?'

'Um . . . The short answer is no.'

'We need to know who the *JZ* executioner is. Stramm is the one to tell us.'

'She'd never tell me. She wouldn't even admit she knows what *JZ* is. She also claimed she and Emily Selby were just friends.'

'There's no chance she would relent and talk to you?'

'If I got close enough to put a question to her, my suspicion is she'd put me in traction before I got my mouth open.'

'I'll drop that one back in Philpott's lap.'

152

'Good. Now I think I'll hang up, C. W. Suddenly I'm getting sleepy.'

'Don't you want to know what Sabrina found out about the Arab shooter?'

'Another time. If I miss my sleep on this cycle, I may have to wait twelve hours before I'm ready again.'

Sabrina was in the pale blue kitchen of her apartment on East 93rd Street, standing at the big butcher's-block counter that divided the room. She had made coffee and was pouring it into a dark green porcelain cup.

'This sensation is not loneliness,' she told herself firmly, 'I'm just out of time-whack.'

She had been feeling like this since she got back from Morocco. The expected pleasure of returning to her own home had not crystallized. She had the distinct feeling, at that very moment, that all of life was happening elsewhere, and she had somehow landed in a pocket of limbo.

She took her coffee to the couch and sat down. She picked up the TV remote and switched on the set. As soon as the picture appeared she began clicking. Women, she had read, were not so prone to channel-hopping as men. Sabrina could hop with the best of them.

None of the images that flashed past appealed strongly enough to make her want to stop and watch. She switched off the set and sat back, inhaling the aroma of the coffee, staring at the dark night sky beyond her windows.

She tried to imagine how different her life would be if she had gone into teaching. She had wanted to teach, once, but opportunity was a powerful side-tracker. After some post-graduate time at the Sorbonne she travelled in Europe for a couple of years, and on her return to the USA she was recruited by the FBI. That had something to do with her father: George Carver was a man with a lifelong career in politics ('. . . in the machinery of political life,' was how he described his work) who had perhaps wanted a son. Sabrina took the job because it smacked of adventure, something she felt her life might need now she had decided to come home. While she was at the FBI

153

she discovered she had a talent with firearms. She also learned she was good at martial arts. Gradually the thoughts of a life in teaching were submerged. By the time she was gently head-hunted and won over by UNACO, Sabrina was decidedly a woman of action, with a robust, well-preserved spare-time passion for languages and European literature. Now, the thought of tenure at a small, picturesque campus seemed very attractive.

She drained her cup and took it back to the kitchen. She washed up, put out the lights and went to the bedroom. Now that she faced it, she felt desperately tired. Her shoulders ached and her legs still felt sluggish, a hangover from the time she spent cramped and dehydrated in the stinking room in Morocco. Sleep and rest for her poor muscles, she thought, would put a whole new shine on her outlook.

She sat on the side of the bed and smiled at the picture of her mother and father on the night table. George and Jeanne Carver lived in Florida now, she hardly ever saw them since George retired. Occasionally they would come and stay for a few days, so Jeanne could have an opportunity to see the shows and George could mingle with his old friends for a while. But they didn't come often enough, and when they did they always believed they were intruding on her life.

'If only you would,' she told the picture.

What she felt now was a familiar sensation she privately called her amputee state: not belonging with anyone and not wanting to belong, but feeling cut off nevertheless. Or it was simpler than that: she was merely sorry for herself.

'Self-pity is a crime against your person,' she said firmly, and stood up. 'Snap out of it.'

All the same, she found it hard not to feel melancholy as she got undressed and put on her nightdress. Emotionally, she made a habit of keeping the wick turned low. Early in her career at the FBI she had had an affair with a sub-controller who turned ugly when she showed signs of falling in love with him. In the end he set his wife on her. Nowadays, beyond superficial friendship, she was wary of men, and she made a point of avoiding the ones who were not entirely free from other attachments – which was difficult to do, because they always said they were.

The telephone rang. She picked it up.

'Sabrina,' Whitlock said. 'I hope I didn't wake you.'

'Nice try, C. W., but no. You should have waited another twenty minutes.'

'You know I wouldn't call at this hour unless it was important.' Sabrina's other line started ringing, then the fax machine cut in. 'I can hear that,' Whitlock said. 'It's from me. A summary of what Mike found out when he visited Erika Stramm's apartment. Read and digest.'

'Why am I getting all this attention so late at night?'

'Because there's a problem. It needs handling and Philpott thinks you're the very person to do the job.'

'Tell me,' she said.

'Erika's response to Mike's break-in was hostile.'

'No kidding. Are you saying she caught him?'

'Apparently. Anyway, Mike did manage to purloin a computer file with the stuff I've just faxed to you, but there's a crucial gap in the information.'

'And crucial gaps are my specialty.'

'We don't know who the killer is, the executioner, the one who's behind two murders that we know of. As things stand between Mike and Erika Stramm, there's not a chance she'll tell him anything.'

'But you believe she'll tell me?'

'Well the chief thinks so.' Whitlock paused. 'And yes, I think so, too. I've always admired your, how shall I put it, delicate powers of persuasion.'

Sabrina took a moment to consider what he had said, then asked simply, 'When do I get the travel details?'

'You have them already. They're at the end of the fax. Keep in touch. And be careful.'

'Sure. You too.'

Sabrina put down the phone. She smiled again at the picture of her parents. It was odd the way events worked on her moods. She had just been told she had to get out there and risk her neck again. Because of that, she no longer felt cut off from anything.

155

TWENTY

Russ Grundy, stout and ruddy-featured, was squeezed into a corner in the back of a big white van with BENTINCK'S WINDSHIELD REPLACEMENTS painted in blue on the side. It was parked in the street behind the offices of the Transit Authority building in downtown Fort Worth, next to the bus station.

'It's busy along here, which is good cover, and the traffic doesn't affect the equipment,' Russ told C. W. Whitlock. 'I'm within a mile of Chadwick's house, which is perfect, and if I need to move closer for any reason nobody is going to notice or care.'

Whitlock had arrived by bus, which he believed was still the best way to travel when a low profile was important. He had entered the van by walking through the bus station from front to back and climbing in as if he owned the vehicle. He sat now on a tiny swivel stool at the opposite end of the van from Grundy. Both sides of the interior were packed with electronic equipment. Where Grundy sat was a small bench with tuning gear, speakers, tape machines and headphones.

'I'm really grateful to you and Mr Philpott for this little diversion, C. W.'

'Glad we can all help each other. How are you working this surveillance, exactly?'

'Most of it's way beyond you – no offence – but putting it simply, I'm aligned with a tight information band set up between this van and the target. The ventilators out on the roof are my focusing receivers. This baby,' he patted an oblong black-and-red box beside him, 'collects and co-ordinates. It picks up from two bugs in Chadwick's house, and a third one in his office, another mile out beyond the house. So far, he hasn't been near the office.'

'How did you get the bugs in place?'

'Respect my secrets, C. W., and that way I'll respect yours.'

'You remembered it's telephone calls we're interested in?'

'Of course I did. So that we don't have to record every sound that gets made in the place every minute of the day, the recording equipment is triggered by the first dialling tone each time a call is made, and it switches off again when the line-cancel tone sounds. This is *really* sensitive equipment, C. W.'

'Can you tell what numbers are being called?'

Grundy put on a pitying face. 'I could do that before any of this stuff was invented. Some guys can do it just by listening near the phone. The tones tell you the country and area codes, and the numbers. They get logged separately.' He pointed to a cassette deck. 'Chadwick's dialled quite a few in the last, ah . . .' he looked at his watch, 'nine hours.'

'Can you transcribe them for me?'

'Sure. This thing makes a printout.' Grundy flipped a switch on the front panel. A moment later a strip of cash-register paper began to appear from under the machine. 'How long have you got, C. W.?'

'I get a return trip on the same bus I came in on. A couple of hours yet.'

'You'll have time to listen to some of this.' Grundy put a small DAT tape player in front of Whitlock and inserted a tape. 'Plug in the headphones at the side.'

Whitlock listened. For a time it was fascinating, hearing Chadwick in his own home, believing he was alone, talking business on the telephone. But it was dull stuff, business talk of a kind that conveyed nothing beyond its own narrow content. After twenty minutes Whitlock decided he would switch off, make his apologies and leave with the tape player and the other three tapes. Then the tape suddenly began to hiss and squeak. He put the machine on pause and pulled off the headphones.

'It's gone strange,' he told Grundy.

'Let me listen.'

Grundy squeezed his way along the van, wedging himself in beside Whitlock. He put on the headphones, activated the tape and sat frowning. Then he paused the tape again.

'Son of a gun,' he said. 'He's masking the call.'

'Masking it?'

'The old-fashioned way. Running water. He probably took the phone into the bathroom and turned on the taps.'

'You think he knows about the bugs?'

'No. He's just leery, like every sharp crook that ever was. They don't trust their own shadows.'

'So we don't get to know why he thought this call important enough to screen?'

'Who says?'

Grundy removed the tape from the player and took it to the other end of the van. He put it into an elaborate-looking cassette deck with six circular dials above the tape compartment. He rewound a few inches of tape, played it, and made adjustments to scales underneath the dials.

'I'm screening out the frequency of running water, which should leave only the voice sounds.'

He rewound the tape again, adjusted three of the six scales, and switched on. The tape went through the machine silently.

'Why can't we hear anything?' Whitlock said.

'I'm in scouring mode. You'll hear it in a minute. The rig knows now what to listen for, so it'll stop the tape automatically at the end of the overlay sound.'

After a timed three minutes and forty seconds the tape stopped. Grundy rewound it to the point where the hissing noise had started.

'Now listen to the difference.'

He switched on. Music poured from the speaker. It was an instrumental of 'Fool on the Hill'.

Grundy slapped his forehead.

'He used music, too?' Whitlock said.

'Yep. This Chadwick isn't your average paranoiac, C. W. He's up there with the wild-eyed conspiracy-theory crowd.'

'Can you eliminate the music?'

'Yes,' Grundy said.

Whitlock looked at him. 'But?'

'But the speech could disappear with it. It depends how much variance there is between Chadwick's voice and the notes and harmonic combinations that make up the music.' Grundy looked at his watch. 'This could be a long job, without any guarantee of success.'

'How long?'

'Well, with music I have to do things manually, grading out the music by fine stages until I get down to the vocal range. And I'll have to work from copies, because the technique rules out error-free procedure. Two hours, maybe.'

Whitlock sighed. 'OK. Go ahead. I'll wait.'

'Remember, no guarantees. I may come up with nothing.'

'We'll get nothing unless you try.'

That evening Whitlock called Philpott on the scrambler line. He explained about the masked recording.

'It took two and a half hours to clear off the music.'

'What did it leave?'

'Chadwick calling an architect in Berlin. Viktor Kretzer.'

'Really? Kretzer's on Emily's list.'

'I know. We have a clear recording of Chadwick telling Kretzer not to communicate until further notice.'

'Marvellous.'

'But better still,' Whitlock said, 'we have a little nugget at the end of the call. Chadwick tells Kretzer that some armaments are due to complete the round trip and come back to Germany, where they were born. The consignment is one item short of the batch Mr Gibson originally purchased, he says, because the Arab was given the gun to use on the job in London. How's that for serendipity?'

'To quote the psalmist,' Philpott said, 'my cup runneth over. You realize that apart from this being Grade A evidence, it means I won't have to do any blind bluffing with Chadwick and Pearce?'

'Of course.'

'I'll pass on my thanks to Grundy in person. Meantime I've skulduggery to get on with. And, indeed, so have you.' He laughed softly. 'Don't you just love it, C. W., when fate takes its foot off your neck and lets you score the occasional goal?'

*　　*　　*

159

Chadwick had reserved a table at the Casa de Oro at Fairmont in Northwest Dallas. When Philpott arrived, Chadwick and Pearce were already seated. He saw them watch him as he came across the blue-and-amber-lit dining room. There was tension in the way they sat, square-shouldered, necks stiff.

'Gentlemen . . .' They stood and Philpott shook their hands. 'I hope I'm not late.'

'Not at all.' Chadwick waved to the chair opposite. 'Sit down, Mr Beamish.'

'Derek.'

'Derek. Sit down and we'll get you a drink. I hope you like Tex-Mex cooking.'

'I adore it,' Philpott lied, smiling. He reached for the leather-covered menu. 'I wonder, do they do blue corn enchiladas?'

'Why, yes, I believe they do,' Pearce said. 'You've some experience of this kind of food?'

'I travel in Latin America.' Philpott threw them a meaningful look. 'One soon develops a taste for the culinary styles of such regions.'

They talked about food and drink and other superficial matters until the waiter came and took their order. Then Chadwick waded in with business.

'We've had time to think about what you told us,' he said, 'time to get it into some kind of perspective. Now we need to know the level of nuisance we're likely to be dealing with. This Jonah Tait, is he what you would call the persistent kind?'

'In what sense?'

'I mean, in your knowledge of him, does he frighten easily?'

'I suspect he doesn't frighten at all.'

'But has he been tested?'

'A man like him is constantly up against opposition in New York. He doesn't back off.'

'So we can't just lean on him and hope to get results.'

'I wouldn't say so.' Philpott sipped his wine. 'It's the kind of situation where a man like Harold Gibson would have known what to do.'

The risk in saying that had been calculated. Chadwick and Pearce could easily be offended and even alienated. It was more likely, Philpott believed, that they would agree with what he implied, that Gibson had been the action man in their outfit.

'He always knew the remedy that would fit the case,' Chadwick said. 'I have to hand him that.'

'Part of my reason for coming to Texas, as you know, was to shadow Mr Tait,' Philpott said. 'I was not sure what I would do to obstruct him, but I did know I had to be on hand to try *something*, should he get out of hand.'

'So what's he doing right now?' Pearce said. 'We know he's staying out at the Comfort Inn on West Kingsley, but his movements are pretty low-key.'

'He's putting the finishing touches to his book. He's got your pictures, he's got the names of local institutions and individuals, he has details of times and dates he needed to fill out the text.'

Chadwick sat back, absently massaging his stomach. 'This book, could it harm the reputation of anybody besides Harold Gibson?'

'It could hurt all of Mr Gibson's associates, and not just their reputations,' Philpott said. 'If I may be blunt . . .' He paused, waiting for their assent.

'Go ahead,' Chadwick said.

'I happen to know of Mr Gibson's connection with the *Jugend von Siegfried* –'

Pearce slapped the table. 'I told you.' He looked at Chadwick. 'People were bound to find out.'

'Shut it, Emerett.'

'Harold was the business,' Pearce said, 'but he wasn't such a whizz when it came to keeping a lid on. Not a week before he got killed, I said the same thing I'm saying now.'

'People don't know,' Philpott said. 'I promise you that. I know because I am first of all a sympathizer, also because I have access to levels of, shall we say, power play, which are shut off from even the average diplomat.'

'You were going to be blunt about something,' Chadwick said.

Philpott leaned forward. 'A record of payments made to the Siegfried people has fallen into Tait's hands. He intends to use it. I am also reliably informed that he intends to name you both as accessories to the killing of Emily Selby, a White House employee who was shot recently in London by a –'

'By a hired gun that Gibson should never have gone anywhere near,' Pearce said. 'Hell, I *knew* this would all blow back in our faces. The unexpected choice was Gibson's idea of covering his tracks. Looks like it didn't work.'

The food arrived. For ten minutes business was suspended and inconsequential talk was permitted to intervene. They chewed, enthused and reminisced. Chadwick had a long-standing love of down-home Mexican food such as *fajitas, ceviche* and *carne asada*; Pearce said he liked to eat at Mia's, where he could get the best *chiles rellenos* in town. Philpott confessed to a weakness for French cuisine, particularly *foie gras*, shaved black truffles, veal with artichokes, and just occasionally, pepper-edged rack of lamb.

None of them finished his main course.

Chadwick was last to lay down his knife and fork. Abruptly, Jonah Tait was back on the agenda. Chadwick wanted to know, for his peace of mind, how Derek Beamish came to know so much about Tait's movements.

'Every politician knows,' Philpott said, 'that if a man's life encroaches on other people's lives, then that man's life has no real secrets. Finding out the important things, the key facts, takes skill, but it really all boils down to keeping a wide range of contacts, and keeping them sweet.' He held up a hand and counted off the fingers. 'I know Tait's bankers, his printers, the firm of lawyers representing his interests, and the landlord of the property he occupies in Greenwich Village. Collectively they let me know, without knowing they do it, about everything he does and most things he plans.'

Chadwick's head was tilted to one side, as if he was trying to see something on Philpott's face not visible at any other angle. 'You haven't said so, Mr Beamish, but would I be right in assuming this Tait fellow could hurt you as much as anybody?'

'Yes.'

'And you're convinced he plans to hurt us, too?'

'I told you. He could have you facing serious criminal charges.'

'Well, maybe. We have decent lawyers hereabout, and the best of them represent me and mine whenever they're needed.'

'I took that for granted,' Philpott said. 'I still think Tait can do you harm. Try to see it coldly. First he destroys your reputation, then he goes on the legal tack, citing your financial support for organizations engaged in criminal activity – outfits like the *Jugend von Siegfried*, for one. He produces whatever evidence he has about the Emily Selby killing. And of course that starts the police digging, and you know what happens when they do that, they will always come up with more dirt, more long-buried skeletons. Something would be bound to stick, however good your lawyers may be.'

Pearce said, 'When we talked to you before, you kind of hinted you would be prepared to take whatever steps were necessary to put a brake on this man. Were you serious about that?'

'Of course.'

Chadwick said, 'See, we don't have your freedom to move. We're businessmen. We occupy a marked spot on the map, we come under all kinds of scrutiny, most of it friendly, but it's scrutiny all the same and if we change our patterns or make wrong moves, well, people notice. You, on the other hand, you've kept yourself close, you move around the globe, nobody has tracers on you.'

'Tait has.'

'Tait, he's different, and what I'm saying is, you're in a better position to do something about him than we are. You can take action without being watched while you do it.'

'I suppose so.'

'What would it take to stop Jonah Tait?' Pearce said.

'Well . . .' Philpott pursed his lips. 'Something extreme, I'm sure.'

'Mother of God,' Chadwick said. He was staring across the restaurant. 'It's him.'

Philpott nearly smiled at the timing. C. W. Whitlock was striding across the room, heading straight for their table. He wore a black leather jacket and a black crew-neck sweater. His expression was blank, but his eyes looked angry.

'Hi there,' he said, stopping at the table. He rested his fingertips

163

on the stiff white cloth. 'Pardon the interruption, I'll only detain you gentlemen a moment.'

'What do you want?' Pearce snapped.

Whitlock smiled at him. 'I'm leaving this fair city tomorrow and I thought I should stop by and thank you in person.'

'For what?'

'Copy. An embarrassment of copy. More, maybe, than I can use.'

'I think I speak for the others as well as myself,' Philpott drawled, 'when I say I don't know what the devil you're talking about.'

'Yes you do, Mr Beamish.' Whitlock flashed his smile again. 'You all do. I came here to put the finishing touches to a book about a profoundly bad man, and I have to tell you I got everything I came for. Rest assured, all three of you have a place in the text that should guarantee you some kind of immortality.'

'Just you back off,' Pearce snarled.

Whitlock shook his head. 'I'll tell you something. There was a point when I was two-thirds the way into the book and I thought, maybe I'm being way too hard on these guys. But now I see you here, and I catch the rancid atmosphere of bigotry and graft, I'm glad I checked every fact and put down every word.'

'Just go away, will you?' Philpott said.

Whitlock stepped back and nodded to all three. 'Don't move,' he said. 'Let me remember you like this.' He laughed and walked away.

For a couple of minutes nobody spoke. Chadwick filled their glasses with wine, snatched up his own and drank it in three gulps. Philpott took a sip from his glass. Pearce had his hands over his face. When he brought them down he was staring at Philpott.

'We need to talk,' he said. 'Urgently.'

Two hours later Whitlock had a telephone call at his hotel.

'Me and the boys talked it over,' Philpott told him. 'We reached a decision.'

'Yes?'

'I'm going to kill you.'

'Well, you're the boss. I'll put my affairs in order.'

'I think they would sooner have had their own man do the job, but I couldn't let them loose on you, could I? Besides, they're pretty scared of anyone looking in their direction just at the moment, and in the end they even agreed to defray my considerable expenses for the job. I promised them something clean, with no reverberations.'

'When should I clear out?'

'I suggest you get back to New York overnight and do some co-ordinating on my behalf. As of some time early tomorrow, you cease to exist.'

'Anything you need?'

'Some penta-methylenediamine. Street-name cadaverine.'

Whitlock thought for a moment. 'Grundy could get you some. Should I call him?'

'No need, I'll talk to him myself. I have another job for him.'

'A word of warning about the cadaverine,' Whitlock said. 'Don't even open it until you need it. And don't open it in the hotel under any circumstances. Is there anything else?'

'Nothing at all. I'll just say goodbye and RIP, old chap. Bang goes another alias, eh?'

'Plenty more where that came from,' Whitlock said.

TWENTY-ONE

Andreas Wolff lived in a top-floor apartment in an elegant eighteenth-century building which overlooked the Hermann Gmeiner park in the Freyung district of Vienna.

'From my work table,' he told Mike Graham, 'I can look into the park and see the children playing in the Wendy houses and gambolling around the nice green open spaces over there. Gmeiner worked most of his life in the service of orphans, you know. He was quite a guy.'

Mike's initial impression was that Wolff himself was a pretty extraordinary person. He was a robustly middle-aged man who exuded compact, restless energy. He had wiry grey-black hair above a wide, furrowed brow; when he spoke his eyes moved incessantly behind the lenses of his glasses, and when he described something his long-fingered hands made shapes in the air. He insisted Mike call him by his first name, and showed no surprise when Mike explained he was an undercover agent attached to the United Nations. 'I already have two murderous-looking police marksmen in residence, so a murderous secret agent will fit the setting very well.'

From that point on, it had been difficult to get Wolff to address the matter of his security. After a conducted tour of the sprawling apartment he insisted Mike try out one of his prototype computer games. After that he decided it was time for coffee. They took their cups to the spacious sitting room where the police bodyguard sat in easy chairs, looking uncomfortable as they pretended to read newspapers with their machine pistols on the floor at their feet. At Mike's request they had been told he was an American computer engineer engaged on collaborative work with Andreas Wolff. When he arrived they had inspected his ID which backed the impersonation.

166

'Life is so damned short,' Wolff said now. His words were clipped and meticulously delivered. He stood by a tall window, watching the traffic down on the Börseplatz. 'I could use three lifetimes, no problem, just turning my games from wild ideas into software. And in between I could maybe use up another couple of seventy-five-year spans to deal with the serious stuff.'

'ICON,' Mike said.

Wolff made a sour mouth. 'I sometimes wish I'd never gone near the thing. You can't imagine how those security codes disrupt my sleep.'

'I'd assume they command a lot of brain space.'

'They sprawl. And apart from that, they constitute a severe discipline. One I did not seek. I am tied to it now of course, and in many ways I find it fulfilling. The new protocols are moving towards a kind of digital perfection. I can sense it. I can even visualize the completed project before I have written the finalizing code.'

'You're saying the protocols aren't finished? I thought they were at the testing stage.'

'They are being tested, that is true,' Wolff said, 'but the test stage is a period with a lot of ruthless chopping. More code has to be written, and that has to be seamlessly incorporated into the body of software which has just undergone merciless surgery.' Wolff jerked his arms upwards, slopping coffee on the back of his hand. 'I take some measure of *Frohsinn* from the effort – glee, you understand?'

'From facing the challenge?'

'Quite so. It is good to take on such substantial difficulties, such threats to the symmetry of my reasoning processes. And it is a deep pleasure to overcome them, to win. But I feel it is endless work. As one challenge is cancelled another springs up.' Wolff turned from the window and grinned at Mike, showing large even teeth. 'Worst of all are the occasions, late at night, when I realize how much of my precious time is being eroded.'

Mike looked at his watch.

'And your precious time, too,' Wolff said, 'is being eaten away. I'm sorry, I respond to visitors the way children do. With a kind of excitement that travels in all directions. Come, let's sit down and we can discuss your business. I assure you again, the sharp-shooters don't have a word of English.' As they sat at a table by the window Wolff added, 'Their German isn't much good, either.'

Mike explained his masters' anxiety that Wolff's security might not be good enough. 'The possible threat to your life has gotten more serious, too.'

'You mean it's not just the possibility of criminals eliminating me, to make sure they have the time to break open ICON once and for all?'

'Well, no.'

'I must say I find that threat a trifle hard to take seriously. It's the kind of thing criminals might talk about doing, but going to the trouble of doing it means stepping beyond whatever safety they've created for themselves. I think perhaps the criminals are not so organized and not so well informed that they would consider killing me a worthwhile risk.'

'I'm not so sure.'

'Listen, Mr Graham, I have fathered a few rumours about a computer genius who is even now overtaking me in the field of computer data security. A lot of people already believe that no matter what happens to me, the future of ICON is going to be in very safe hands.'

'There will be plenty of people who won't believe a word of it,' Mike said. 'They're the ones who take the trouble to dig down to the truth, which means they're also likely to take the trouble to blow your head off.'

Wolff shrugged. He was obviously not convinced.

'Anyway,' Mike said, 'the new threat is something different.' He took out a sheet of paper and unfolded it. 'You'll see your own name on that list. Do you know any of the other men?'

Wolff took the list and frowned at it. 'Him,' he said, jabbing the paper with a long finger. 'Rudolf Altenberg. I don't know any of the others.'

'How do you know Altenberg?'

'Against my better judgement, and under pressure from my ex-wife who is a friend of Altenberg's wife, I devised a computer

168

system for him and I personally installed it in his home. A very sophisticated system, I might say. It's better than anything I've got myself.'

'Have you mingled socially with Altenberg?'

'Now why do you ask that?'

'To be blunt, the men on that list are Nazis.'

'Except for me.'

'Well . . .'

'I'm not surprised Altenberg's a Nazi. He's a very unpleasant man with terrible taste in books and music. So why do you suppose I am on that list?'

'Somebody thinks you're a Nazi, I guess.'

'And why is there a list at all?'

'It's a hit-list. Two people on it are already dead.'

'That is gloomy news, Mr Graham.' Wolff looked towards the window. 'Somebody could really be after me, then.'

'It wouldn't be wise to doubt it. Tell me, why would anybody get the impression you're a Nazi?'

'Because of my association with Altenberg?'

'Maybe.'

'I would assume so,' Wolff said. 'We attended social gatherings together. He insisted on a couple of visits to functions, he wanted to introduce me to people he said were now beneficiaries of the computer system I had designed for him. He was really just showing me off, of course, because I'm rather famous. Tiresome, very tiresome.'

Mike wasn't sure if he detected evasiveness. Wolff seemed to want to dismiss the topic and move on.

'You can't think of any other reason why somebody might think you're a Nazi?'

Wolff's eyes hardened. 'No,' he said. 'Just try to accept that.' He looked away.

'I think we should tighten your security, anyway,' Mike said.

'I don't agree.'

'It can't hurt.'

'What I have is adequate. I am hampered enough, I don't want any more restraints.'

'These guys are not adequate. They would be halfway out of

their chairs and reaching for their guns at the point when a competent assassin would blow them away.'

'Is that the threat I face? A trained killer?'

'It seems so. We have a description and we're trying to track him down, but until we do, you definitely need to be shielded better than you are. I know it means offending the local flatfoot tribe, but we can't take feelings into account.'

Wolff stood and walked to the window again. 'Come and look,' he said, pointing. 'That building over there, on the far side of the park, is the stock exchange. A busy place, every room occupied by clerks and other functionaries. A sniper operating over there is outside the bounds of likelihood. And that is the only building which looks directly towards this one.'

'Even so –'

'Downstairs, as you know, is a team of very fastidious security people who have emergency switches that can barricade stairways and disable elevators. Nobody who is even faintly suspicious is going to get up here, and security always check with me first, even when it's my old mother who calls.'

'I got past them with a phoney ID,' Mike said.

'But first they showed me your face on the security monitor, didn't they?'

'And you thought I looked honest, and you let me come up. I could have been an assassin.'

'I let you come up because I know perfectly well who you are.'

Mike blinked at him. 'What – because I made an appointment?'

'No.' Wolff smiled. 'Use your imagination. If you were a layman, as I am, with occasional access to classified UN files, as I have, wouldn't you take a look now and again?'

'Oh.'

'So,' Wolff continued, 'in the *extremely* unlikely event of somebody making it to my apartment door, I think there's just enough vigour in those two to make holes in him, should such a thing become necessary.'

Mike thought it over. Finally he nodded. 'I'll pass on what you say. In the meantime, be careful. Don't go out alone. If you

170

plan to move around let us know, we'll get you a shadow. Two shadows if we think you need them.'

Mike turned from the window. One of the marksmen was staring at him. It was the same look, he thought – half curious, half absent – that cows gave passers-by.

'Remember what I told you, Andreas. Don't rely on your troops. Stay alert.'

An hour after sunrise, two men in a black Ford pickup were parked 180 metres from the service yard of the Comfort Inn in Dallas. They were a fat man called Chuck and a thinner, younger one called Billy. Both were employees of Don Chadwick. For this surveillance job they had been equipped with high magnification monoculars, through which they watched a borrowed station wagon with false plates parked near the service elevator of the hotel.

'Here we go,' Chuck murmured.

They watched as Philpott got out of the elevator, opened the station wagon tailgate and stepped back into the elevator. He bent over and hoisted one end of a rolled carpet and began dragging it towards the vehicle.

'Lord save us,' Billy said. 'No real puzzle about what he's totin' there.'

The carpet was obviously heavy and unwieldy. They could see sweat shine on Philpott's face. He dragged the roll between his arms until the midpoint touched the edge of the tailgate, then he let go. The carpet dropped with a bump that Chuck and Billy could hear. Philpott bent again, picked the other end of the carpet up off the ground, readied himself behind it with spread feet, and pushed. The roll slid into the station wagon. Philpott folded it over, shut the tailgate and got in behind the steering wheel.

'Just leave a good space behind him,' Chuck said as Billy started the engine. 'There won't be too much traffic on the road this time of day.'

Philpott drove out on to West Kingsley and turned right, travelling south. At the first major dip in the road he looked in the rearview mirror and saw the black Ford pickup hanging back,

171

a couple of hundred metres behind. As he took the turning for Trinity River and the Greenbelt Park, the mobile telephone in his pocket beeped twice. He took it out, thumbed the green button and put the phone to his ear.

'Is it all right to speak?' a voice said. It was C. W. Whitlock.

'How are you doing that?' Philpott demanded.

'Sorry?'

'You're dead and rolled up in a carpet in the back of this vehicle I'm driving.'

'You're on your way, then?'

'Bowling along, some distance ahead of a not-so-subtle tail.'

'I wanted to be sure things were going as expected.'

'As *hoped*, not as expected. I'm too steeped in wariness ever to expect much. Is anything happening there that I should know about?'

'There's a message from Sabrina.'

'Any developments?'

'Nothing yet. She's in Berlin. Observation convinces her that Erika Stramm goes nowhere without her bear-like escort.'

'Keep me posted on her chosen line of action. I trust her judgement.'

'Very well.'

'I'll turn the phone off in another hour or so. If you've anything urgent to communicate after that, it'll have to wait. Oh, and by the way, Chadwick paid cash. We now have a fat anonymous donation for whatever charity comes out of the hat.'

'Well done,' Whitlock said.

'I'll be in touch as soon as matters here are concluded.'

'Right. And if I could just ask . . .'

'Yes?'

'When you dispose of the remains, be gentle with me.'

TWENTY-TWO

At three in the afternoon Erika Stramm and her companion, Gregor Bryusov, returned home from a luncheon appointment. It was a good lunch and they had both taken a lot of wine. They had been the guests of a magazine publisher with a flair for mingling business and pleasure, and in the course of the meal a deal had been struck. Erika would write a series for the intellectual monthly *Deutsch Herzfeuer*, a ten-part study of the transforming effect of socialism upon the arts in Germany since 1946. A commission like that, she told Gregor in the taxi home, was like being paid to play with her favourite toys.

They talked intensely as they entered the apartment, each overlapping what the other said, but in the gloom of the hallway Gregor suddenly stopped talking. He pointed to the strip of carpet between the hall and the door to the sitting room. A single nylon thread lay coiled against the dark fibre, glinting in the dim overhead light. Since the American journalist broke in, Gregor had taken to fixing a thread across the sitting-room doorway each time they went out.

Erika kept talking, her face serious now as she watched Gregor step carefully into the sitting room. He switched on the light, walked to the centre of the room and stood there, looking slowly round.

The bedroom door off the sitting room was half open. It had been closed when they left. Gregor took a leather cosh from his pocket, hooked his thumb through the thong and silently wrapped it around his wrist. He crossed the room and kicked open the bedroom door. It flew in against the wall with a bang and swung back.

Erika came into the sitting room. She saw Gregor step through the bedroom doorway. He moved out of sight, towards the fitted wardrobes along the left wall. She heard him open a door. He grunted, just once, then there was the unmistakable sound of a body falling.

'Gregor?'

She went to the bedroom door. There was no sound. She put one foot forward, using her leg as a prop, and leaned into the room. Gregor was lying face-down in front of the wardrobes. Erika turned her head to look behind the door.

'Can we do this peacefully?' Sabrina said.

She came forward, her arms extended to the sides. She was in her black worksuit and rubber-soled boots, her hair clipped tightly behind her head. Erika moved back a pace, tensing herself.

'I only want to ask questions. They are important, and answering them will not hurt you or impinge on your liberty.'

Erika looked at Gregor's motionless body. She could see he was handcuffed.

'I don't have to talk to you.'

'Well maybe you do.'

Abruptly Erika jumped back, pulling a knife from the pocket of her jeans. The blade flicked open, long and thin.

'Any questions that get asked,' she said, 'you'll be answering them.' She jerked her head at the sitting room. 'Get in there. Now!'

For an instant Erika looked down at the knife, positioning it in front of her. When she looked up Sabrina's fist was an inch from her nose, moving fast. It hit her with a snapping sound. She fell. Sabrina stepped out from behind the door and kicked her twice, hard, in the ribs. Erika tried to scream but she had no breath. She began to gulp, trying to suck air into her stricken chest.

Sabrina shook the knife from her hand, took her by the ankles and dragged her into the sitting room. Erika pulled back her leg, trying to aim a kick. Sabrina let the leg drop and jumped on it with both feet. Now Erika did scream. She doubled over on the floor with her knees curled to her chin, clutching her injured calf.

'Right then, ups-a-daisy.'

174

Sabrina got behind Erika and took her by the armpits. She hoisted her into a straight-backed chair, pushed her hands through the slats and slipped on a pair of handcuffs.

'There.' Sabrina came round in front, wiping her hands on the legs of her worksuit. 'You and the boyfriend are a matching set now. You were both a lot easier than I expected.'

'You won't get away with this,' Erika panted. 'You or the other one, Miles or whatever he calls himself.'

'Please, spare me that.' Sabrina tucked a loose strand of hair into the clasp at the back of her head. 'I just did get away with it. Didn't I?'

'That's what you'll pay for,' Erika said. The pain of Sabrina landing full-weight on her shin had brought tears to her eyes; they had flowed freely down her cheeks, taking a quantity of mascara with them. 'I'm talking about later.'

'Do you want me to make it rougher still?'

'You wouldn't dare harm me.'

'I've already harmed you. And your friend.'

'What did you do to him?'

'Given the difference between his weight and mine, and given the fact I knew I had to deal with two of you, I played dirty pool, Erika.'

'What did you *do* to him?'

'Knocked him out with a blast of CS.' Sabrina held up the silver canister, then dropped it back in her pocket. 'He went down like he'd been shot. In a couple of minutes he'll come round and he'll be fine. For the time being. If you don't answer my questions, I'll take it out on him.' She went into her pocket again and brought out a hypodermic syringe, the needle capped and in position. 'Pentothal, Erika.'

Erika looked shocked.

'And don't tell me I wouldn't dare.' Sabrina nodded at the syringe, which contained yellow-tinted water. 'There's a big overdose in there.'

'You're a crazy woman!'

'Well, you obviously know that when the subject's heart is really pounding, a big dose can bring on a spectacular brain seizure.'

'You could kill him!'

'Yes, I could.' Sabrina moved close. She bent down, putting her face level with Erika's. 'Shall we talk?'

'What the hell do you want with me? I don't *know* anything.'

'You have information I need. Please don't wear down my temper by denying it. Listen – I won't come to harm for any of this. But your boyfriend could. Don't doubt me, that would be a bad mistake.'

'What do you want, for God's sake?'

'The name, address and timetable of your assassin.'

Erika said nothing. She lowered her head.

'Am I to take it you're refusing?'

'Why do you want to know this?'

'I work for an organization that has to stop what you're doing to the men on Emily Selby's list.'

'What organization?'

'I can't tell you. But in spite of what you think is evidence to the contrary, we are on the side of the angels.'

'A Nazi would have no difficulty saying that.'

'Erika, I don't like Nazis. Did you ever hear of a neo-fascist called Klaus Schneider?'

Erika nodded. 'I heard of him. Was he a friend of yours?'

'I brought him in.'

Erika stared. 'That's easy to say.'

'The details of how he was caught were never made public,' Sabrina said. 'But I bet you know what happened.'

'Perhaps I do.'

'So. Schneider was on a bench at Unter den Linden on a warm night in August 1992. He was waiting for a consignment of stolen heroin which he planned to sell below the going price. It was one of his ways of raising funds for the cause. At the appointed time a young woman arrived and he followed her into the bushes to make the exchange. Except she turned on him, beat him up, stripped off his clothes and tied him to a tree. Then she took a Polaroid and sent it to his compadres, those who thought he was the new Führer. They got the picture with a note saying the same would happen to them. Dispersal of the group was my mission. It worked.'

176

Erika shrugged. 'The details are correct, but you can't prove you were the woman.'

'I swear on my mother's life, I was.'

'Then why object when we take serious action against the fascists?'

'Because you're into wholesale slaughter, and there's no obvious proof that you're targeting the right people.'

'But we are.'

'To say that, you must have substantial proof, or at least enough to get a legitimate investigation going. Why not hand over your evidence to the police?'

'Conventional investigations are too polite and too prone to end in flabby liberal leniency. Our way is better.'

'Erika,' Sabrina leaned close again. 'I can't spend any more time arguing. I have a job to do. I need to know who your hatchet man is. I'm prepared to do what it takes to get an answer. I wasn't kidding about the Pentothal.'

Erika was staring into the bedroom. Gregor had come round. He lay coughing feebly against the carpet.

'I don't want you to hurt him,' she said, the hardness gone from her voice.

'Then talk to me.'

For a long moment Erika stared at Sabrina. Then she nodded. 'Take the cuffs off him. Give him water. Then I'll talk to you.'

'You want me to let him loose before you've talked?' Sabrina shook her head. 'I don't think so. Not until –'

'It's a promise!' Erika whispered hoarsely. 'A promise. I never go back on a promise! Now in the name of God help Gregor. Help him!'

The black pickup was parked on a rocky bluff high over a stretch of open land between two dense clumps of woodland. The sun was high and the temperature inside the pickup, in spite of the windows being open, was 92 degrees Fahrenheit.

For more than two hours Chuck and Billy had sat behind the dusty windshield, observing Chadwick's station wagon parked on the open ground below them, its grey-and-blue paintwork baking in the heat.

177

'All that time in a wagon in this heat with a dead man,' Chuck said. 'That guy ain't natural. What kind of man could put up with that?'

'He's English, don't forget.'

Since parking the station wagon Mr Beamish did not appear to have moved. He had simply stopped on the dirt road linking the clumps of woodland, the same dirt road that led right through that sector of the Greenbelt Park. When he stopped he switched off the engine, sat back behind the wheel and folded his arms.

'He does have air-conditioning in there,' Billy said. 'But I don't think that would give him too much protection, not after all this time.' He groaned. 'I promised Mr Chadwick I'd clean the inside of that wagon after this character's done with it.'

At that moment Malcolm Philpott, sitting in the station wagon, could see what the two men in the pickup would have to use their scopes to identify, a small bulk-liquid transporter with a fat blue chemical tank on its back. It approached along a branch road and came slowly down the hillside to the spot where Philpott was parked.

The driver was Russ Grundy. 'Mr Beamish?' he called.

'That's right.'

'Are we being watched?'

'Yes we are. Get into your part, Russ. You have a keen-eyed audience up on the hill over there behind me. Please don't look in that direction.'

Grundy got out. He was dressed in the uniform of a US State Trooper. He came across to the station wagon and held the door as Philpott got out.

'What do I have to do now?'

Philpott pointed to the back of the station wagon. 'There's a roll of carpet in there. In the interests of verisimilitude, there are two half-filled plastic sacks of water taped to the centre of the roll. I want you to help me carry that carpet over to your empty tanker and poke it in through the lid on top, which of course you will first open.'

'Can you tell me why I'm dressed like a lawman?'

'Why do you ask? Do you need to know what your motivation is?'

'No. I'm just eaten up with curiosity.'

'In my experience,' Philpott said, 'it's the really baffling visible evidence that burrows deep into people's credulity. I mean, what in heaven's name is a state trooper doing driving a tanker? And what's he going to do with the carpet-wrapped corpse he's loaded into the tank?'

'It's bizarre, I'll give you that.'

'Thank you.'

From the pickup high on the bluff Chuck and Billy watched through their scopes as the ominous roll of carpet was man-handled on to the pickup and slid, after some struggling, down into the tank. They watched the trooper close the lid, get down, shake hands with Beamish, and drive away. After a couple of minutes Beamish drove off in the opposite direction.

'I'll be real glad when this day is over,' Billy said to Chuck.

Back in Dallas Philpott parked the station wagon at a quiet spot near his hotel, as arranged with Chadwick. Before he closed and locked the door, he sprinkled three drops from the phial of cadaverine Grundy had obtained for him. Within seconds the unmistakable odour of decaying human flesh began to fill the interior of the station wagon. He shut the door quickly.

'Mission accomplished,' he whispered with satisfaction. He'd enjoyed this little jaunt. It felt good to be back in the field again. As he walked back to the hotel he whistled softly, thinking ahead to a hot bath, a fine dinner, then a late flight back to New York.

TWENTY-THREE

'Memories threaten me,' Uli Jürgen said. 'I hate the way they invade my present.'

'Really? How strange.'

Marianne Edel was on a high-legged stool in the centre of the bare-floored studio, her face and her uncovered shoulders mercilessly sunlit by tall windows and wide fanlights. When she spoke she tried not to move.

'How else would you make contact with memories?' she said. 'They have to invade the present before you become aware of them.'

'They always seem to challenge my safety. So I try to leave the past undisturbed.'

Jürgen stepped back from his easel and put down the brush he had been using. He smiled at the canvas, being careful to frown at the same time, so he would look self-critical. The picture pleased him. It gave him a secure, competent feeling. All his good commercial work did that.

'I think we are finished, Frau Edel.'

At six sittings over four weeks he had painted a perfect likeness of his sitter, which any half-adequate portraitist could have done. But he was Uli Jürgen, so his picture was much more than a likeness. He had been described as an artist who could invest a portrait with the spirituality of its subject. The picture of Marianne Edel was a true likeness invested with a dozen ingenious falsehoods – at the eyes, the mouth, the jawline, the neck. Her skin sagged and wrinkled in exactly the places it did in reality, but in the picture the sagging and the furrows were softer-edged and looked more like silken drapery than tired epidermis.

'May I look at it now?'

'Well . . .'

Individually the falsehoods were unremarkable, but the collective effect was to flatter Marianne Edel shamelessly, and brilliantly. A stranger looking at the picture would see a convincing harmony of line and tone and colour which suggested, powerfully, that the vigour and sexuality in the image must be a true reflection of those qualities in the sitter. Uli Jürgen had known Marianne Edel only a little over a month, but he doubted she had ever looked half as good as his creation.

'Yes, come and look,' he said.

She stepped down carefully from the stool and stood beside him. For a minute they were silent, he thinking about his meeting later with his accountant, she bedazzled by a talent that could make her resemble so strongly her own idea of herself.

'You are a genius,' she said.

'Oh, come now.'

He cringed within himself as she impulsively threw her arms round his neck and kissed him on the mouth.

'You darling!' she exclaimed, and kissed him again.

Jürgen held his breath and waited for it to be over. The woman was fifty, heavy for her size and not well preserved. Facially she bore an unflattering resemblance to the actor Jon Voight. She had stale breath and bad taste in perfume. But she was rich, and Jürgen never repulsed money or anyone who came bearing it, however objectionable.

'You think your husband will like it, then?' he said as she released him.

'He will adore it. When can I take it home?'

'It should remain here another ten days, at least. But if you are really impatient to remove it to your home, I can have it taken there two or three days from now by someone who knows how to handle freshly-finished canvases. He can hang it for you, too.'

'That would be splendid. Can you arrange that for me?'

'Horst will be here later to pick up some other work. I will organize everything with him then, and call you to confirm.'

Marianne Edel took her coat from the stand by the window. Jürgen helped her put it on.

'You are so well organized for an artist,' she said. 'And more of a thinker than I would have expected.'

'A thinker?' Jürgen smiled cautiously. 'What makes you say that?'

'You've told me so many interesting things on my visits here. And what you were saying just now, about memories, that is so haunting.'

If she had not been a client he would have laughed. In the circumstances he stared neutrally into his coffee cup. The observation about memories was entirely for effect. He had read some of it somewhere and made up the rest.

'My husband says you're the living image of Freud, you know.'

Jürgen looked at Frau Edel. 'Freud?'

'Your beard, the broad forehead – and the way you hold a paintbrush when you look at the canvas, it's just the way Freud held a cigar.'

It was the first time he had been told he looked like a Jew, and it stung. He looked pointedly at his watch.

'I must go,' said Frau Edel. He accompanied her to the door. 'Do call me as soon as you have made arrangements to have the portrait delivered.'

'Of course.'

She kissed his cheek one more time before she left. He closed the door softly behind her, making a sour face at the panels.

'Freud, indeed.'

The telephone rang. He hurried across and picked it up. It was his accountant's secretary, reminding him of his appointment.

'Tell him not to worry,' he said, 'I haven't forgotten. I'll get there on time, I always do.'

There was a sharp tap on the door. Horst, he thought, or the Edel woman had forgotten something.

He crossed the studio and opened the door. A stranger was there, tall, blue-eyed, with very fair hair. He had a confident smile.

'Herr Jürgen? I came for the package.'

'I'm sorry? The package? There must be a mistake.'

'That's it.' The young man pointed to a cardboard box halfway across the room.

'No, it isn't, I –'

The young man pushed past Jürgen and entered the studio. He stopped in front of the portrait of Marianne Edel, staring at it.

Jürgen came away from the door, frowning, confused.

'That is rubbish,' the young man said, still smiling.

'Get out of here,' Jürgen said. He took the young man by the arm. 'Right this minute, or I call the police.'

The young man pulled his arm free and slipped the other hand into the pocket of his tweed jacket. He pulled out a black snub-nosed revolver.

'Here is a fact, Uli Jürgen. In 1942 the painter Samuel Weiss was kicked out of his Berlin studio, two streets away from this spot, and his canvases and paints were thrown out of the windows on to the road. Weiss was then made to wear a placard listing his alleged crimes against humanity, and while he was paraded around the little park near his studio, the Nazis made a bonfire of all his paintings.'

The young man waved the gun at Jürgen, making him stand in front of the portrait of Marianne Edel.

'Another fact. Samuel Weiss was estimated to be one of the foremost experimental painters of the thirties. His name was mentioned alongside those of Schwitters, Hodler and Kandinsky. He illuminated the world with his vision. You, on the other hand, call yourself a painter, an artist, and yet you have never displayed a talent for producing anything more elevated than sophisticated posters.'

'What is your point?' Jürgen demanded. 'What do you want with me?'

'Weiss finally died after being blinded and having his hands and his spirit broken in Belsen. That was his fate, after having lived his entire life in poverty. You, an ungifted hack, have brought no light into the world, have never been poor, and are about to die rich. My point, sir, is that everyday life bulges with sickening ironies.'

Jürgen had turned white.

'Suppose you at least try to die the death of a true artist,' the young man said.

'I warn you,' Jürgen said, 'you will find yourself in great trouble.'

'Not me, sir. I am not about to suffer like so many people have suffered at the hands of you and yours, your sidekicks, the brotherhood with its benighted faith in the power of thick-headed bullies to prevail.'

Jürgen felt his bowls loosen. He swallowed against the dryness in his throat. He remembered the telephone call from Viktor Kretzer, warning him to be on his guard.

'Here is your chance of redemption, Uli Jürgen.'

The young man extended his arm suddenly, pointing the gun at a downward angle. He fired. Jürgen stood where he was, half-deafened. His right arm was numb and felt incredibly heavy. He looked down and saw half his hand was gone. Blood trickled freely on to the floorboards.

'You are an artist,' the young man said. 'Try to think like one. This context is unbearable, yes? You paint with your right hand, it is the instrument of your expression. But it is gone. It cannot be used so your art is effectively silenced.'

'You bastard,' Jürgen said weakly.

'Enmeshed in such *catastrophe*, what does the true artist wish for at once, as a matter of reaction?'

Jürgen stared at the bright intelligent eyes, the fixed smile, trying to read salvation from this nightmare. Pain suddenly surged along his arm and his stomach lurched. He doubled over and vomited.

'So what does the true artist do? What can he want now, bereft of his *raison d'être*?' The young man snapped his fingers. 'If he is a determined artist who would wish to express himself in spite of the most major of setbacks, he would say, to hell with this, I will teach myself to paint with my other hand.'

In an instant his arm was outstretched and the gun pointing downwards. He fired a second time, blowing off the thumb and first two fingers of Jürgen's left hand. Jürgen staggered back, reeled for a moment, then dropped to his knees in the puddle of his vomit.

'Now we have the position of ultimate despair. Discount any deranged impulses to learn to paint with the feet or the mouth. You have lost the ability to express yourself. Can you feel that, the sense of loss, the black hole of despair?'

Jürgen tried to say something but managed only a grunt. Shock had put his body into tremor. Blood gathered in pools on the floor on either side of him.

'You want to die. Am I right? You know life holds nothing for you any more. Tell me, Uli Jürgen, have I made you feel that?'

Jürgen looked at the end of the barrel, thinking how small it was, how insignificant for something so terrible.

'Do you feel the way poor old Samuel Weiss must have felt, after they had taken away his vision and his means of expression?'

The young man pulled Jürgen to his feet and stood him in front of the easel again. He raised the gun.

'In the end he must have *longed* for death.'

The young man fired the gun into Jürgen's face.

TWENTY-FOUR

Sabrina poured a large cognac and handed it to Erika as she came out of the bedroom. Erika drank it in two swallows. Sabrina poured another. This time Erika sipped.

'He's asleep,' she said.

Gregor had gone to bed. The CS gas had made him sick. Erika had overcome his apparent desire to fight, and told him firmly that he needed rest. In the end he felt too ill to resist.

'I didn't realize how attached I had become,' Erika said.

'It can be a surprise.'

'I thought, if he dies, I'm going to die too.' She looked at Sabrina.

'I need you to keep your promise, Erika.'

'Go to the kitchen, we can spread things out in there.'

Sabrina prepared coffee while Erika made a telephone call. By the time the coffee was ready, a motorcycle courier was at the door with a satchel. Erika brought it to the kitchen and put the contents on the broad worktop. There was a thick book bound in black leather, a photograph album, and handwritten notes on hundreds of sheets of paper, stapled together in batches.

'This material is kept at the home of a magistrate,' Erika said. 'This is the first time it has been out of that place since it was gathered together.'

Sabrina touched the hard leather cover of the big book.

'That is a catalogue of crimes committed by the *Jugend von Siegfried*. It's the accumulated records of more than two thousand acts of brutality, robbery, fraud, coercion and murder, committed over a thirty-five-year period.'

'These are their own records?'

'Copies, yes. Hard won, I promise you. It has cost time, money

186

and labour, and at least one co-operative lawyer's clerk was killed for helping us.'

'What are the pictures?'

'The guilty men and mementoes of some of their victims. The collection means very little, unless your own heart is caught up in what they did, and what they still do.'

'And the bundles of notes?'

'Interview material, mostly the testimony of victims.'

'It looks like a labour of love. Or hate.'

'What astonishes me, even now,' Erika said, 'is that the records exist. They are so damning. Nazis have this self-destructive compulsion to record everything they do. They can't make a move without making a record of it. They have to leave their mark, like dogs at lamp-posts. During the war, they spent fortunes in time, money and manpower just keeping their records straight – the very records that hanged dozens of them.'

'It looks like a well organized collection.'

'It is brilliantly done. The method of accumulation and cataloguing was devised by Emily Selby's father, Johannes Lustig.'

'Your father's cousin.'

'Yes. To me he was Uncle Johannes. He also carried out the early research work. As time passed and we became more organized, the research was co-ordinated by myself and the other members of *Juli Zwanzig*. We only became a group with a name after Uncle Johannes died. It was his wish.'

'I know.'

Erika sighed. 'I suppose I should have guessed.'

'Are you all activists? Or are you mainly fund-raisers and co-ordinators?'

'I am an activist against Nazis in general,' Erika said. 'Journalism is my chosen means of attack. The others raise money, as you surmised. They fund lectures and publications to keep alive the truth of what happened to whole generations of Jews, and they do what they individually can to give our movement shape and spirit. But at the core, *Juli Zwanzig* has physical aims –'

'To kill off the surviving members of the *Jugend von Siegfried*.'

'That is correct. Uncle Johannes insisted nothing less would do. We lacked the stomach, individually and collectively, for such a course of action, but that didn't mean it was wrong. We needed to find a person who could consummate our aims.'

'You had no moral problem with that? Hiring a killer?'

'No problem at all,' she said defiantly. 'Just remember, we live with the knowledge that year in, year out, the *Jugend von Siegfried* systematically undermine, sabotage and actually kill Jews as a matter of policy. They do it subtly, without even communicating directly with each other. Unopposed, they would never stop. Somebody has to stop them, somebody has to punish their iniquity.'

'They're not bomb-proof. You have evidence here that the police can use against them.'

'Uncle Johannes did not want them handed over to the law. To extract the kind of justice he called for, we needed someone who hated the Nazis as much as we do, and who was capable of killing.'

'So who does that? Who's the mysterious young man with fair hair and blue eyes?'

For a moment Erika looked as if she would not say. But the understanding between them was clear, and she had given her word. Sabrina watched her head bow a fraction, the only sign that this was capitulation.

'He is Einar Ahlin. A Norwegian.'

'Why him?'

'Two years ago he came to Germany vaguely intending to do harm to the new Nazis. We diverted his attention to the old Nazis instead.'

'Norwegians have no fond memories of the Third Reich.'

'This Norwegian especially. Einar has a troubled history. Very troubled. He is an epileptic with personality problems who just happened to be born into a family touched by tragedy. His grandparents were tortured to death by the occupying Germans in Oslo during the war. Their daughter's life, as a consequence, was shadowed until the day she died.'

'Einar's mother.'

Erika nodded. 'She committed suicide in 1989. For nearly fifty years she kept her hatred of the Nazis burning and the fire passed into Einar at an early age. Many people would regard his obsession with punishing Nazis as pathological.'

'But you found it convenient.'

'Read the facts any way you wish,' Erika said. 'He believes in what he does. I believe in it too. I am happy to fund work which achieves an end we both passionately seek.'

'These records could probably put the remaining Siegfried boys in jail for the rest of their lives,' Sabrina said.

'You think that now I should hand them over to the police?'

'It would be the civilized thing to do.'

'That brings us back to retribution,' Erika said. 'Is a desire for proper redress so uncivilized? Justice on the biblical scale is the only real kind. These bastards have spent their lives from childhood working against Jews. They have wreaked misery, calamity and death on people they did not know. They have to pay for that. The enlightened liberal answer, life imprisonment, does not meet the bill. They have to pay with their lives.'

Sabrina noticed that the passion was gone from Erika's voice. She was spouting the words, but now there was no force of conviction behind them.

'Where is Einar Ahlin?'

'I've no idea.' A spark of defiance still flared, demonstrating once more the passion of Erika's commitment to her cause.

'Come on, Erika.'

'I promised to co-operate, I didn't promise to deliver anyone's head on a plate. Besides, it's true, I don't know where he lives. When we meet it's on neutral ground. He works from an address list Emily put together, and picks his targets from the order they appear in the picture.'

'What picture?'

Erika opened the album and pressed it flat at a ten-by-eight sepia-toned enlargement. It showed Adolf Hitler, standing on a rain-swept, bombed-out street, saluting a group of young boys.

'The *Jugend von Siegfried*,' Erika said. 'Photographed in 1945, on the very day they were inaugurated.'

Names had been entered in white ink next to everyone in the picture. The first boy on the left was Karl Sonnemann. The next one was Stefan Fliegel; beside him was Uli Jürgen.

'Einar broke the pattern when the American showed up.'

'Harold Gibson?'

'Yes.'

'How did he know about him?'

'Emily sent me e-mail about the man and his organization, all gathered from notes she'd found – they were for a paper Uncle Johannes had been preparing at the time of his death, about Americans providing financial support to a Nazi organization in Berlin.'

'And you showed the e-mail to Einar?'

Erika nodded. 'He is like a ferret with anything like that. He took the information to himself, worked on his own research.'

'Did you know he was planning to eliminate Harold Gibson?'

Erika shook her head.

'You don't have any control over this guy at all, do you?' Sabrina said.

Erika said nothing. Sabrina looked at the picture again. 'Uli Jürgen,' she said. 'That name rings a bell.'

Erika nodded. She pointed to the radio on the corner of the worktop. 'Uli Jürgen. There was a bulletin. He was found dead earlier today.'

Sabrina caught Erika's gaze and held it, trying to communicate to her the seriousness of the situation. 'Listen, Erika, I want you to understand something. This situation that you have created has got much bigger than just your personal vendetta. Other people's lives are at risk and that could have serious implications for world security. So I'm going to ask you again, and I want a straight answer this time: what do you do if you need to contact Einar Ahlin?'

Erika paused, searching Sabrina's face. Apparently impressed with her gravity, she said reluctantly, 'He has a girlfriend. She passes messages between us, both ways.'

'What's her address?'

Erika took down a pad and pencil from a shelf above the worktop. 'Her name is Magda Schaeffer.'

'Remember,' Sabrina said, 'if the address is wrong, I'll be back.'

'It's correct, you have my word.' Erika scribbled an address in Oranienstrasse. 'It's a one-room flat above a little nightclub. Magda works there, she's a stripper.'

Sabrina put the paper in her pocket. She looked at the photograph again. The name of the boy standing next to Uli Jürgen was Andreas Wolff.

'Do you have a scanner?' she said.

'What for?'

'For these records.' Sabrina slapped the book. 'I want copies. Quickly.'

'I don't think that's any part of our deal.'

Again there was no conviction. Sabrina felt the protest was a token.

'Why did you let me know they exist, Erika? Why did you have them brought here?'

'I wanted you to see them, to understand their part in what we do.'

Sabrina shook her head. 'You wanted me to force an issue. You still want the Siegfried gang attacked, but you know damn well Einar's going to get caught long before he gets around to killing them all. And your chances of finding another Einar must be one in a million.'

'I know nothing of the sort.'

'Please, Erika, credit me with a little intelligence. Your killer is an extrovert, he puts on the high profile every time he makes a hit. He'll get taken out before he's halfway through Emily's list.'

'We have a mission –'

'You know that pretty soon your only hope will be to let the law do the job for you, because your assassin will be a goner. And I think that after the fright you got today with Gregor, you want to draw back from the physical stuff sooner rather than later.'

Erika was silent for a moment, then jerked a thumb at the door. 'There is a scanner in my office along the hall.'

'Come and help me.'

Erika set up a word-processing program on the computer and Sabrina used the flatbed scanner to transfer copies of the book pages on to the screen. The completed copy file was very large.

'How do you plan to get all that on to a disk?' Erika said. 'The high-capacity removable drive is broken.'

'I won't take a copy away with me,' Sabrina said. 'I'll send it to a safe box. Let me use the keyboard.'

She called up the modem, made contact with her communications area and tapped in her UNACO password for Mailbox Access. The padlocked box came up. She put in her personal access code. The lid of the box opened. She addressed the *Jugend von Siegfried* file to C. W. Whitlock and uploaded it. The transfer took three minutes. When it was complete, she typed out a terse note, labelled it MOST URGENT, and addressed it also to Whitlock.

'And now I get out of your life,' she said.

'Can you guarantee that?'

'No. But I've no desire to have anything more to do with you. Barring any sidewash, we're through with each other.'

At the door she said, 'I understand your mission, Erika. But you haven't been cheated out of anything. It's true what I said, your executioner's luck can't hold.'

Erika flapped her hand, perhaps accepting that. 'My feelings about what has happened are – ' She hesitated. 'They're complex. Mingled. To know how I feel, maybe you would have to be a German Jew.'

C. W. Whitlock was in the corridor outside UNACO's copy room. As he punched the red button on his mobile and dropped it in his pocket Philpott stepped up behind him.

'There's a communication for you from Berlin,' Philpott said, pointing to the door of the Secure Communications Suite. 'Shall we look at it?'

They went in and Whitlock sat down by the console. When he had ascertained the Mailbox file was from Sabrina, he punched in DIRECT PRINT and stood by to wait for the printout.

'Can you give me a running translation of the stuff coming out of the printer?' Philpott asked.

Whitlock nodded. For ten minutes without pause, he sight-translated from the sheet of paper unreeling on to the carpet. He read summaries of fraudulent transactions which had resulted in Jewish businessmen being ruined. He read gloating descriptions of evictions, midnight batterings, a gang rape of a Jewish woman and two murders. After the description of the second killing, Whitlock stopped.

'I think I want to take this stuff in smaller doses from here on,' he said.

'Quite.' Philpott started rolling up the ribbon of paper. 'Our dear girl has struck gold of a particularly nauseating yellow. Let's get translators down here to deal with this. I'll fix a meet with the Federal German Legation.'

He glanced at the monitor. 'Why is that blinking, C. W.?'

Whitlock looked up. 'Damn.' He hit the button marked READ. 'It's a separate communiqué. She probably meant us to read it first.'

Sabrina's message flashed on to the screen, short and to the point: *Wolff may be next on the list.*

'Talk to her as soon as you can,' Philpott said. 'Then alert Mike.'

TWENTY-FIVE

'Uli Jürgen,' Wolff said, repeating the name, his voice husky on the telephone. 'I heard about the murder on the radio, and the name rang a bell then. Now you mention it, I believe a member of a group I met at a restaurant on Leipziger Strasse was called that. It was one of those occasions I was being shown off by Rudolf Altenberg. Jürgen was talkative, something of a show-man as I recall.'

'He was on the list,' Mike said. 'He was also standing next to someone with your name on an old photograph that the assassin works with. That's what I called to tell you. It's a picture of all the people on the list taken when they were boys.'

'It occurs to me,' Wolff said, 'that maybe that group I met were the people on this list. All about the same age as myself, all acting as if they *weren't* a group. They didn't sit together, and they said nothing about being connected in any way, but at the same time they acted as if they hadn't seen each other in ages and were having trouble concealing their pleasure. It's odd how a thing like that shows.'

'Do you remember anything else?'

'Lots of photographs were taken. It was a charity affair, I think.' Wolff paused. 'My God.' He snapped his fingers, making a cracking sound on the line. 'I had forgotten it completely . . .'

'What?'

'Two different people, members of that coterie – if it was a coterie – told me I had the same name as a boyhood friend of theirs, now sadly dead.'

Mike groaned. 'Good old mistaken identity.'

'Oh no, they didn't think I *was* their friend.'

'No, but the person who made up the list did.' Mike had no

doubt Wolff was telling the truth. 'You're the right age to have been in the Hitler Youth.'

'Only just.'

'These men were the last of the chosen,' Mike said. 'You've been seen in their company and by a nasty coincidence you've got yourself lumped with them. That's bad for your reputation, but it's worse for your long-term prospects.'

'I find it hard, accepting that I am at risk.'

'Well, you'll have to. You could be high on the list by now. I want you to stay put and don't move far from the guys looking after you.'

'Whatever you say.'

Mike rang off, then he put through a call to Philpott in New York and told him about his conversation with Wolff.

'We've been digging in the news archives since we got the records from Sabrina,' Philpott said. 'We found that a Berlin businessman called Andreas Wolff, born in Munich in 1934, died in a motoring accident in 1982. Significantly, a newspaper account of his funeral reported that among the pallbearers were Erich Bahr and Klaus Garlan.'

'Who are both on the list.'

'So the real Wolff is dead and our man is being mistaken for him.' Mike heard muffled voices in the background. 'C. W. is in the process of suggesting to the Austrian police that they double their efforts to protect Wolff,' Philpott said. 'Have you contacted Sabrina yet – I assume you *are* in Berlin?'

'I'm in Berlin, but I haven't been in touch with Sabrina. I'm about to do that.'

'As soon as anything happens, for good or ill, let me know.'

Mike went directly to a bar off Kantstrasse, near the Kurfürsten-damm. Sabrina was waiting, sitting alone at a table by the door. Her hair was combed down, touching her shoulders. She wore a dark blue linen dress with a flared skirt; around her shoulders she wore a silk shawl.

'Going somewhere special?' Mike said, sitting down.

'I made an effort to look civilized, that's all.' Sabrina poured him a glass of wine from the carafe on the table. 'That's *Scheurebe Kabinett*. Not bad.'

'Why did they want you to stay in Berlin?' he said. 'Did somebody think maybe I couldn't cope on my own?'

'Keeping me here is like parking a car handy to where you might need it. C. W. thinks Philpott wants the case resolved within the next twenty-four hours. If it comes to a showdown rather than a routine arresting of guilty parties, I suppose it makes sense to have us both where the action's likely to break out.' She sipped her wine. 'Care to bring me up to speed?'

Mike told her about his conversation with Wolff. 'What's the lead you have on the assassin?'

'It's his girlfriend. Magda Schaeffer. She's a stripper at a club in Oranienstrasse. I've bought you temporary membership. The show doesn't start until eleven.'

'Even if we corner this guy, he isn't going to throw up his hands and tell us we've got him fair and square,' Mike said. 'That's way too low key. If he goes down, he'll be fighting all the way.'

'He won't be the first one.'

'I had a dream about him,' Mike said. 'It was jumbled, but he had just blown away somebody, in a fairground. I was going right up to him and he was standing there with the gun still smoking in his hand. I was getting ready to put an armlock on him. He turned and he had this terrific smile. I smiled back, completely won over in spite of myself, and he brought up the gun and shot me in the heart. The pain woke me up.'

'This is no time to talk about death-dreams,' Sabrina said.

'Are there good and bad times?'

'It's what my friend Pratash believes.'

'Pratash. I don't think I've had the pleasure.'

'He's a mystic. Or I think he is. I met him in Calcutta. He told me he was drawn to my emanations.'

'Which always look nice when you wear light clothing.'

'He wasn't coming on to me, he was serious. A little, old, deeply serious man. He believes the world is a great big mistake and that the Creator will one day realize this and start it all over again from scratch. In the meantime, we should keep our heads

196

below the parapet. One way of doing that, he told me, is never to think of danger, or dwell on dreams of jeopardy or death, at a time when real danger is likely to occur. He says such behaviour stimulates disaster.'

'I suppose we all have our spiritual authority,' Mike said. 'I haven't settled on mine yet, but Ralph Waldo Emerson might just fit the throne. Here's an example. You know I love speed.'

'Real speed. Not chemical speed.'

'Real speed. I use speed as recreation, but I also use it to tune myself for challenges that come up in the job. I believe that life rewards those who move fastest, and that speed is sometimes a kind of magical cloak. Emerson said, "In skating over thin ice, our safety is in our speed." Now how's that for a guru tuned to my own needs, huh?'

'I'm sure he'll serve you well.' Sabrina held up her glass. 'To Ralph Waldo.'

Mike picked up his. 'And to Pratash.'

They drank, watching each other over the rims of their glasses. Sabrina was caught by the moment's warmth, the clarity of good feeling between them.

'Tell me something honestly,' she said. 'Are we really friends? At heart, beneath all the top show?'

'I would say so, yes.'

Sabrina could not bring herself to ask any more.

'And I'll tell you something else,' Mike said. 'Just this one time. The past hasn't finished with me yet. But one day it will. I'll be liberated, if that's the word. And when that happens, maybe you'll detect a change or two.'

'You mean that one day we won't automatically bunch our fists at the sight of each other?'

'Something like that,' Mike said.

They smiled again. So did the woman behind the counter.

In theatrical terms, the on-stage act performed by Magda Schaeffer contained plenty of conflict and a good measure of tension, but it was entirely lacking in imagination.

Magda swayed and splayed to electronic music on a tiny area of spotlit floor. At appropriate intervals, with apparent

197

reluctance, she lost parts of her costume. As each item fell away from her body, her own excitement seemed to increase. As the minutes passed, however, her timing deteriorated and the pretence of sensuality gave way to vulgar posturing. In the end, what began as an apparent attempt at improvisational, sensual dance, ended up as old-fashioned downmarket striptease, with the audience roaring for her to take off the final wisp of material. When she did, it was to a scattering of applause from a crowd already losing interest.

Mike saw no need to waste time on niceties. Ten dollars bought him the complete co-operation of the bar-tender who promised that as soon as Magda was decent, he would arrange for her to join Mike at his table in the corner.

Less than five minutes after her act concluded she slid into the chair opposite Mike's. She was wearing a white T-shirt and jeans and carried a small grab-bag which he assumed contained her costume.

'I hope you liked the show, Mister –' She fluttered heavily darkened eyelashes at him. 'What should I call you? My name is Magda, by the way.'

'And I'm Mike.' He tried to guess her age. Twenty at most, he decided, but already raddled and weary-looking. 'And, yes, I enjoyed the show. You have a very lovely body.'

'Thank you.'

He watched her lower her eyes. It amused him how women in the skin trade always came on so fluffy and demure, as if anything indelicate might cause them to blow away on a wave of affronted modesty.

'Was that your only performance for the evening?'

'My only one here,' she said. 'Two nights out of six I do a speciality act at the Saucy Sailor, across the road.'

'Speciality act?'

'That's right.' Again, she lowered her eyes demurely. 'It's different to what I do here, and it costs more to see. But customers say it is worth the extra.'

'So you'll be going there now?'

'As soon as I've had a drink.'

Mike took the cue and waggled a finger at the barman, who

had been waiting for a sign. He had the drink poured ready. When he brought it across Mike saw him wink at Magda – a sign of confirmation, Mike assumed, that here was another soft mark.

'Cheers, Mike,' she said, and swallowed the whisky as if it was a thirst quencher. She leaned across the table. 'If you want, I can see you after I finish across the road.'

'That would be nice. But I'm an impatient person, Magda. What if I made it worth your while to cancel your show at the Saucy Sailor, just for tonight?'

She frowned at that, but the frown looked as counterfeit as her smile. 'I would lose my pay for the evening . . .'

'As I said, I would make it worth your while.'

'I would also have to provide a substitute act. Otherwise I would no longer be a friend of the management, you understand?'

'How much for your stand-in?'

'Dollars?'

He nodded.

'Fifty.'

He produced a wad, peeled off five twenties and put them on the table. 'That takes care of you both.' He pushed the notes towards her. 'For the moment,' he added, making her flutter her eyes again.

Arrangements for Magda's deputy were made through the barman, who did not appear to find the transaction unusual. Magda had another drink, then coyly suggested they go upstairs to her place, where it was quieter.

It was certainly quiet, Mike observed as he followed her into the tiny room. It was also airless and incredibly shabby. He had been in poorly furnished rooms that nevertheless said something good about their occupants; this room, with its litter of empty food containers, grubby glasses and full ashtrays, simply said that Magda Schaeffer was precisely the charmless slut she had appeared to be the moment the spotlight came on.

'Sit down,' she told Mike. 'I won't be a minute.'

He sank into a dusty old armchair that creaked under his weight. Magda disappeared behind a curtain hung across one end of the room. When she emerged she had two drinks in her hand.

'I hope you don't think I do this often. I only let you come up here because I like you.'

'I'm flattered.'

She drew a nail-bitten fingertip along the rim of his ear. 'What would you like me to do?'

He smiled. 'Stand up,' he whispered.

She eased away from him and stood back, watching him from behind lowered eyelids. Mike got to his feet. He reached under his jacket and pulled out his revolver. He pointed it at Magda's throat. She gasped and backed away.

'I don't do sick stuff,' she said.

'But I do.'

'I'll scream!'

'Do that, and a second later you're dead.'

'Please, don't hurt me.'

'I have to say I'm shocked, Magda.' Mike backed off a little, keeping the gun levelled on her. 'This is no way to treat your boyfriend, is it? Entertaining strange men for money.'

'I have no boyfriend.'

'He's called Einar. Einar Ahlin.'

She stared at him, her mouth moving uncertainly. 'Who are you?'

'I'm Mike, remember? I was asking you how you square this kind of behaviour with your boyfriend.'

'Einar doesn't mind.'

'Hard to believe, Magda.'

'I'm his girl, but we don't . . .' She shrugged. 'I hold him in my arms sometimes. When he cries. That's all. We are not physical.'

'Where is he?'

'I don't know that.'

'Tell me where he is.' Mike wagged the gun at her.

'I swear I don't know. He tells nobody. He comes here a lot, but I don't know where he goes.'

'Do you know what he does?'

She swallowed.

'Magda?'

'He kills people.'

'He told you?'

'He always tells me.'

'You must have some idea where he is when he isn't here.'

'I don't know where he goes. All I know for now is that he is away on work. Professional work.'

Magda glanced at the tiny fireplace. 'He has a safe, in there.' She pointed to a metal plate with a small door at its centre, set into the firebricks at the back. 'He put that there, he keeps the key for it on a chain round his neck.'

'What's in it?'

'His schedule, he calls it. He likes to take one week for each job. He puts a single name on each week of the diary.'

'A week for each killing?'

She nodded. 'He has a diary with seven days printed on every page, and on each page he writes a name from a list he keeps.'

'Why does he keep the diary in the safe?'

'It's his only private space in Berlin. That's what he said. He said he'd make a private space, and he did, and when it was made he put his diary in it. He says it is something orderly. The pages are his life's schedule, he said. They are sacred to him, so he keeps them apart from the world.'

Mike knelt before the empty fireplace. He picked up the small steel poker by the hearth and pushed it under the lower edge of the metal plate. He jerked the poker backwards and particles of brick fell away from the edges. Two more hard tugs on the poker and the plate sprang loose. He reached up under the edge and felt a book. He pulled it out and took it to the coffee table.

'This is the schedule?'

'Yes.'

Mike riffled through the pages, looking for the one for the current week. When he found it he saw a single name written diagonally across the page. It confirmed what he had feared.

The name was Andreas Wolff.

TWENTY-SIX

'The big companies are all turning to out-sourcing,' Don Chadwick said. 'The little outfits are fast becoming the well-head for new jobs and opportunities.'

His luncheon guest, a plastic-casings manufacturer called George Winship, was nodding steadily, but his attention was elsewhere. They were at a table on the roof restaurant at Don Giorgio's, a mile south of Waxahachie.

'The small man like yourself has a lot to offer in terms of employment and direct creation of cash. It's just a pity you're so vulnerable.'

'Mr Chadwick, forgive me interrupting, but I've been looking out over the parking lot there, and I'm sure somebody is paying uncommon attention to your car.'

Chadwick stood up, shielding his eyes against the sun. He had come in his classic MGB, one of his extensive collection of British cars.

'It's a fraction to the right of the ticket machine over there,' Winship said, pointing.

'Oh, yeah.'

Two men were standing in front of the car. One was writing in a notebook. Chadwick reached into his inside jacket pocket and took out his mini-scope.

'You always carry one of those?'

'Yep.'

'I heard of people being arrested with things like that on them,' Winship said.

Chadwick put the scope to his eye and turned the focus ring. He saw the two men looking into his car. He could clearly see their faces, their frowning expressions. He moved the scope down. They wore good shiny shoes and they had briefcases

202

standing beside them. They didn't look at all like thieves.

'Want to call the law?' Winship said. 'I got my mobile.'

'No, I think we'll just hold on a second before we do anything.'

'Looks like they're coming across,' Winship said.

'What?'

'Those guys that were nosing into your car. They're coming this way.'

Chadwick watched as they approached the restaurant. They stopped a short distance in front of the awning and spoke to a waiter. He nodded several times and pointed to the roof without looking up. The men disappeared under the awning.

'We'll soon see what this is all about,' Chadwick said.

He tried to smile at Winship but found he couldn't. Anxiety had gripped him so quickly he hadn't gauged how severe it was. He cleared his throat, took out his handkerchief and dabbed his brow just as the two men appeared. They spoke to the waiter at the desk and he pointed to Chadwick. They came across. Up close they seemed very tall. They had the kind of serious, no-nonsense faces that appeared never to have been touched by smiles.

'Donald Chadwick?' the taller one said.

'That's me. How can I help you, gentlemen?'

The tall one produced a small black leather folder and flipped it open. On one side was an ID card with his picture; on the other side a badge glittered.

'I'm FBI Special Agent Louis Cole. This is Agent Hubert Mullins. Could we speak privately, Mr Chadwick?'

'I'll be down in the bar,' Winship said, out of his chair already. 'If anybody wants me, just call.'

When he had gone the FBI men sat down. Agent Mullins was obviously used to being silent. He sat back, visibly withdrawing from the confrontation, becoming atmosphere.

Louis Cole folded his hands on the table and looked squarely at Chadwick. He was blond and broad-shouldered, not at all the kind of wimp Chadwick had heard the FBI recruited.

'Do you have any idea why we want to talk to you, Mr Chadwick?'

'None at all.'

203

'Well, I'll tell you straight off. Two days ago certain documents came into the possession of the FBI. They paint a detailed picture of your involvement in the financial affairs of the late Harold Gibson of Dallas.'

'Harold was a dear friend,' Chadwick said, trying to keep his voice steady. 'We did business together over a period of years, and Harold was a board member of several companies within which I have executive standing.'

'The financial matters detailed in the documents refer to money raised in this country and gifted to an illegal organization in Germany.'

'I know nothing about that.'

'I have to tell you, Mr Chadwick, that as a result of other matters raised in the documents, we have already impounded files, ledgers and diaries relevant to the company trading as Lone Star Realties and another called Chadwick, Pearce Associates.'

Chadwick looked astonished. 'How did you get those papers? They're private, they're locked away.'

'We have special powers under the Constitution, Mr Chadwick. The three banks and the firm of accountants involved were all very co-operative, as the law requires them to be.'

Chadwick's mouth had gone terribly dry. 'What – what about my associate, Mr Pearce . . .'

'He is already co-operating with us, as of ten o'clock this morning.'

Chadwick wet his lips. 'I think I want to have my lawyer with me before I say anything more.'

'That is your right. Now we'd like you to accompany us to the Bolton Rooms Hotel in Dallas. You can call your lawyer from there. We have an operations room set up in the hotel and a couple of my superiors would like to ask you some questions.'

Superiors. His *superiors*. There were men on the case loftier and more nerve-rattling than this one.

They stood up. Chadwick took a wad of bills from his pocket and peeled off three. He put them under a water glass. 'Off the record, Agent Cole, would you say my position is serious, at all?'

'I would say so, yes.'

As they went down the stairs Agent Mullins spoke. His voice was soft and so close that Chadwick felt its warmth on his ear.

'You're looking at a real long stretch,' he said.

Philpott sounded rattled. The call had brought him awake too suddenly. As a result of that, he informed Mike Graham, he would probably never get back to sleep.

'The position with Andreas Wolff is critical,' Mike said. 'He's due to turn up here in Berlin at ten o'clock this morning as a celebrity guest at a computer games fair. That's in two hours time, and the minute he shows he's going to be a wide open target for *Juli Zwanzig*'s hit man.'

'You haven't been able to trace this Einar Ahlin?'

'We've nothing to go on. Apart from his dippy girlfriend, nobody knows him. He has no buddies, there are no places he hangs out – we don't even have an address where he puts down his head at night. The girlfriend doesn't expect him to show up at her place for at least another two days. We're clueless.'

'Then Andreas Wolff must not be allowed to appear in public. He must be made aware he is this lunatic's prime target.'

Mike ran his gaze around the hotel room, breathing steadily, holding down the temptation to start shouting.

'Sir,' he said, 'that issue is what prompted this call in the first place. It's the very matter I raised when you picked up your phone. Wolff won't play ball. I just spent ten minutes on the phone trying to convince him of the risk he'd be taking. When I spoke to him the time before, he got the picture, he could see the kind of danger he was in. But now he's had time to sit and think about it and he believes as long as he's surrounded by people, he'll be safe.'

'What makes him think that?'

'He believes the assassin is a fastidious type. He only harms his targets, he won't risk other people's lives.'

'That's rubbish.'

'I told him about the car bomb, but he said that had been timed to go off when no one else was around. I said I knew different, but he wouldn't listen. The fact is, Wolff just won't duck down out of view. Especially when ducking down means

205

cancelling a public appearance at a computer fair. Events like that are his idea of the big time.'

'What about the Stramm woman? Wasn't Sabrina able to alert her that Wolff is a wrong target?'

'Erika Stramm is missing from home. Not been seen since early yesterday, and her only close contact, the Russian guy Gregor, is mystified.'

'There's one slim hope,' Philpott said. 'We managed to get both main Berlin daily papers to run stories about Wolff in connection with the computer show. Both pieces cover his parentage, his background, there's even a few childhood pictures. Maybe Ahlin will see a paper and get the message.'

'Maybe.'

'I presume Wolff will have a proper team of marksmen covering him while he's in Berlin?'

'Afraid not,' Mike said. 'The Austrian clodhoppers are coming with him. National pride, all that stuff.'

'Then you'd better cover him yourself, Mike. Get Sabrina on the job and as many sharpshooters from the Berlin police as you can persuade to do us an unofficial favour.'

'Believe me, sir, I'll do all I can to protect Wolff.'

'I don't want him coming to any harm. God, it's unthinkable.'

Mike was about to say 'trust me', but he lacked the confidence to back reassurance on that level. 'I'll keep you informed, sir. Sorry I broke into your sleep time.'

Philpott mumbled something and hung up. Mike finished dressing, decided to skip breakfast and got reception to call him a taxi. Before he left his room he strapped on a shoulder holster and loaded up his Harrington and Richardson Defender, a five-shot .38 he kept as a memento of his days with Delta. Apart from its sentimental associations, the weapon had a 3-inch barrel, which gave reassuring accuracy over medium-to-long range.

Half a kilometre from the place Mike was staying, Sabrina Carver emerged from her hotel at one minute after nine and got into her taxi. Twenty seconds later, as the cab pulled away, an inconspicuous grey Opel across the street started up and slipped into the stream of traffic three vehicles behind Sabrina's car. The driver of the Opel was Einar Ahlin. Beside him, tightly belted in and angry, was Erika Stramm.

'There is no need for this,' she said as they clipped a red light to stay close to Sabrina's taxi. 'I've told you, keep the money. I'll even give you a generous laying-off bonus.'

'Not the point,' Ahlin snapped.

Erika stared at him. It was ironical that he looked so much like the ideal of the people he hated. Today, wearing a black leather jacket and black polo shirt, he reminded her of a photograph she had seen of the arch-Nazi Reinhard Heydrich, relaxing with Hitler and Eva at a lodge by the Baltic.

'I think you have forgotten the basis of our relationship,' Erika said. 'I employ and specify, you carry out my instructions and get paid for doing so.'

'I think perhaps you have not properly understood the relationship in the first place,' he said, keeping his eyes on the traffic. 'You gave me the opportunity to embark on a mission against specific vermin. I was grateful for that, I am still grateful. But you cannot expect me to dismantle my determination.' He glanced at her, his eyes wide. 'You can't expect me to chop the legs off my will. I am on a set course and that is that.'

She had never seen him like this. Before, he had displayed an easy-going temperament, a smoothness of style that added a fine sinister edge to his desire to slaughter Nazis. Now he looked like a bare-fanged fanatic.

'Why am I being treated like a prisoner, Einar?'

'You are not a prisoner,' he said curtly.

'You won't let me do what I want. You've insisted I be here with you today. You've curbed my freedom and I call that being treated like a prisoner.'

'You're here with me because I want you to be close when the subject is hit. I want you to experience the zest of the event, the rightness of what I do. Then perhaps you will understand that I must carry on, and that it is in your interests as well as mine that I do.'

'You read that article in the paper, for heaven's sake. This man Wolff is not a target. He's nothing to do with the *Jugend von Siegfried*. Anybody can see that.'

'Any idiot might believe it, Erika, but it doesn't fool me. That stuff is just more snow, more cover for a Nazi as rotten as the rest of them.'

The previous day Einar had come to the bar where they met once a month to perform the small ritual of lunch and the handing over of a cheque for his services. When Erika told him she had decided to let the authorities deal with the remaining members of the *Jugend von Siegfried*, he had gone very quiet. He would not eat lunch and, when finally she announced she was leaving, he would not let her go. He had used no violence against her, but she knew it would come to that if she tried to get away.

'You should learn to absorb the messages and the lessons of omens,' Ahlin said now.

'I don't understand that kind of talk.'

The previous evening, as they left the place where they had met, Erika saw Sabrina. She told Ahlin who she was, and felt compelled to spill it all, the coercion, the acceleration of what was probably inevitable. Ahlin had driven slowly along the street, following Sabrina until he found out where she lived. He had then booked a double room in a cold-water hotel opposite the much nicer place where Sabrina stayed. They had spent the night there, taking turns at watching the front of the hotel.

'The police will be on the case very soon,' Erika said. 'You should pull out before that happens, before they're swarming all over the Nazis.'

Ahlin expelled air between his teeth. 'I might as well have said nothing to you,' he said. 'Try to get it into your skull, I don't care about the police or anybody else. I have a job, a God-sent job, and I'm going to carry it through.'

'Then do it without me.'

'You stay and you witness this one hit. That is important, I told you why.'

'I want to go home and see Gregor.'

'He will wait. This won't.'

He swung the car round a corner by a wide-fronted conference centre and parked it at the side of the road.

'This is the place.'

He pointed behind them. Erika looked and saw Sabrina get out of her taxi and enter the building.

'Didn't I say so, when you wanted to argue during the night? Didn't I say this woman would attach herself to the man Wolff? They are all part of a whole, don't you see?'

'Why follow her? You were coming here anyway, it was in the paper where he would be today.'

Ahlin gently eased Erika's fingers away from the buckle of her seatbelt. 'We are not going in there.'

'Why not?'

'Too many people, too much protection around Herr Wolff. I only ever tempt fate so far, and no further. We will follow him when he leaves.'

'How will you see him in among the crowd?'

'He is a protected person. He will come out while the show is busy. It will be quiet out here.' Ahlin smiled thinly. 'Rely on my judgement, Erika.'

'You still haven't told me why we followed the girl.'

'I wanted to see if my instinct was right,' he said. 'And it was. She is part of what we oppose, she is integrated, whatever her motives.'

'So?'

'So I will break my working rule.'

'What does that mean?'

'I will kill both Wolff *and* the girl.'

Wolff left the exhibition centre at one o'clock. An armoured Mercedes Benz saloon, property of the Viennese police, was driven up to the front door and he came out with his two lumbering bodyguards behind him. Mike and Sabrina hung back, watching his flanks, guns cocked and ready under their coats. Another two marksmen were at windows on the second floor.

As soon as Wolff was in the Mercedes Mike and Sabrina got into a police Volkswagen which had been hastily rented, together with its driver, after tight bargaining in the refreshment room. Five hundred dollars to the police widows' fund would let them have the car, driver and the use of a long-range rifle for six hours. Anything after that would be subject to fresh negotiation.

'Where are they taking him?' Sabrina asked as they raced along back streets towards the north of the city.

'A hotel in the Mühlenbeck district,' Mike said. 'It's out of the way, on a quiet street. He has offered to work on finishing the ICON security programs while he's in Berlin, and he's had a load of computer equipment installed in a top-floor suite at the hotel. I suppose we should be grateful for that.'

'What's security going to be like?'

'The Austrians have agreed to two extra marksmen in the building with him. They're from the Berlin police, both hot-shots.' Mike patted the heavy rifle on the seat beside him. 'I'll be in the next building with this baby.'

'And I'll be watching the door, as usual.'

'Don't be bitter, Sabrina.'

When they reached the hotel the Mercedes drew up close to the door and Wolff was hurried inside. Sabrina moved into the front passenger seat beside the police driver. Mike went to the warehouse next door to the hotel, where police had arranged that he should have a window seat looking directly into Wolff's suite.

He called Sabrina on the mobile and confirmed he was in position. 'It's tidy,' he said. 'The goons are sitting at either end of Wolff's work table, watching him do his stuff. The extra marksmen should be here in a few minutes. I'm ready to go ballistic if anything irregular happens.'

'And I'm striking up a friendship with a nice German boy in the front seat of a cop car,' Sabrina said. 'What happens after today? Is Wolff going back to Austria?'

'He stays here until blue eyes is in custody. The wheels are turning. The police will be looking for him soon, so it won't be long.'

A hundred metres from the hotel, Einar Ahlin was standing by his Opel, using a foot-pump to inflate a tyre he had manually deflated as soon as he stopped.

Erika sat in the front of the car, behind the steering wheel, coping with a new level of stress. On the way across the city, tailing the Mercedes through heavy traffic and along narrow back turnings, Ahlin said he had decided she could no longer simply pay for his services, she had to be practical in her condemnation of the *Jugend von Siegfried*. She must stick with him.

She wound down the window. 'What are you going to do now?'

'Wait to be inspired,' he said, watching the hotel. 'I think we can move closer.'

He finished inflating the tyre, put the pump in the boot and got in beside Erika. She drove along past the front of the hotel. There was no sign of the big Mercedes.

'God,' Erika said suddenly. 'It's her.'

Ahlin looked at the car they were passing. Sabrina was perfectly visible, sitting in the front with the police driver.

'Now do you understand about omens?' Ahlin said. 'Stop the car!'

Erika drew in to the side and braked. Ahlin jumped out and walked back to the police car. Erika watched him in the rearview mirror.

'Lunatic,' she murmured.

There was a strong impulse to run, but she knew it would never work. He would find her, and she didn't want to think what he would do then.

'Out!' Ahlin snapped, jerking open the driver's door of the police car. 'Out now! Out!'

The young officer scrambled out and as he straightened up by the open door Ahlin hit him on the side of the head with the barrel of his revolver. The officer dropped without a sound. Sabrina had the other door open when she felt the pressure of the gun in her back.

'Come out slowly,' Ahlin said. 'Very slowly.'

She slid across the seats and got out. As she did, a police armoured vehicle appeared and drew in at the side of the hotel, near the entrance to an alley running behind the building. Two men carrying rifles and wearing dark combat suits got out. Almost at once the vehicle moved off and disappeared round the corner.

'Who are they?' Ahlin said. 'Tell me or I'll shoot you.'

211

Sabrina told him they were the reinforcement guard for Andreas Wolff.

'Go across. Speak to them. Improvise. Understand?'

Sabrina brought up her arm sharply, almost knocking the gun from Ahlin's grip. He held on to it and simultaneously grabbed her hair. He tugged once, hard, making her yelp.

'Try anything like that again,' he muttered, 'and I won't bother with warnings, I'll shoot you. Now speak to those men, and remember I'm right at your back.'

She crossed the road, waving to the marksmen. Ahlin walked three paces behind her.

'Are you going up to Herr Wolff's suite?' Sabrina asked the marksmen in German. 'Perhaps I can show you the way.'

They stared at her, scowling, puzzled.

'You must forgive her,' Ahlin said, pushing her ahead of him, smiling, emanating charm. 'She talks without thinking.'

When he was close enough he shoved Sabrina aside, knocking her down. He brought forward his revolver, pushing it in a marksman's face.

'Drop your guns,' he hissed. 'Do it now!'

They dropped the weapons. In a single sweep Ahlin hit one man in the face with his revolver, breaking his cheekbone, and swiped the other across the chin with the butt. Both men went down. Almost casually, watching Sabrina scramble to her feet, Ahlin crouched and hit each man on the temple with the chamber of the revolver.

'Help me,' he told Sabrina, waving the gun.

He stood by, keeping the gun trained on her as she dragged one unconscious man then the other into the alley behind the hotel.

'Now I'm going to become a police sureshot,' Ahlin said. 'And you're going to be my pretty helper, yes?' He pointed to one of the marksmen. 'Strip off his combat suit.'

Eight minutes later, as Mike sat watching through his peep sight, he saw the main door of Wolff's suite swing open and a police marksman come in. Only one.

'Better than none . . .'

He continued to watch as the marksman said something. The

others in the room, Wolff and his two bodyguards, turned and stared at him.

Several things happened in rapid order. The two Austrians were on their feet, reaching for their guns. Wolff leaned across his work table, picked up three or four optical storage disks and pushed them down the front of his trousers. The police marksman levelled his sub-machine-gun and shot the two bodyguards. As they fell, one of them smearing the wallpaper with his blood, the marksman grabbed Andreas Wolff by the shoulders and head-butted him in the face. Dazed, Wolff let himself be dragged to the door.

Mike couldn't get a clear shot in. He grabbed the rifle and ran, taking the stairs to the ground floor three at a time. He got outside in time to see the police Volkswagen scream away from the kerb. A woman was at the wheel. In the back Einar Ahlin was just visible. He appeared to be tying Andreas Wolff's hands.

Sabrina called out. Mike turned and saw her kneeling on the pavement at the side of the hotel. Her hands were bound behind her back. Blood ran from a wound on her arm.

Mike eased her to her feet and undid the cord on her wrists. 'He shot me when he came out,' she panted. 'Nearly missed. I never knew I could roll so fast.'

Mike held her close. 'I don't want to sound callous,' he said, 'or uncaring, but there's no time to pamper you right now.' He looked up and down the quiet street. 'I didn't expect him to kidnap Wolff. I have to get after them.'

'Do something for my arm and I'll come with you.'

Mike took a handkerchief from his pocket and folded it in a strip. He wrapped it round her arm, tied a secure knot, patted her shoulder and pronounced her cured.

'Or as good as.' He shouldered the rifle. 'Now come on. We've got to steal something faster than a police Volkswagen.'

TWENTY-SEVEN

For an hour after clearing the Berlin city limits Erika Stramm drove steadily north-east, keeping to main roads, only making diversions when the traffic became heavy and slowed her down.

'I hope you know what you're doing,' she told Einar Ahlin. 'The police could pull us over any time.'

'The police will be looking for this car in the city,' Ahlin said. He was still in the back seat, sprawled beside Andreas Wolff, who sat awkwardly, his hands taped behind him. 'That is why I showed you the fast route out. The police would presumably throw up road blocks, but I've timed measures of that kind in a number of cities, Erika. It takes a minimum thirty minutes just to get three blocks in place. We were out in eighteen minutes. Ergo, the police are wasting their time, which is always a soothing thought.'

'They won't just be looking for us in Berlin,' Andreas Wolff said. 'This little kidnap merits a nationwide alert.'

'Again, an unwieldy thing to implement,' Ahlin said. 'But facts and figures have no place in this. My instincts are what matter. My instincts and the way I use them to sustain my run of fortune.'

'In my view,' Wolff said, 'you should put yourself in the hands of a competent psychiatrist.'

Ahlin sat forward. 'It is stupid to confuse mental hyper-acuity with mental disorder,' he said.

'I never do that,' Wolff said. 'You're mentally disordered. There's no doubt about it.'

Ahlin punched Wolff on the mouth. The impact jerked Wolff's head sideways against the door pillar. As he straightened up Ahlin punched him again. Wolff grunted, pursing his lips to stem the rush of blood from his mouth.

'Don't speak again,' Ahlin told him. He looked over Erika's shoulder at the road ahead. 'What did the last sign say?'

'Gristow, eighty-two kilometres.'

'In that case I think you should drive a little faster.'

It began to rain, big drops exploding on the windshield.

'You're sure about this boat?' Erika said, putting her foot down a fraction, making the car surge forward. 'How do you know you'll be able to use it?'

'It is mine, so I am sure I can use it.'

Erika said nothing. Ahlin interpreted her silence as disbelief. 'I stole it, you see. I decided that my destiny, if I had any, would be in this country, and as I have been a good sailor since childhood, I decided I would travel here on the water. I picked the nicest launch I could find at Arendal, in south-east Norway. It was stocked with fuel and food, it had the latest navigation equipment. It even had an armed guard.' Ahlin laughed softly. 'He was the first man I ever killed. I knew I had to do that. My fitness to fulfil my destiny was being tested.'

'And nobody came after you?'

'Probably somebody did. But they would have been looking for a white launch registered in Oslo. After I crossed the Skagerrak, and before I made it down the Kattegat to the north coast of Germany, I stopped at a rundown Swedish yard and for a small price they changed the registration and identity of my launch, which is now an attractive sea-green.'

'How can you be sure it's still where you left it?'

'Because I see it quite often, Erika. I live on it. I like to stay at a distance from cities. I regularly hitch rides out of Berlin so I can sleep in my own little bunk. I can usually be in Gristow in two or three hours. Hitching in the other direction is even quicker.'

'What are we going to do when we get there?'

'You asked me that already,' Ahlin said.

'I'm asking you again. I have a life and I'm concerned about the turn it's taking.'

Ahlin picked up a rag from the floor. It was oily, the kind of rag that might have been used to wipe the spark plugs. He dabbed it to Andreas Wolff's bleeding mouth.

'We will walk the last kilometre to where the launch is berthed,' he said. 'That will be after we have ditched this car.' He leaned forward and spoke close to Erika's ear. 'Before we lose the car, you're going to use its radio to transmit a very important message.'

For more than an hour Mike had driven a stolen motorcycle a full 50 metres behind the police Volkswagen. Earlier, gridlocked traffic had slowed the Volkswagen's approach to the fast northern route out of the city, giving Mike time to spot the car break away from the herd and take a sudden detour the wrong way down a one-way alley. He followed and had been behind the Volkswagen ever since.

The bike was a big Kawasaki, a courier's machine, scarred and battered, with a 500cc engine and enough poke in the acceleration to make it easy to manoeuvre. The crash helmet, on the other hand, was half a size too big. Mike had jammed a folded newspaper up the back to make it fit. Sabrina was on the pillion seat, her Burberry trenchcoat buttoned to the top, her head tucked down to conceal the fact she had no helmet.

Once he was used to the machine's handling Mike drove steadily, keeping himself behind other vehicles on the straight, weaving forward or dropping back to keep the space between them constant. The first few times Erika detoured he did the same, until he realized she was following a main route northeast. After that he timed his speed to dovetail close behind her each time she rejoined the major highway.

'All right back there?' he shouted as the rain began to lash them.

Sabrina inched closer, getting her face near the gap at the bottom of his helmet. 'I'm fine, but I noticed we've been skidding. Is everything OK?'

'The tyres are worn from too much heavy cornering. Try to ignore it.'

As they passed the 50 kilometre signpost to Gristow the traffic became noticeably thinner. Mike dropped his speed, letting the Volkswagen get a good 200 metres ahead of him. Two minutes past the 30 kilometre marker a thunderstorm broke. Lightning flashed and danced over the highway. Even above the roar of the bike's engine the thunder was a thudding rumble, like blows on the ears and ribs. A couple of times the bike lost its purchase on the road and sailed towards the shoulder. Each time Mike corrected and regained control, grateful that Sabrina knew to sit motionless and let him do everything.

A kilometre outside Gristow the Volkswagen left the road. It turned sharply along a rutted farm path towards the north-west shoreline, 3 kilometres away. Mike slowed until the car dipped out of sight, then he followed, chugging along at a trotting pace, listening to Sabrina mumbling with relief as the circulation came back to her hands.

At the top of an incline Mike stopped and straddled the bike, holding it upright. He took off the helmet.

'They're heading for somewhere on the shore,' he said, looking at his watch. 'What time do you make it?'

'Three-twenty.'

'We still have satellite time.'

Mike kicked down the bike's support and climbed off. Sabrina swung her legs to the side and flexed her ankles vigorously before she risked putting her weight on her feet.

'Such fun, a biker's life,' she muttered, rubbing her hands.

Mike took the heavy rifle from his right shoulder and transferred it to his left. He shook the loose water from his hands, took out his mobile and tapped in the satellite code. At the contact signal he thumbed the automatic dial code for UNACO and pressed the phone close to his ear. After ten seconds of whistles and pops he heard the faint but undistorted voice of C. W. Whitlock.

'It's me, C. W. Mike. I thought the old man would appreciate a rundown.'

'He already has one,' C. W. said. 'The Berlin police have worked out what happened. One of the Austrian bodyguards lived long enough to give them the meat of the story. A number of small assumptions have taken care of the rest – including one about a messenger's bike that went missing from outside a café just after the shooting. Did you take it?'

'Would I do a thing like that?'

217

'Is Sabrina with you?'

'She is. I have to tell you C. W., we have no idea what Einar Ahlin is up to. As far as I can tell, he's got Erika Stramm driving the stolen police car with himself and Andreas Wolff in the back, and they're heading for the shoreline at Gristow.'

'Hang on, Mike . . .'

'Don't be long. Satellite time's tight.'

'What's happening?' Sabrina said. She was mopping her hair with her scarf.

'No idea.' Mike looked at the sky. 'The rain's stopping. On the other hand . . .' He looked off towards the east. 'There's more thunder and lightning on the way.'

'Terrific.'

'How's your arm?'

'Sore.'

Mike laughed.

'What's funny?'

'You look like a half-drowned refugee in an expensive raincoat.'

Whitlock came back on the line. 'Erika Stramm has used the radio in the stolen police car to issue an ultimatum,' he said. 'It was routed to Interpol and they just channelled it to us. We got it while she was still talking.'

'What does she want?'

'I have a transcript.' Whitlock cleared his throat. 'Statement begins, "*Juli Zwanzig* gives notice that in three hours' time the man Andreas Wolff will die, and the German Navy's experimental station at Stettiner Haff will be blown up, unless one million US dollars is handed over in direct exchange for Wolff at a place and time to be specified in one hour, by which time the authorities should have been able to make the funds ready for transfer. This demand is modest, unmotivated by greed, and is generated purely by the need of *Juli Zwanzig* to continue its mission." End of statement.'

'We're probably no further than a mile or two from where they are at this minute,' Mike said. 'We'll go after them, but reinforcements at some stage would be a comfort.'

'The German authorities already got a rough fix on the radio signal,' Whitlock said. 'We can pass on something more precise. Hold down the hash mark and the star buttons simultaneously for a count of ten. I'll take a fix on your position.'

Mike did as he said. At the end of ten seconds he heard the phone beep.

'That's recorded and on its way to the proper authorities,' Whitlock said. 'Now, while your skin and Sabrina's are precious to us, you understand it's Wolff we're most concerned about at present.'

Mike said, 'When the shooting started back at the hotel, I saw him grab some optical disks and stick them down his pants.'

'The ICON protocols,' Whitlock groaned.

'It might have been better for ICON if he'd left them,' Mike said. 'If Ahlin realizes what he has in his hands, it could be worse than catastrophic.'

'I don't even want to visualize that,' Whitlock said.

'We'd better get moving, C. W.'

'Keep in touch.'

Mike pocketed the phone and told Sabrina what Erika had said.

'Her voice,' she said, 'but Einar's words, I'll bet.'

Mike started the bike. 'I have to admit, I have the worst kind of gut feeling about Ahlin.'

'Me too.' Sabrina waited until he righted the bike then she climbed on. 'The way I feel about him,' she said, 'is like the sensation you get when you see a terrorist turn and look at you, and you realize your gun is back at the hotel.'

'I know that sensation,' Mike said. 'There's a technical term for it.'

'Yeah?'

'Blind terror.'

The sky turned steadily darker as they drew near the shoreline. Mike eased the bike along rutted tracks and over increasingly stony hillocks, watching all the time for a sign of the Volkswagen. The rain was starting up again when Sabrina slapped his shoulder.

'There,' she said, pointing out to sea.

Ten metres beyond the end of a jetty the boot and part

of the rear end of the car's roof were visible above the water.

'I hope he didn't leave anybody in there,' Mike said.

He drove on for another five minutes, picking up speed as the shingled road became smoother. A number of small boats lay at anchor along the way, covered with tarpaulins, abandoned until the city sailors arrived at the weekend.

Sabrina slapped Mike again. 'That boat along there. The big green one. There are lights on board.'

The launch was moored against the side of a flimsy one-lane jetty. Down in the state room Andreas Wolff was propped in the curve of a padded couch facing aft. At the dining table Einar Ahlin sat opposite Erika Stramm. He explained their position as if it had been ordained long ago.

'They will know where we are, or roughly where, because they will have taken a lock on the broadcast signal. Police radios permit that kind of trace, which was the only reason we used it. Delay, when it comes time for the exchange, will be minimal.' He took a cellular telephone from his pocket. 'When you talk to them again, you will use this.'

'So you want them to come here,' Erika said.

'I want them to see Wolff,' Ahlin sat back and clasped his hands behind his head. 'We will be some way out by then, but they will be able to satisfy themselves it is him. They will then float out the money in the small boat they will find by the jetty, and when it reaches us, we release Herr Wolff. They will rejoice and give great sighs of relief as they help him out of the boat in which he will be returned to the shore. He will still have his hands bound, of course, and his mouth will be taped.'

'Why?'

'So he cannot warn them he is sitting on a bomb.'

Ahlin pointed to a grey metal box on a shelf by the door. It was a 15-centimetre cube; a stemmed handle stuck up from the top. The handle was broad and flat-topped.

'Pushing down the plunger does nothing. Releasing it again does. *Boom!*' Ahlin threw his arms in the air and laughed. 'I built that myself. Originally I intended to use it to despatch Mr Gibson, the American. But I decided it would be better if something so

220

potent and – I confess it, so unstable – did not travel too far before it was used.'

He leaned across and patted the side of the bomb casing. Erika stared at Andreas Wolff. His eyes looked sunken with despair.

'What about the threat to blow up the naval yard?'

'Sheer nonsense,' Ahlin said. 'But they must take a threat like that seriously.' He nodded at Wolff. 'People are valued, of course, especially clever ones like him, but property and investment and secrets – oh, they must be protected above and beyond all else. The threat to blow up the yard guarantees delivery of the million dollars. A side benefit will be that a pleasing number of police and security forces will be deployed at the naval yard to no good end.'

Ahlin reached out and touched the bomb again, stroking it this time. 'It is a big charge,' he said, 'a huge one really, so when Herr Wolff stands up, there will be a lot of damage, many casualties, and an overriding confusion, during which we will speed away.'

Erika looked ill. 'I don't want to go anywhere. I just want to see Gregor. I want to be with him more than anything.'

'First you must come with me.'

'Where? Norway?'

'I'm sure that is what the authorities will think. But no. We will just go round the corner, geographically speaking. Remember, we have a job to finish in Germany. So we will creep back while the forces of law and order are looking for us everywhere but Germany, and we will complete the grand mission. After that . . .' Ahlin shrugged. 'After that I don't know. Maybe by then I will have devised another mission.'

Erika looked at Wolff again. He was very pale. He sat staring at the floor.

'I'm scared,' Erika said. 'You'll get us killed.'

Outside, Mike and Sabrina had inched their way on deck, leaning along the rail, setting up a minimum of movement. Mike tiptoed to the forward state-room porthole and put his eye to the edge. He turned to Sabrina and nodded. He eased the rifle off his shoulder and readied it. Sabrina pulled out her pistol and thumbed off the safety. They went down the six steps to the state-room door on their toes.

Mike looked at Sabrina. He gently grasped the handle of the door and began to mouth a countdown from five. Sabrina nodded on each count. On *two* Mike eased the door open a fraction. On *one* he kicked it hard.

The door burst open with a crash.

Ahlin jumped back, nearly falling. Erika screamed and Andreas Wolff jumped to his feet. Mike leaped into the room holding the rifle at waist height. Sabrina was two paces behind him, standing on the bottom step, her pistol aimed at Ahlin's head.

'Freeze!' Mike yelled. 'Don't move! Not a muscle!'

Ahlin's eyes rolled. He swayed, looking as if he might faint. He sank slowly to his knees. Mike was three paces away as Ahlin went down. When his shoulder hit the floor his hand snaked into his jacket pocket and pulled out a shiny silver pistol.

'Watch it!' Sabrina yelled.

Ahlin fired at Andreas Wolff before Mike got to him. The bullet hit Wolff in the middle with a splintering sound and he fell back across the couch.

Mike's rifle butt clipped Ahlin on the chin. He landed unconscious in the corner. Mike snatched the pistol and pocketed it.

'Let's go!' he yelled, pushing Erika towards the door. 'Move!'

He took Wolff by the arms and pulled him to a sitting position. Wolff's eyes opened and he winced.

'I don't think the bullet went into you,' Mike told him. 'How do you feel? Can you stand up?'

Wolff nodded, gasping to pull in air, pointing to the waistband of his trousers.

'The disks,' Mike said. 'I know.' He pulled Wolff to his feet and pushed him through the state-room door. 'Help him walk,' he told Erika.

'Watch that box,' Erika called back out as Sabrina led them out on to the jetty. 'It's a bomb. Reflex detonator, I think.'

Mike hoisted Ahlin off the floor by the armpits and leaned him against the wall. He pat-searched him then slapped his face

222

until he came round. When the blue eyes fluttered open Mike spun him away from the wall and out on to the stairs.

'He's coming up, Sabrina,' he shouted. 'Keep the gun on him and shoot him if he puts one foot wrong.'

Mike shouldered the rifle and picked up the bomb. He carried it up on deck and set it carefully in the prow. As he straightened, Sabrina cried out. He saw her stumble aside, then he was pushed violently from behind.

'Move aside, Mr Yankee Hero,' Ahlin rasped, staggering past Mike.

He turned and before Mike could grab him he sat on the bomb. The plunger went down with a grating sound as it took his weight.

'Now then,' he said, swaying, touching the side of the hull for support. 'I think you and I should stay right here.'

'I don't think so,' Mike said. He turned. 'Get on shore, Sabrina. Run!'

'If I stand up,' Ahlin said, 'you'll come to paradise with me. Nobody can run fast enough to dodge this touch of nemesis.' He slapped the bomb beneath him. 'Care to take me up on that?'

Mike said nothing. He looked at the others, at the far end of the jetty now, edging on to the path. Wolff moved slowly, staggering as Sabrina and Erika urged him to walk faster. They were still too close.

'If you try anything, I'll stand up at once.' Ahlin clasped his hands behind his head. 'Tell me now, does this seem oddly relaxed?' He raised his eyebrows. 'It *does* look laid-back, no? But in fact it has a purpose.' Ahlin brought his hands away from his neck. The right hand held a revolver, identical to the one he used to shoot Wolff. 'A jacket collar pocket. You have encountered it before, surely?'

He laughed and raised both arms above his head. Mike made a grab for the pistol. Ahlin threw it from one hand to the other.

'Erika!' he shouted.

She turned. Ahlin fired the pistol at her. She dropped at Sabrina's feet.

'For treachery!' Ahlin shouted, wincing as Mike tore the gun from his hand.

Sabrina knelt and touched Erika's neck. She looked up and shook her head.

'You killed her,' Mike said.

'She deserved it. So do you, Yank. Don't fret, it won't be long.'

Mike sighed. He eased the rifle up on his shoulder. 'You're a savage, Einar. I'd like to break all your fingers, one after the other. But that would put me too close to your league.'

'So what will you do?'

Mike reached out and put his hand flat on Ahlin's head, pressing down hard, keeping him seated. He pushed him back sharply. He was leaning on the hull, supported on either side by boxes.

'A little anaesthetic.'

Mike slid his hand down off Ahlin's head and along the side of his neck. Ahlin's hands came up to defend himself but Mike's arm wouldn't be deflected. His fingers went under the collar of Ahlin's shirt and found the brachial plexus. He squeezed. Ahlin's head dropped forward. Mike stood back a second, then turned smartly and crossed the deck. He leapt on to the jetty and ran to the others.

'Ten minutes, I'd say, before he comes round. How are you doing, Andreas?'

'I could be much worse,' Wolff croaked. 'I also could have had more luck.' He looked at Erika lying by the jetty. 'Perhaps we all could.'

'It's been one of those days.' Mike crouched to pick up Erika's body. 'Help Andreas up the hill, will you, Sabrina? While there's a lull, I think we should get ourselves to a safe vantage point.'

Four minutes later a police firearms unit arrived. They brought with them a senior officer, who carried an attaché case with a million dollars in used bills.

Mike explained the situation. The tension among the policemen ebbed.

'There's nothing to do but wait,' Mike said.

Erika's body was put on a stretcher, covered with a blanket and placed in the back of the police wagon. The marksmen took up positions on the hill overlooking the jetty, their tele-sights trained on the unconscious man in the launch. Mike sat on the grass talking quietly to Andreas Wolff, who was feeling sick.

As the minutes ticked away Sabrina realized some of the men were moving further down the hill.

'Stay back!' she warned. 'That's a big charge he's sitting on!'

Some of them took notice. Others froze where they were, re-positioning their guns, re-focusing their sights.

From where Sabrina stood she could see the launch clearly. She didn't want a close-up. She could make out Einar Ahlin's shape in the prow. She could see him moving. Ahlin's neck straightened, he rubbed the back of his head, then cupped both hands over his eyes. As his hands dropped away he looked up at the hillside.

'He doesn't understand what's happening,' a policeman said. 'He's dazed.'

'I hope he stays that way,' Sabrina said.

She saw Ahlin rub his eyes, as if he might sink back and go to sleep again. Then abruptly he stood up.

Everybody seemed to stop breathing. Ahlin stood motionless, looking round at where he had been sitting. He stiffened visibly, then took a step away from the prow.

The bomb went off with a blinding gold flash. A second later the roar travelled up the hillside and behind it the shockwave, bending bushes, knocking over a gun tripod and whipping off hats and spectacles.

Debris began to land like rain. The air was filled with cloudy vapour. Some of that, Sabrina thought, was Einar Ahlin. He was now what explosives experts referred to as pink mist.

'So it's over,' Andreas Wolff said. 'One less lunatic, making space for one more.'

TWENTY-EIGHT

'The police are here, so are the medical services, and there are one or two people I suspect are Federal German Security,' Sabrina told Philpott over the mobile phone. 'It's a circus. Thanks to Mike's touch of ingenuity with Einar Ahlin, it's a very grisly circus. There's nothing left of the boat, apart from flotsam.'

Philpott asked how badly Wolff was hurt.

'The bullet hit him right in the software, sir. Four metal-and-plastic laminated disks of it. Didn't even break his skin, but I think he's going to have a badly bruised abdomen.'

'Did those four disks represent all of the security protocols?' Philpott said. He sounded grim.

'I haven't asked yet. But considering the amount of data even one of those disks can hold, I would imagine he'd get everything on to four of them.'

'Maybe he had back-ups.'

'Opticals are pretty secure. People don't tend to make extra copies.'

'Well thank you for poking those rays of golden light into my day,' Philpott said. 'Call me back when you have more to report.'

'I certainly will.'

'Next time we speak I'll have details of your next mission.'

'It's cooking already?'

'C. W. is on the case. You know what they say about there being no rest for the wicked.'

'Why should that apply to a virtuous soul like me?'

Philpott grunted. 'Any other time I'd enjoy this light-hearted blather, Sabrina, but in view of what's likely to happen to ICON, you'll pardon me if I remain grumpy. Call me soon.'

'Very good, sir.'

226

Sabrina put away the mobile and went to kneel beside Wolff, who was still sitting on the grass.

'I hope you won't mind me raising something like this so soon after your ordeal,' she said. She looked quickly at Mike, who rolled his eyes but said nothing. 'It's about the software you had tucked under your belt. Was that all of the work you were doing? I mean, was everything on those four disks?'

Wolff nodded. 'Frankly, that is why I feel so sick.'

He pushed his fingers down the top of his trousers and fished out a few shards of the broken disks the medics had missed.

'All gone,' he sighed. 'All gone.'

'The grim truth,' Mike said, 'is that your life was saved at the expense of ICON's next generation of security.'

Wolff stared at him. He looked puzzled.

'I'm sorry. I don't follow . . .'

'I just said that ICON security has perished in the process of –'

'Perished?' Wolff stared at Mike wide-eyed. 'ICON security? Never. Not a chance of it. Not as long as I breathe.'

Mike and Sabrina looked at each other. Mike looked at Wolff.

'I don't understand, Andreas. Those disks, weren't they the upgrade security files, the ones you've been working on so hard?'

'*Tcha!*' Wolff looked at Mike as if he was an idiot. 'The security codes are my discipline,' he said, tapping the side of his head. 'I make notes, sure, but the programs, the routines, they evolve all the time, and because they do they require volatile storage.' He tapped his head again, more forcibly. 'They were generated in my skull, and they will stay there until they are perfected and transferred to the network.' Wolff pulled a few more particles of plastic from the waistband of his trousers. 'These disks contained my new masterpieces,' he said. His voice was hollow and sad.

Mike frowned. 'You mean games?'

Wolff nodded. 'Four of them. All beauties. All gone.' Wolff looked at Sabrina with agony in his eyes. 'I spent three years working on them. They were my creations, my children.' He shook his head, desolated beyond comforting. 'Three years of dedication. Three years of my life, for God's sake.'

Mike did his best to commiserate.

Sabrina turned away.

It had been a hell of a day.